At The Wake

Michael David MacBride

СКУНС

DEDICATION

As always, to my family

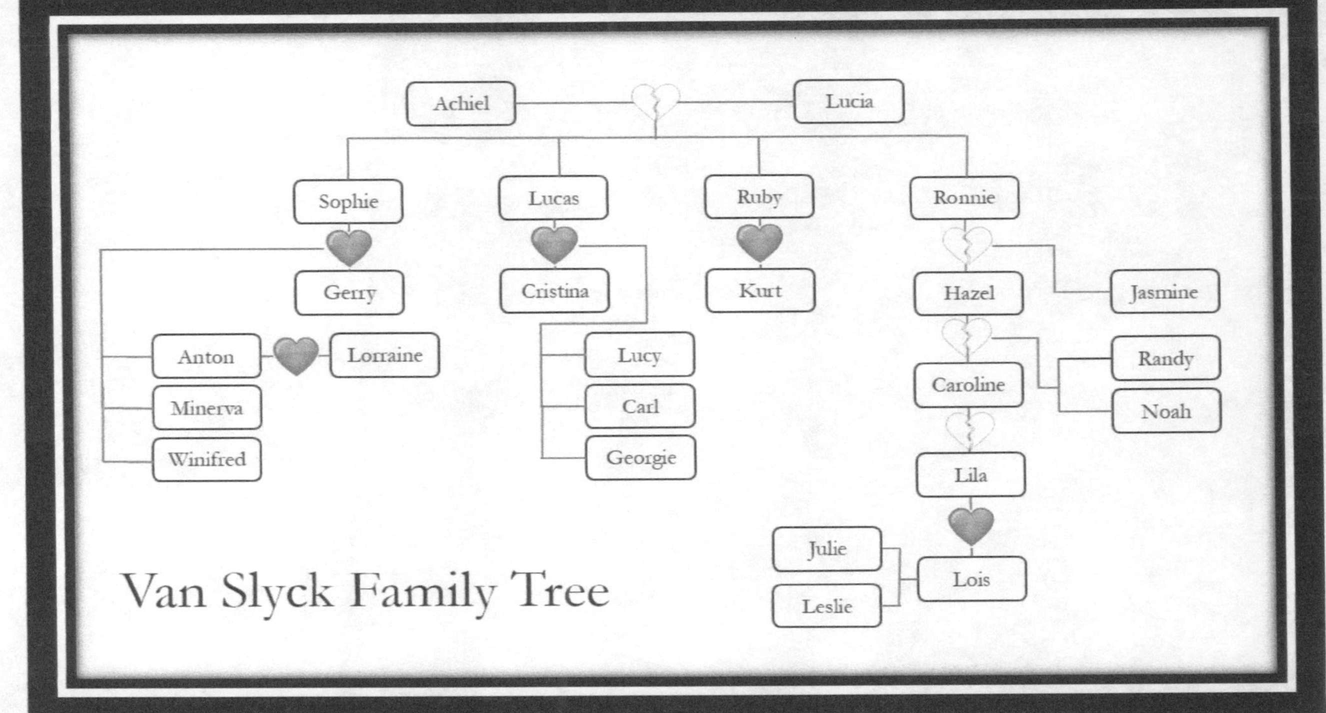

Van Slyck Family Tree
Achiel
Lucia
Sophie
Lucas
Ruby
Ronnie
Gerry
Cristina
Kurt
Hazel
Jasmine
Anton
Lorraine
Lucy
Caroline
Randy
Minerva
Carl
Noah
Winifred
Georgie
Lila
Julie
Lois
Leslie

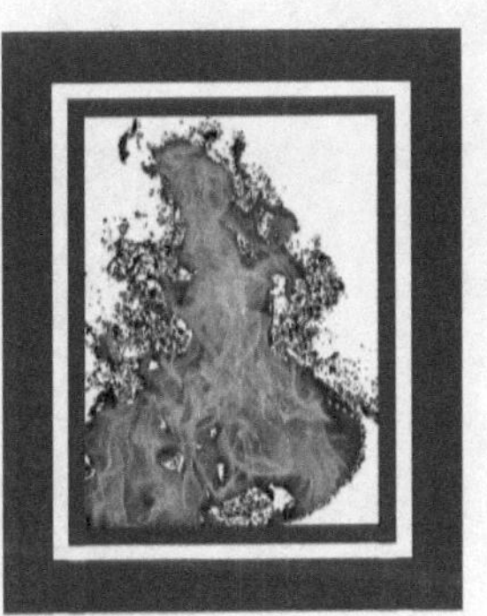

PART I: AT THE WAKE (2001)

When Achiel Van Slyck killed Clifford Ellis, it wasn't quite the definition of a premeditated murder, but it was definitely in the gray. At the time, Achiel claimed he had brought his .243 rifle with the intention of shooting animals only. After all, he and his sons were spending the day hunting on their own property, but had he also intended to kill Clifford that day?

Clifford and Achiel had a long uncomfortable history, and on more than one occasion Achiel had said, with various witnesses present, that he would, in fact, "Kill that son of a bitch one day." So, did he do it? Did Achiel actually lure Clifford onto his property and then kill him in cold blood in front of Achiel's children? It didn't seem that hard to believe. People who knew Achiel could attest to his temper and his supernatural ability to hold a grudge longer than anyone else they knew. They also knew Achiel was creative and devious in his revenge.

For instance, there was the neighbor who had accidentally (though Achiel would dispute the accidental nature of the claim) killed one of Achiel's favorite hunting dogs, Blackie. Achiel and the neighbor had words, but the neighbor apologized and believed the matter resolved. Imagine his surprise when he returned home from a camping trip up north to find every tree on his ten-acre property cut down. There was no absolute proof that Achiel had done this, but the timing was more than coincidental.

The neighbor drove over to the Van Slyck property and knocked on the flimsy-framed screen door. Achiel responded to the knock by laughing at the man standing on the porch and walking back inside the house. The neighbor was left standing there wondering what to do. He could enact his own revenge. Those trees were expensive. His father had planted many of them, and they had stood on the property some thirty or forty years. How much would it cost to replace them? And then there was the matter of the stump removal. Perhaps, the neighbor thought, he should have the stumps professionally removed and then have the bill sent to Achiel. But again, there was no actual evidence Achiel had chopped down the trees. What if this only angered the man more?

Still, he couldn't help but be a little amazed at the creativity of the chopping down of every single tree on his property. If nothing else, it must have taken a long time. In the end, he returned to his home, and he worked to remove the stumps himself. He chopped the wood and burned it in his fireplace for years to come. He planted more seeds, and he never once set foot on the Van Slyck property again.

This wasn't the only story about Achiel that spread around the village of Lewes. There was also the one about how Achiel burned down a rival's welding shop in 1954. Freshly back from Korea, Achiel and his (then) friend Eddie Davis set up welding shops on either side of Lewes. In truth, Eddie's was just over the border and into Gilbert, but since Gilbert didn't have its own post office or ZIP code anymore, everyone thought of it as part of Lewes.

Eddie and Achiel had known each other before the Korean War, but they really got to know one another after they wound up in the same unit during the war. Their idle chitchat, as with most men, revolved homeward. They talked about their families and what they would do after the war. They were surprised to learn they each had a knack for welding. In Eddie's case, welding was something he picked up in high school and then picked up again in the Army where he worked repairing damaged equipment and providing patchwork welds on bridges and infrastructure. Achiel's interest in welding came from his father, who had a welding shop in Belgium before they moved to the United States. Achiel literally grew up on the trade.

The two men agreed that Lewes was big enough to sustain two welding shops as long as the shops were located far enough apart. The men bought property on opposite sides of town, each assuming people on the east half would visit Eddie's, and the ones on the west half would visit Achiel's.

When the work began to pile up, each man was gracious enough to send extra work the other man's way. They even assisted one another on particularly difficult jobs, though it was often Eddie who required the assistance and far less often Achiel.

As it became more and more obvious that the United States was going to enter the conflict in Vietnam, the two men found themselves at one another's shop talking about whether they would re-enlist. Achiel was almost certain he would. Eddie was less certain.

"What do you mean?" Achiel asked. He was surprised.

"I've spent enough time overseas," said Eddie. "I've got a great shop and am happy. Why upset the apple cart?"

"To serve your country? To kill. For some excitement?"

Eddie finished a drink of his beer. "I've had enough of all that."

"So," said Achiel. "What? You're just going to sit over here and let everyone else fight your war for you?"

"I'm not sure this is really my war," said Eddie. "You and I, we're almost thirty."

"I'm twenty-eight."

"Right. We're almost thirty," said Eddie. "This is a young man's thing. I served. I did my time. Let someone else fight now."

Achiel didn't have a response to that. He wasn't one for cursing or name-calling, but Eddie's comments were filed away for later use. That later use came less than a month later.

Eddie's phone rang at 2:17 AM. He rolled over and answered.

"Your shop is on fire." The voice said, and the line went dead.

Eddie didn't want to believe it was true, but the voice didn't sound like it was joking. It didn't sound like a drunk teenager prank calling or any of the voices of his friends who he could imagine might be getting out of the bar right about now and having a little fun. So, Eddie crawled out of bed without disturbing his girlfriend and went to the shop. It was indeed on fire. Eddie was not an expert on fires, but it looked like the fire had been going for quite a while, and the shop looked past the point of salvaging anything. Still, he drove to a pay phone and called the fire department and then returned to the shop to wait.

A full moon illuminated everything around the fire as Eddie paced around the outer ring of the shop. At times the heat from the fire pushed him further away, and he wondered if any of his gas cylinders had exploded. Eddie was wary of all gases and assumed they all could and would explode, but even if the gases weren't flammable, he assumed the pressurized tanks were ready to blow at any second.

Finally, he heard sirens coming in the distance. He stopped his pacing and took several steps back, away from the building. He would let the professionals—well, the volunteer Lewes squad anyway—take care of the fire. As he removed himself a distance from the fire, he saw the outline of a man standing on the other side of the property. The man appeared to be staring in Eddie's direction. At first Eddie wasn't sure if the man was facing the fire or him, and then he saw the man's nose. They locked eyes and the man threw a gas can at the fire. It covered the distance between the man and the shop easily and landed almost squarely in the middle of the fire. At first, Eddie thought the tank was empty but then he realized it couldn't have flown quite so far if it had been. Now, there would be an explosion.

It didn't happen immediately, and Eddie realized he had been holding his breath while staring at the place where the gas can landed. When the can exploded, Eddie looked up to see bits of metal flying through the air. It was only then he realized the other man was no longer standing there.

Eddie watched the firemen put out the fire and eventually he crept back to his house and into his bed. His girlfriend Valerie stirred slightly as Eddie tried to fall back asleep, but sleep wouldn't come. He got up and made some coffee. As he was pouring his first cup, the phone rang. It was Achiel.

"Heard you had a fire," said Achiel.

"Yeah," said Eddie. "I was going to call you in a little bit."

"No need. News spreads fast around small towns."

"No, not about that. I figure you already heard," said Eddie. "I was going to see if I could work out of your shop for a while, until I figure everything out."

"No," said Achiel.

"No?"

"I had a fire, too."

"What?"

"Shop burned completely out. It's the damnedest thing."

"Both welding shops in one night?" Eddie said incredulously.

"I guess."

"Wow," Eddie said. He wasn't sure what else to say. He was completely mystified by this whole thing. Who would want to burn down the only two welding shops in town? As best as he could figure, he didn't have any enemies. Well, at least not any that would resort to arson.

"What's your excuse now?" Achiel's voice shook Eddie out of his thoughts.

"Excuse for what?" Eddie asked.

"Not re-enlisting."

So, there it was, another instance where Achiel was probably the guilty party, but no one could prove it. Signs at the fire obviously pointed to arson, but unfortunately for Eddie, there were also indications that he might have started the fire himself. No one could verify the late-night, or perhaps more properly early morning, phone call. He had done nothing to try to stop the fire himself, despite having a fire extinguisher and several buckets in his truck and a river full of water behind the shop. No one could vouch for Eddie's whereabouts after midnight when Valerie was asleep. While there were no charges brought against Eddie, the insurance company was not going to pay out anything to reimburse him for his loss either.

Eddie tried to recoup his losses while Achiel headed overseas. The town commended Achiel's patriotism in the face of his tremendous loss of the welding shop. Achiel seemed to be taking it all in stride. Furthermore, he was seeking no damages from his insurance company.

"Why would I?" he said, when a reporter asked. "I'm headed back overseas to serve my country. Whoever burned that place down did me a favor. Now I have a clean break."

Eddie's claim that his friend had burned his shop down to get him to re-enlist only made Eddie sound crazy. Eventually, he became a regular at the bar, repeating the story of arson that other regulars at the bar only half-believed. His girlfriend left him. Then one night, drunk and walking home because his license had been revoked and his vehicle impounded from repeated attempts at drunk driving, Eddie was struck and killed by a semi whose driver thought he had hit a deer and didn't bother to stop.

LUCIA

What can I say about my husband? I met him in the factory. He was a welder, and I was on interiors. I was from Sicily, and he was from Belgium. We both lived through the war and knew what it was like to survive. This was important to me because no one here knew what it was like to live through a war. They only watched it on the TV or read about it in papers and books. They didn't know what it was like to be hungry because of the war.

His dad hated me, but he hated most people, so I didn't care. Wanted his son to marry a good white Flemish girl. He didn't like that my skin was dark—not black, but like I had a good tan all the time. He didn't like that one bit, but my Achiel didn't care. He loved me and married me, and his dad disowned him. That was it.

Back then, Achiel was a looker. Whew. He was. That hair. That smile. And those eyes. Blue, blue eyes. When I was growing up in Sicily, all the girls loved Sinatra and Crosby because of their blue eyes, but Achiel, he had *blue* eyes. Do you know, he told me once that if I went blind, he would give me his eyes? And he loved his eyes. His eyes were the most important thing to him. He could see things so far away. And so clear. He would read me signs as we drove and could make out the words before I could barely start to see the letters. He wrote to me from the Army saying he didn't even need a scope, but the Army gave him one anyway.

He was also very, very good driver. I'm sure his eyes helped with that. He could see things and knew how they worked, and other drivers were like that. He'd see them and know what they were going to do before they did it, and he'd cut that way and get around them. Always made me scared. Boy, he liked to drive fast though. He'd cut like this and turn and weave through spaces where I didn't think we'd fit. One time, the tire blew out on the highway, and he was jerking the steering wheel this way and that. We were hauling a trailer and didn't have that, what do you call it? Oh. Power steering. That was before the power steering. But we didn't crash or hit nothing.

He had a temper. When he drank it was bad, but he almost never drank, so that was good. But he had a temper anyway. When our first child was born and the nurse told me it was a girl, I was afraid to tell him. I made the nurse go tell him. But he surprised me. He was so sweet and asked if we could name her Sophie after his mom. His mom died before I ever met her. I didn't love the name Sophie and had hoped we'd name the baby after my mom or me, but Achiel asked so nice, and his mother always looked sweet in that picture Achiel had in his wallet. So, we had Sophie.

When our second came around, it was my turn to name the baby. I wanted to name it after my mom. Luciana. My mom was a wonderful person that I loved so much. But it turned out to be a boy, so I picked Lucas. My little Lucas looked just like my mom. He had her skin and her hair.

Seeing her here in my little boy just made me love my sweet little boy all the more. No surprise, Achiel did not like the name I chose, but the hospital was a safe place from Achiel's temper. I wasn't sure what would happen when we got home, but by then I think he forgot he was mad about it.

When Achiel's brother Ronnie died, Achiel went crazy. He fought people at work and everywhere. He got fired. Boy, he drank so much. And his temper. Now Achiel just had his dad, and they still weren't talking. When we had our third child, and it was a boy, Achiel named him Ronnie after his brother and that seemed to sort Achiel out.

Our last one, little Ruby, I don't know where she come from. I mean, I know. But I thought we were done with children, and then, another. The name, Ruby, was his idea. No one we knew had a name like that, it just come to him. And that was that.

He stopped the drinking, but then that thing with that girl started. She was one of Sophie's friends from school. She's the whole reason Achiel did what he did to her dad. Cliff. Now, that one was a drinker. Phew. I don't know that I ever saw him when he wasn't drunk or drinking. He was always going around causing trouble. Doing little things. Saying things he shouldn't. I'm sorry he died, don't get me wrong, but he was a bad one. Achiel and him never got on well and were always yelling at each other. We had property right next to Cliff's property. I wanted to sell that property, but Achiel kept saying he was going to build something on it. He had this idea of this big house on all this land. I kept saying, "We have a house and a bunch of land over here." But Achiel wouldn't hear it. He liked that property over there more, and he wanted to build the house himself. He'd walk around our house and point out this and that and say, "Whoever built this house was a damned fool. When I build our new house, everything is going to be level. And the foundation isn't going to have these cracks. And our doors are going to be solid wood, not this."

I don't remember what he called it. Something about particle? I don't know.

LUCAS

I helped cut down the trees. What ten-year-old boy would turn down a chance to use a chainsaw? It was '64, maybe? Ronnie was born that year, and Dad had just gotten home from Vietnam a year before. Old man Harper used to like to come hunt on our property. Dad somehow always knew when he'd be there. Dad would get his bb-gun with that Army-issue scope on it, and he'd set it alongside the cabinet between the kitchen and the dining room. Then later, we'd be doing whatever, and he'd casually stroll over, open the window, level the gun on the window frame (we had those windows where you could either raise the bottom frame or lower the top one, he'd always lower the top one), and take a shot. He'd adjust, shoot again, repeat, and then close the window, set the bb-gun down back against the cabinet, and come back to us with whatever we were doing. Mr. Harper never complained, so he must not have gotten seriously hurt, but it was Dad's way of saying, "I see what you're doing."

When Dad was in Vietnam, Mr. Harper hunted our land, and no one stopped him. Mom didn't care, and

Sophie and I were too young and too inexperienced with our guns to care either. I certainly wasn't the shot that dad was. Sophie was a good shot, but I think we all felt vulnerable with Dad being away. Anyway, the trouble started while Dad was gone. As the story goes, Blackie (our family dog) was in the brush one day while Harper was hunting on our property, and I guess Harper thought Blackie was a deer. Maybe Harper knew it was Blackie all along and wanted an excuse to kill our dog. Blackie could be a bit of a nuisance as he roamed free and didn't listen to anyone except for Dad.

When Dad came home from the war, he noticed Blackie was missing right away. He did his usual whistle, that high-pitched thing he could do with his fingers that Blackie usually responded to immediately, but Blackie didn't come. I was the one who had to tell him, and somehow, even though I had nothing to do with it, I got the beating. This was always the way with him. He always killed the messenger. Then again, I was never his favorite. I got Mom's olive skin, and who knows where I got this curly hair from, which definitely didn't help. But, you know, there's a cousin that looks just like him. Plus, Mom had put up a stink about wanting to name me Lucas after her mom. She, as far as I know never really fought for anything, suddenly wanted to name her first son after her family and not after her husband. It must have surprised Dad because he didn't argue. Then again, maybe I didn't look enough like a Van Slyck for him to put up a fight about having a namesake of his own.

When my little brother Ronnie came around, the "oops" of the bunch, Dad was more intent on honoring his own dead little brother. It's almost funny to think about it now, but I remember one of those times he was beating me, he kept saying how Mom had an affair with some black guy and that's where I came from. The idea of Mom having an affair was ridiculous, but the claim was even more ridiculous coming from Dad, who himself actually had affairs. At least the one with that Ellis girl. Probably others. Anyway, after Dad got through beating me for Blackie being shot, he sat down with me and said he had an idea about how to get back at Harper.

It's weird. You'd think I would have hated him, but all I ever wanted was make him proud. I crawled under the cars with him when he went to change the oil. I learned how to weld by watching him. When he opened his mouth, I listened. So, when he told me his idea for revenge, and mentioned I could use a chainsaw, of course I said yes.

"This is going to take a little time to do right," he said.

He called Harper that night, and Mr. Harper came over to apologize. The way Dad was yelling at him, I thought Dad was going to kill him on the spot. Eventually they quieted down and talked normal, and Mr. Harper went back home. Dad walked into the living room and saw me sitting on the couch. He nodded at me and kept going down the hall.

Honestly, I kind of forgot about the whole thing by the time Dad finally came and told me it was time.

"For what?" I asked, and he shook his head. I followed him and decided I'd figure it out as I went. We went into the barn, and he handed me these big leather gloves.

"Put them on," he said. I did.

Then he pulled down the chainsaws, and we loaded them, along with the gas tanks, into the back of the truck. It took two days to cut down all the trees. By the time I cut through my third tree I was ready to be done, but I knew Dad didn't want to hear about how my hands ached or how my arms were tired, so I just kept going. We started close to the house first, and, as the day went on, we worked our way out toward the road. You'd think a neighbor would have seen us as they drove by, but if they did, no one said anything. I didn't see anyone either, but then again, I was trying not to get crushed by falling trees. And Dad, like with everything, didn't care. He had the attitude of a man who was supposed to be there cutting down trees. He acted just as natural as could be. When we were done, it was like one of those pictures out of a history book where the lumberjacks are standing around, and trees are felled everywhere in the now desolate landscape.

If this were any other dad—well, if this were any other dad, we wouldn't have done this whole thing in the first place—he would have thanked me for all my hard work and maybe rewarded me with my first beer. But Dad wasn't one for sentimentality. We went back to the house, put the chainsaws and gas tanks away, hung up the leather gloves, and went inside. I kept waiting for him to say something, but he didn't. Instead, he went into the bathroom and flossed his teeth.

He flossed his teeth after every meal. He was obsessive about it. He always said that flossing was more important than brushing.

"Do you think we had time to brush our teeth in Korea?" he would ask. "Hell no, but I flossed every chance I got. And look at my teeth."

He said the same thing about Vietnam. There were times when I swear he went days without brushing even after he got home, but he never skipped flossing.

The night we cut down all the trees, I'm not sure if he brushed or not, but I remember him flossing as I waited my turn for the bathroom. I had to piss so bad. I wasn't paying attention to much else, but I watched him meticulously work the floss between each tooth, then rinse the floss in the sink and hang it over the toothbrush holder.

Dad wasn't necessarily cheap, but he saw no reason to get rid of something if it still worked perfectly well or could be repaired. He was good with his hands and could fix most things, so we didn't throw away much.

I wasn't there when Mr. Harper finally came home from camping and knocked on the door, but Sophie was, and it's one of her favorite stories. The short version is that he came, knocked on the screen door, Dad walked by and laughed, then left him standing on the porch for a while. The way Sophie tells it, she could almost see the gears in Harper's mind turning trying to decide what to do.

After the trees, I helped with most of Dad's errands. Even if I had wanted to say no, it wasn't really like I could. We killed people's cats and dogs, dug up yards, burned things down, gutted deer and left the guts around on people's porches. I'm not proud of it, but at the time it was the only way to be with Dad when he wasn't angry or beating me. He loved the hell out of Sophie, but he never asked her to do any of those things. Dad never thought of Sophie as anything other than a girl, and even if he thought I was some kind of bastard freak, at least I was a man and supposed to do that kind of thing. Maybe he wanted to protect Sophie and didn't care if I was caught and arrested? We never were, but, you know, it's something I hadn't thought about before saying it just now. It might have been that he didn't want Sophie to end up like me, and in that sense, it worked. She turned out alright. Things could have gone better for me, but they could have gone a lot worse, too.

SOPHIE

She was my friend, so of course it disturbed me. Obviously, Miriam never told me she was fucking my dad. I found out like everyone else in our family, when Mr. Ellis came over and punched Dad in the face on Mother's Day. Mom's family was there. Everyone was sitting at the table. When the door opened, we just assumed it was someone we'd forgotten about who had been invited and was showing up late. Mom started to get up, probably feeling bad that we'd started to eat without whoever it was.

It happened so fast. It wasn't a very good punch. I'd gotten in my share of fights and hit better than he did, but Dad wasn't expecting it.

"You son of a bitch!" Mr. Ellis said. "You fucked my daughter!"

Dad didn't say anything. He just rubbed his cheek where a bruise was forming, and it had split open. Blood smeared onto his hand. What could he say? Either Mr. Ellis was drunk as usual and needed to calm down, or Dad actually was responsible. But Mr. Ellis started to cry and made it easy on Dad by leaving on his own and driving away.

As you can imagine, Mr. Ellis' visit changed the tone of the dinner. We finished eating in silence. Mom and her family wouldn't look at Dad, which wasn't really all that unusual, but I couldn't stop staring at him. He just sat there, pushing food around on his plate, looking all thoughtful. The ham at the end of his fork plowed through the vegetables and skimmed across the gravy from his potatoes.

I'd never seen anyone hit Dad and get away with it. But then, Dad didn't always get back at people right away. In fact, he was probably sitting there planning his next step. If what Mr. Ellis said was true, and I was pretty sure it was, Dad wouldn't have any reason to take revenge on Mr. Ellis. This wasn't like the time when Dad killed the Rogers' dog and left it on their front porch because they couldn't keep their dog on their property and Dad was tired of stepping in their dog's shit. The only thing Mr. Ellis had done was embarrass Dad at a family meal by announcing something he had done wrong. Despite the wrong being committed by my dad, I was sure he would find some injustice in it and Mr. Ellis would end up paying for it.

Finally, Dad set his fork down, got up from the table, and went to his room. Mom got up quietly and did the dishes and poured coffee for her family. They sat there drinking their coffee in silence like nothing had just happened, and that's how I knew it was all true. How could Miriam never tell me? Worse, how could she do that with my dad!?

Lucas was probably too little to understand it all, and Mom was pregnant with Ronnie, but I immediately wondered if Mom was going to divorce Dad. Back in 1964, people didn't get divorces like they do today. She was Catholic, and he was, just what was he? He never went to church. I never saw him do anything religious at all. Mom went to church every Sunday, and still does to this day. But Dad, I don't think he believed in anything but himself.

Back at the table, my mom and her family were now talking quietly over their coffee, speaking in Italian as they often did, and I couldn't follow. I could only pick up bits and pieces that they weren't happy about "him," but I couldn't string together enough of the Italian words and phrases to make sense of what was going to happen. Would we move in with my mom's family in Livonia? What school would I go to? I had just started high school. I had friends. If we moved, I wouldn't know anyone. Then again, did I really want to go to a school where people would eventually find out about my dad and Miriam? What would everyone at school say?

My mind drifted away from the Italian conversation taking place at the table back to memories of Miriam and me. She was one of the few friends who ever came over to play. Sometimes Mr. Ellis would bring her over in their station wagon, but more often we took turns riding bikes to each other's house. Dad always talked about how one day we'd have a house on the property closer to the Ellis house, and I always thought that would be great. The other property was practically across the street from them, and Miriam and I would be able to play whenever we wanted.

In the meantime, Miriam and I had learned to navigate the dirt road between our houses. It was a long ride, but the dirt roads weren't too bad. I'd take Holmes down to Old Farm, and then Old Farm over to Tietz. Sometimes there was a dog by that house on the corner of Old Farm and Tietz, but usually he was tied up. If he was loose, and he got too close, I'd kick him in the nose or right under his chin. That was one thing Dad taught me that came in handy. He always said if I was going to be riding around on my bike, I had to know how to defend myself. I usually rode my bike to Miriam's because she had Barbies. I wasn't sure how the Ellises could afford to buy her all that stuff because it never seemed like Mr. Ellis worked. Miriam said it was because she was an only child, and her parents didn't have to worry about buying other kids presents. As much as I liked the idea of getting more toys, I loved having a brother (and then two when Ronnie came around).

When we were younger, we'd have tea parties, even though I'd never had tea before. It was fun to get all her dolls out and set them up around a table. Sometimes we put water in the cups, and other times we'd just pretend to pour and sip. Sometimes her dad would come in and join us. Even then I knew he was a drunk because Mom and Dad always complained about Mr. Ellis' drinking, but he was always nice to me. He'd sip the tea and play along with whatever we were doing. Mrs. Ellis would be there sometimes and sometimes not. She had a job, but honestly, I can't remember what it was. We were like a big happy family, and Miriam was like my twin.

Tea parties didn't last forever, and we moved onto listening to music and dancing and talking about boys. Back then everyone loved Elvis Presley. Miriam had all his records. I preferred Johnny Cash and The Kingston Trio. Dad liked Johnny Cash, too, so I listened to his records over and over again. When I wanted to hear the Trio, I had to borrow 45s from kids at school or wait for the songs to be played on the radio. Once I borrowed Douglas Massey's 45 of "O Ken Karanga" and wore out the B-side with "Where Have All the Flowers Gone?" Doug didn't mind too much because he thought "O Ken Karanga" was a hoot and "Where Have All the Flowers Gone" was a downer.

If I had money like Miriam, I would have bought my

own copy to listen to again and again. We didn't get paid to do chores, Mom and Dad didn't have the kind of money for an allowance for us. When I did have money, from a birthday or something, I would save it for something special. I didn't know what that something special was, but I knew I'd know it when I saw it. When I first heard "Love Me Do" on the radio, I knew that was it.

Miriam loved "Please Please Me" but said "Love Me Do" was too "out there." I'm still not sure what she meant by that. After seeing the Beatles on the television, Dad made it clear that he was not a fan of the Beatles and "all this noise." I, however, was most definitely a fan of them. Especially George. His eyebrows made him look so serious, and I loved his voice and how he could play that guitar. We only had one record player in the house, and if I wanted to hear "Love Me Do," I was going to have to spend my savings on it and make sure Dad didn't hear me playing it.

Sometimes when I was over at Miriam's, Mr. Ellis would go into town. Occasionally, he'd ask us if we wanted to go. When we were younger, we wanted to go get candy from the store. Once we started liking music, we always went to the record store. It wasn't a record store like you're probably thinking of though. It was like a part of another store that happened to sell records. And they weren't organized into all these different categories, they were just alphabetized. After I made the decision that I was going to buy the Beatles' record, I made sure to take all my change with me every time I went to Miriam's.

I must have gone over there five or six times before her dad finally asked, "I need to go to town. You girls want to come?"

And boy did we ever. Miriam was dying for "Sugar Shack" and "Surfin' USA," and I desperately wanted "Love

Me Do." It turned out to be a great day because the store actually had a copy of the record I wanted, and it didn't even cost me all my money.

I couldn't wait to play it when I got home. Mr. Ellis drove us back to their house, but rather than staying to listen to what Miriam bought, I raced the rest of the way home on my bike. Mom and Dad were over at Nana's house in Livonia, so I played my new record over and over again. I didn't know when they were going to be home, but for once I didn't really care. When it started to get dark, I hid my record and put everything right back where it had been. Mom and Dad got home a little after eight, and for once they both seemed really happy. They were laughing, Mom was still pregnant with Ronnie, and Dad was holding Lucas' hand as they came through the door. That was the first weekend in May 1964. Two weeks later, it was Mother's Day, and Dad was getting punched in the face.

RONNIE

By the time I turned fifteen, Dad had already been in prison for four years for the incident involving Clifford Ellis. I think I missed Dad more than anyone else, but then again, I was so much younger than Sophie and Lucas. Sometimes I'd find myself thinking about him and remembering shooting at the range, or hunting, or how good he was with his hands. He'd call sometimes, and he wrote, but his writing was hard to read. I think he sometimes paid someone to write his letters because the handwriting was different and clearer.

At first, Mom took us to visit him every month or every other month. We always made a point of going on big holidays, his birthday, and Mom liked to go on their anniversary. By the time I turned fifteen, we were only visiting maybe twice a year, and he called and wrote a lot less. Generally, he only called when he wanted something. Usually, he needed some money in his commissary account, or asked about how the fight with the builders who were supposed to be building our new house was going, or sometimes, if I answered the phone when no one else was around, he'd ask me to keep an eye on Mom. He wanted to know if she was seeing anyone and if she stayed out after work and that sort of thing. She wasn't and didn't, so it was easy to answer him truthfully. I didn't feel like I was really spying on her by answering Dad's questions about her whereabouts.

I never knew what to tell him about the builders, so if he started asking about them, I just passed the phone to Mom. Just before he was put away, the foundation for the house on the property near the Ellis property had been poured. Dad didn't like the work the builders did and tried to sue them to make them redo it. Well, at first, he wanted them to redo it, but later he wanted them to redo it and refund his money. After he ended up in prison, I think the builders didn't take him seriously anymore and ignored his letters. He had to tell Mom what to say and get her to go and talk to them, and then she had to deal with the courts. She never felt comfortable in front of people like that, but even behind bars Dad had a way of making people do what he wanted, especially Mom. Eventually, we lost the court case, which meant we had to pay their legal fees and deal with Dad being pissed about the shitty foundation. Of course, eventually we lost the property, too. But that came much later.

Dad called on my fifteenth birthday, which I thought was nice, but then I realized he forgot how old I was.

It was hard knowing what to say over the phone to someone you might never see again.

He kept asking me when I was getting my license and if I was going to drive his '70 Nova. I didn't know what the right answer was. Was he going to be mad if I said I was going to drive his car? Or would he be mad if I said I didn't want to drive his Nova? I didn't think I could win, so I told him that Sophie gave me two records for my birthday. She and Dad used to listen to music together, so I thought maybe it was a safe topic. But he didn't care that she gave me John Cougar's *John Cougar* album, or the Cars' *Candy-O*. I shouldn't have expected him to understand why the Cars or John Cougar mattered to me.

The Cars album wasn't as good as their first one, but wow the art on the cover was sexy. The model, Candy Moore, she was a looker. I tried to find out more about her, but we didn't have the internet back then, and the librarians weren't very invested in helping me find information about a model who posed for art on a record by the Cars. The song "Candy-O" was pretty good, but I played the first song "Let's Go" and the last song on the second side "Dangerous Type" more than anything on that album. I guess Sophie had seen the Cars live and they had played some of the new songs. She said the songs were much better live than they were on the album. Anyway, she knew how much I loved their first album and figured I'd like this one, too. She was always good to me.

The real prize from that birthday was the John Cougar record, even though he couldn't seem to make up his mind about what he wanted to be called over his career. First, he was Johnny Cougar. I guess the record company made him go by that. Then he reinvented himself as John Cougar, which is when I first heard about him. Then he became John Mellencamp, then John Cougar Mellencamp, and now I think he's back to John Mellencamp. Regardless, in 1979, he was John Cougar, and, man, could he rock. I don't even know how many times I played "I Need a Lover" that year, or years since, but it's safe to say it was my theme song before I really knew what a "lover" was. I just liked the way it sounded. He took the sound of the Cars and blended it with something that was more like Springsteen or the Rolling Stones and made, in my mind, the perfect song. Even today when I hear it, it gives me goosebumps. There are only a handful of songs that do that for me. When I did eventually get my license and drive Dad's Nova, I had an 8-track of *John Cougar* and later 1982's *American Fool.* I know everyone loved *Scarecrow*, but *American Fool* had "Hurts So Good" and "Jack & Diane." Even if the rest of *American Fool* sucked, which it didn't, those two songs would have sealed the deal for it being the greatest album of all time.

But I'm getting ahead of myself. One of the things I loved about "I Need a Lover" was that there are two versions of it. If you heard it on the radio or bought the single (with the fairly sleepy "Welcome to Chinatown," though the last minute of that song is pretty good), you got the 3 minute 44 second version. If you listened to it on the album, you got the full 5 minute 35 second version. What's missing in the single or radio version? An almost two-minute intro of rocking guitars. I remember blowing my friend's mind when I played him the album version. He'd never heard it before.

Anyway, that's what I remember about my fifteenth birthday. John Cougar, the Cars, and talking to Dad. After I told him about the albums Sophie gave me, Dad asked if Lucas was around, which I thought was weird because he usually didn't want to talk to him, especially after what happened at the trial. Maybe they were patching things up. I called for Lucas and then let the phone hang by its cord as I went to try to find him.

MINA

Look, I know we're not supposed to speak ill of the dead, but Achiel always knew how I felt about him, and him being dead doesn't change my mind. He was an evil, evil man. Yes, he had a tough life. He lived through the war. Me and my sister Lucia did, too. We didn't go around killing animals, burning things, and killing that poor man. Maybe the poor man was trouble, too, but he didn't deserve to be killed that way. That man's family. I can't help but think about the poor girl that Achiel ruined. And then to kill her father. It's nice that some of you have good things to say about Achiel. I mean, I can't believe anyone is *all* evil, but from what I saw, well, I can only say what I saw. And none of it was good.

And, even though nobody is saying it, I know you're all glad he died before he got out. But, I was worried. If you weren't, you are a fool. That man was going to do something. Who knows what. But he was going to do something when he got out. God saved us by stopping him before he could.

He fought in three wars. You can say that he wanted to

serve his country, but honestly, I think he just liked killing. Maybe the war in Belgium messed with his brain, or maybe his cruel father did. If you live through something like that once, like what we suffered, how could you volunteer to go and fight again? And again? The first I understand. He was just a child living there. He had no choice. He had to survive. I understand that. I did the same, survived. While we didn't have to carry guns because we were girls, well, Lucia was a woman, I was just eleven, I understood even then that you do things because it's war, and there's no choice. But Achiel moved to the States to escape, like we all did, and when war happened again, this time in Korea, he chose to fight. He didn't have to. He chose to. He said it was patriotic, for this new country of his. He left his wife with a brand-new baby—and Sophie, you turned out wonderfully, you know I love you—and he went off to fight on the other side of the world. Patriotic? I don't know. And, if that wasn't crazy enough, he went off to fight again in that Vietnam. And, what a mess that was. I'm certain he would have stayed longer, too, if he hadn't gotten hurt. Something about his back. Who does that? Nobody except someone who isn't right.

Sophie, Lucas, and Ronnie, I'm sorry, but even if you're not saying this, I know you're thinking it. It needed to be said. You all turned out fine and have lovely families. You know I love you with all my heart. But, I won't stand by and pretend this, this man, was something to be admired or that I miss him. He was dangerous and destructive. Good riddance.

RUBY

Hey, everyone. I have something to say, too. I know, everyone forgets about little Ruby. Just because I wasn't there when it all happened, doesn't mean I didn't hunt with him, too. Or have memories or things to share. No, I didn't cut the trees or kill anyone's pets, but you know who helped him pack shells? I definitely did. How about who cleaned up brush and worked in the garden? I know the garden is usually remembered as Mom's thing, but Dad loved it, too. Maybe he did it just for her, I don't know. But, I do know I spent hours out there with him crouched over pulling weeds. And, he was meticulous.

One of the times I got lazy and I'd pull a weed and then drop it, instead of putting it in the bucket. Man, that was a mistake. I'm not going to say he never hit me, but the way his eyes could cut through you made it so he didn't have to all the time. He could speak volumes with a glare. This time, it said: "What? Are you stupid? Pull a weed to leave it to grow right back, because you didn't want to walk a few steps, or carry a bucket?" I guess you learn to know what to expect after a while.

The same for when I overwatered the plants. I was just a kid, I didn't know there was such a thing as too much water. And, it was kind of fun to watch them float as the water puddled around them. At first the water would soak into the dirt, and then it turned muddy and finally it would pool. I was just playing in it. Having fun. Don't remember how old I was.

But, to this day, we have a beautiful garden. No weeds and the right amount of water.

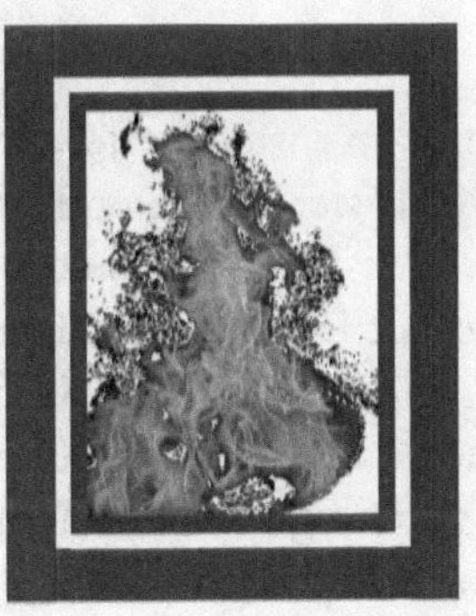

PART II: IN THE CAR

It was easier not to visit, not to take his calls, not to write letters. It was easier to pretend her father had died, or ran off, or maybe just never existed at all. Her father-in-law filled any void her father might have left, and he did a great job of it. Gerry's father, Reuben, was a kind gentleman. When you spoke with Reuben, he listened, and it was the kind of listening where he actually heard you. He wasn't just waiting for you to take a breath so he could interrupt with some story of his own. Reuben caught your eye and held it and actually listened. There could be twenty other people in the room demanding his attention, but if he started a conversation with you, he finished it and put everything and everybody else on hold. That was the kind of listener he was. It was so different from her actual father. With Achiel, it was always hard and there was always an angle being worked. Once he was incarcerated, he only listened to gather information to use later. And when he did use that information, it was almost always to gather more information and, ultimately, to hurt someone with what he learned.

Each time Sophie decided to visit Achiel, first she had to find out which prison he was in because the State moved him around. For the first several years, he was mostly stationary, but after, that it seemed like the State was always moving him around. At first, it was just Jackson State Prison. Technically, it was called Michigan State Prison in Jackson, or Southern Michigan Correctional Facility, but Sophie just thought of it as Jackson State. Achiel was there until 1983, just a few years after the riot, but after that, if she wanted to see her father, which admittedly became a less and less frequent desire, she had to call the Michigan Department of Corrections and ask. She did this so seldom that when she did, she forgot to prepare herself for the barrage of questions. Name? Date of birth? She hadn't celebrated his birthday in so long, the date slipped from her memory, she'd have to look it up. What's his MDOC number? She never had this number handy, but she imagined that loved ones who really cared about their family member would have it memorized. Clearly, she wasn't one of those. And then, only after all the questions were answered, would they provide her with the information she requested: the location of her father.

The visiting hours varied from prison to prison, and based on his behavior in the prison, his number of allowed visitors varied as well. One year, she found out where he was (Mt. Pleasant), filled out the forms, arranged her schedule to make it work, and made the drive (two and a half hours), only to be turned away because he had already exceeded his number of visitors for that month, and the month wasn't even over yet. While she was upset, she was more baffled at just who was visiting him in prison? She knew Lucas and Ronnie occasionally reached out, but what were the odds that they had both gone this month, multiple times, without telling her?

There was also the time when the MDOC staff abruptly announced the need to terminate the visitation hours. Sophie inquired as to why, but there were no answers offered. Instead, one of the guards directly asked her, "How far did you travel to come to visitation hours?" Sophie thought it was an odd question to answer her own question with.

"Over two hours."

The guard shook his head and said, "In miles."

The answer was 140 miles. The guard explained that if she had traveled 400 miles or more, then she would have been allowed to stay. Since she hadn't, it was time for her to go. There were no other explanations offered, and Sophie was escorted out of the prison.

In order to visit Achiel, Sophie had to fill out a CAJ-103, in order to appear on the CAJ-334. The first was the visiting application, and the second was the list of approved visitors. The CJA-103 wasn't a big deal. It only required basic information about a visitor, their relationship to the prisoner, the prisoner's name and number, and whether or not the visitor had any outstanding warrants, was on parole, or was a former inmate. Sophie wasn't sure why the last questions were relevant, but as they didn't pertain to her, she didn't give it too much thought. With those forms filled out, the correct prison identified, the drive made, she then had to provide identification (a driver's license would do). If she wanted to take Anton with her, then it was a little more complicated because then Sophie had to remember to get Anton's "certified true copy" of his birth certificate from the safe deposit box and take it with her.

At first, Sophie felt like it was her duty to take her child to visit his grandfather Her son had a right to know his grandfather, didn't he? So, she went through the steps to make it happen. She sat there in the visiting room with her son on her lap and her father across the table from her.

"Look, Dad, I brought Anton to see you," she'd say.

Achiel would smile briefly and look at his only grandchild, and then begin the usual routine. He complained about the food. He complained about being put in solitary. Whatever landed him there was never his fault. He complained about the gangs in prison. He complained about his cell. He always needed a new lawyer. He was always working on a new appeal. He never failed to complain about some aspect of his original trial. He accused Lucia of cheating on him, of stealing money from him, of being glad that he was away in prison. He called Lucas terrible names and threatened to kill him when he got out. He berated Sophie for not coming more often to see him. The only person to escape his wrath was Ronnie, but Achiel also didn't ask about him or express any interest in how Ronnie was doing, or what Ronnie was doing, or anything about his youngest child. In short, visiting her father was an exercise in emotional abuse, and Sophie always left feeling drained.

It was on the ride home from such a visit (really, they were all such visits), that she decided Anton really didn't need to know his grandfather. What did Achiel have to offer anyway? Wouldn't her son be better off not knowing about him? She still went occasionally by herself, though the visits became annual, then slipped to every three or five years and then not at all. The further apart the visits became, the guiltier she felt and the harder it was to overcome the awkwardness imposed by absence and time. There was still the question of her children, his grandchildren, but she found the less she thought about her father, the less she saw him, the less he was likely to come up in a conversation.

Sophie realized that she was, in a way, keeping Achiel in her life by visiting him and invoking his name. When the twins came along, a year after Anton's sixth birthday, she didn't bother mentioning her father to them. They were the first round of Van Slycks (well, technically Carpenters, since she took Gerry's name) who had no memory of the patriarch of the family, and when they were older, they never asked because they had no reason to. It wasn't exactly like Sophie was hiding anything from them. She always promised herself she'd tell the truth if they asked, but they never did. If Anton had memories of her father, or going to the prison to see him, she really didn't know. Anton had been four when Achiel committed murder, went to trial, and then to prison. Sophie knew she had memories from early in her childhood, but it was hard to know which were actual memories and which were memories formed by people showing her photographs and telling her stories.

Then, one day, Anton came home from school and found her crying in her room. She hadn't even heard him come home, and then suddenly she felt his eyes staring at her.

"What's wrong?" he asked.

He was ten. It might have been a bit young to completely unburden herself on him, but he asked, she needed to tell someone, and he was there. So, she did.

"I had jury duty today, and I was standing there in front of the judge and all the jurors. Did you know they choose a bunch of jurors and then eliminate them until they have the final number they need for the trial? I didn't know that. This was my first time being called for jury duty. The judge calls a juror's number, and then they ask some basic questions. Each lawyer has a chance to ask additional questions, and then they decide if there are objections to that juror or not. So, they asked me if I knew anyone who was convicted of a felony, and I had to say yes. Do you know what a felony is? Well, I guess I'd describe it as a serious crime. There are misdemeanors for things like stealing, and then there are felonies. Felonies are really serious. Like murder."

Then Anton replied, "You know someone who's committed a serious crime?"

Sophie had to answer, "Yes."

Anton asked the next logical question which was, "Who?"

Sophie found her cheeks reddening, just like they had in court when asked, "What relationship did you have with the felon?"

So, she told Anton about her father, about the murder, about him being in prison. She watched his ten-year-old face absorb the information, and then she waited for him to say something, or to ask a question.

She was not expecting him to ask, "But, why are you crying?"

Why was she crying? That was a good question. Was she crying because she felt like the people in the courtroom would judge her based on what her father had done? Was she crying because being asked that question summoned old memories that she hadn't ever fully resolved or processed? Maybe she was crying because she felt humiliated in front of people from her community, even though she knew none of them, and feared they'd go home to their families and spread her family's secret? Maybe she felt relieved because she had an opportunity to speak the truth, instead of hiding it away and telling white lies to avoid what she feared to be awkward conversations the truth would inspire?

She pulled her son to her in a hug and kissed him. Her

tears wet his neck, and his hair stuck to her wet eyelids and lashes. Holding him made her feel better as she tried to come up with an answer to his question.

ACHIEL (1946)

You've told me about Sicily during the war, but now I want to tell you about Belgium. For instance, did you know my last name is Dutch even though we are from Belgium? The "van" basically means "from." A lot of people with van-names have names about where they are from like "from the great river" or from a city or region. For many, the "van" was a status thing, like royalty or wealth. Not us. Our family name meant "from the dirt." Kids would make fun of us, but Dad always told me, "Not dirt. It's grit. And not *from*, it's more like *of*. We're a family full of grit." Then he'd send me out to show the kids my grit. I'm not sure if it's true or not, I never learned to speak Dutch, we spoke German and sometimes French in the house, but it's a good story.

Before my dad and I moved here, my parents had lived in Belgium all their lives. I had two older brothers, but they both died in the first war. It was right at the end of the war. Louis and Tobias. I'm surprised I remember their names. I never met them. I think they were in their early teens when they died. Maybe fifteen and thirteen? It was stupid, really. They went to go see the "wire of death." The Germans had built a fence to keep people from leaving into the Netherlands, and I guess my brothers just wanted to see it. They got too close. Not close enough to be electrocuted, but close enough to anger a German soldier. He shot them. Dad told me that the soldiers brought the bodies by the house and tossed them on the porch and said, "Trying to escape." But they weren't.

It was hard on my mom and dad, and Dad told me he knew it was no time to try to have more kids. So, they waited. In fact, they had forgotten all about wanting to have more kids when I finally came along. It wasn't unheard of, but it was very uncommon that a thirty-nine-year-old woman would have a child, and yet there I was. Imagine their surprise when little Ronnie came along almost three years later.

Like I said, by the time I was born, my parents were old and tired. They had parented two boys only to see them die young by war. They had grown old grieving this loss, and now they were suddenly thrust back into a daily reminder of the two boys they'd already lost. Because they were old and tired, they had no patience for certain aspects of parenting, things like crying and feeding their children.

Basically, crying was not tolerated by my parents. If I did cry, my parents would yell, or hit, or slap, or spank. At first, this brought about another round of crying or intensified my screams. Eventually, I would lose my voice, and soon enough, I learned to stop crying entirely. I accepted food when it was brought to me, and everything else I learned to get for myself. As a result, I learned to walk at an early age. Likewise, I caught onto language very quickly but used it sparingly as my father was quick to tell me that I spoke too much—and so I learned to read instead. Ronnie was a sweetheart. He never complained about anything. I don't remember him crying as a baby, not even once. I guess that's why my mom and dad loved him more. He grew up to be a quiet man, but you've met him, so you know.

When the depression hit Germany, it spread to Belgium and all surrounding areas. Our currency was worthless and was often used as toilet paper. I remember wiping my butt with it when I was toilet trained. We used to trade for things instead of buying things with money. Just like everyone else, we were poor. Dad was old, so no one wanted to pay him to weld like they used to, plus who could afford to pay for welding anyway? Even if he had been young, there were no jobs for anyone.

Mom taught me my next life lesson: *Nimm, was du magst, iss, was du nimmst.* Do you know that one? Take all you want. Eat all you take. Those were my mother's words, as she taught me to steal. Since I was so young, my little body was perfect for slipping under shopkeepers' tables in their stores and making off with goods while the shopkeepers were busy elsewhere. At first, I only stole bread and food. Quickly it advanced to watches, jewelry, and other items of status. No one had money to pay for things, but we could trade for food and other things. Some of the things we kept in a hiding place for when things were better. My parents thought we could sell the stuff and find a better house. In the meantime, I had learned a way to earn the respect of my parents, finally something I was good at.

World War II marked some drastic changes for my family. First, my mother died. She went to bed one night in December of 1939 and never woke up. At least that's what Dad told me and Ronnie when it happened. When we were older, he told me she killed herself with gas.

My father always had been a hardened bitter old man, but now he was angry. He cursed God, and he turned his back on religion. I continued to steal for my father, but I could never do good in his eyes. Every night I would return, and every night I was beaten. Often my father was drunk, but it hurt more when he wasn't. I would look at my father and wonder how I had failed, and what I could do to please him—what I could do to stop the beatings. So, every day, I stole more and more.

The Germans returned to Belgium on May 10, 1940, and by May 28, 1940, Belgium was conquered. I had turned 14 only a few weeks prior, but I was big for my age. I hold the honor of fighting both sides of the war. The first was as a soldier for Belgium when I was too young to really realize much of what was going on. What I did realize was that I didn't have to steal to support my parents anymore, and that the army gave me a gun and permission to kill. The second was when Germany plowed through Belgium. I spoke fluent German, so why not? I fought against the Allies, I shot the Allies, and I murdered Jews. I just did what I was told.

At first, the Germans had me rounding up the Jews living in Belgium. My group knocked on doors, looked in barns, and found as many Jews as we could find. Then the Germans sent all of the Jews to Auschwitz via the Mechelen transit camp. I didn't know what was going to happen to them, and I didn't care. It was a job where people respected me, and I was good at it. I shot some people who tried to escape and killed a few others who resisted. My parents had hardened me by years of abuse, and I was used to living rough in the streets—fighting for food, stealing what I needed. Life as a German soldier was second nature to me. Plus, Dad had already taught me to hate Jews and homosexuals and those Gypsies anyway, so it didn't take much for me to kill them. It was a job, and I was getting paid. I'm sure you had people like me in Italy.

As the war dragged on, I got tired of the higher ranks pushing me around, so one day I walked away and went home. By then my dad was looking for a way to get to the United States, so I found a way to sneak Dad, Ronnie, and me out of the country and to the US.

I know Dad can be hard, but he's just proud. He wants his grandchildren to be all Flemish, and not just half. I think he's coming around. It helps that Ronnie loves you and thinks you're great.

Do you remember our first dance? I'll never forget it. I know it wasn't anything fancy. It wasn't in some big hall or with a live orchestra. I love remembering you coming over to Dad's house. He was out somewhere. It was just you and me and Ronnie. Ronnie was the one who suggested it.

"How about a dance?" he asked.

And you thought he meant you and him. That was so funny. He moved the chairs out of the kitchen, so we'd have room, and practically pushed me out there with you. Then he turned on that Glenn Miller 78 he had. Miller died the year before, right at the end of 1944, so that record came out after he was gone. Anyway, Glenn Miller on the phonograph, I'm holding your hand, and everything else just faded away.

ANTON (1999)

Shit. Looks like everyone's slowing down. Must be some kind of accident. Ugh, it takes forever to get there on a good day. I guess it's going to take even longer now.

Grandpa? What about him? Oh, Grandpa Van Slyck. Sure. I had to figure it out on my own, but after I knew the basics, then they started to tell me stories. I mean, I was told the same stuff you guys were told. At least I assume so. Grandpa did something bad and was in prison. I don't think that Mom and her brothers were trying to hide it from us. I'm sure it was hard for them and probably painful to go through again. I can only imagine what it was like trying to live a normal life after that. In a small town, that stuff spreads so quickly, and people have long memories for stories like that. Plus, you know when someone asks you, "Tell me about yourself" like in an interview or on a date. It's hard to see yourself objectively enough to be able to answer and harder to know what they're looking for, or at least the basic idea of what they want to talk about. I remember asking Mom to "tell me about Grandpa," and she did, but I wasn't asking the right questions. Of course, it's hard to ask the right questions when you don't have the information to begin with.

Anyway, let's see. I heard Mom and Uncle Lucas talking about Grandpa and what they were going to do when he got out, and that caught my attention. I wasn't exactly eavesdropping on them because they knew I was there, but I just made it look like I was more engrossed in my book than I really was. They were talking quietly, so I didn't catch it all, but the gist was that he was up for parole in 2002, and they were starting to freak out. Lucas made it very clear that he was nervous because of what happened during the trial, and Mom didn't do anything to ease his concerns. They both agreed Uncle Ronnie didn't have anything to worry about, but Lucas had reason to be nervous, and Mom didn't know where she stood in the whole thing. That was about all I heard that day, but hearing them talk about the trial made me realize I should be able to go to a court and find the transcripts from the trial. So, I did.

Did you know Grandpa had an affair with a young girl? Yeah, I learned that from the court transcripts. Pretty fucked up. Worse, it was one of Mom's friends. I don't remember her name, but she was the daughter of the guy Grandpa killed. I guess he was having this affair, and then Grandma found out, and he ended it. The daughter told her father. The father pressed charges, and Grandpa went to jail for like a year for statutory rape. Yeah. Well, she was fourteen, or thirteen, and he was, uhm, thirty-eight? I think. I didn't look for the transcripts for that trial, but if I go back to the court I probably will give it a quick read to see if there's anything else interesting. The rape came up in the murder trial because the attorney claimed it was Grandpa's motive. The father, wish I could remember his name, put Grandpa in jail, and Grandpa wanted to make him pay. I mean, he said as much right during the trial. I remember the line from the transcripts:

"And Mr. Van Slyck, isn't it true that you said, and I'm quoting from the transcripts, 'when I get out I'll still know where you live'?"

Not precisely a threat, but it doesn't require reading between the lines too carefully. I know, he must be a psycho. Of course, Grandpa got out of jail, and it was ten years later before he killed Mr. Ellis. Oh yeah. That was his name. Clifford Ellis.

I have some memories of Grandpa, not many though. I was only four or five when he went away. But, I remember thinking he gave shitty Christmas and birthday presents. It's superficial, but as a kid, that's what I remember. The gifts were cheap. You know, instead of a Hot Wheels car, they'd give me some knock-off that they bought at a local grocery store or something. The wheels were skinny, the cars were mostly plastic, and the axles always bent easily. I'm sure it was all they could afford, or maybe they just didn't see the point of spending more money on a toy for a kid that was probably going to break it, or lose it, or forget about it a few hours later.

I do have this memory of sitting on his knee and him bouncing me there and doing the horsey-ride thing. He really did have a nice smile when he actually smiled. The problem is, I'm not sure if I really remember that or it's just because I've seen that photograph. I feel like it's a real memory, but it's one of the few photos of him and me together, and so I don't know how many times I've looked at that photo.

Have you guys seen it? Oh, you should go through Mom's old photo albums. There's some interesting stuff in there, and some hilarious photos of her and Dad. That photo of me on Grandpa's knee is in there. Grandpa's smiling, and I'm clearly enjoying myself, but if you look over my shoulder, you can see Mom, and she looks very concerned. She is not having a good time. Knowing now what she knew about her father, I can't say as though I blame her for being nervous. Grandma and Mom always said he was very good with children. I guess I was at the right age because he seemed to be having fun with me.

We went up there to see them a few times a year, but it was a two-hour drive to get to their house, so we didn't go often. We'd go at Christmas, and birthdays, and sometimes Easter. I think. I remember a picture of me with an Easter basket at their house, so we must have gone at least once for Easter. I remember Mom saying that Grandpa was always at work when she was growing up, but he was always there when I visited with Mom.

He liked telling me stories when we visited. He told stories about cutting people's trees, or killing people's pets, or whatnot. His stories were crazy and as best as I can tell, occurred much earlier in his life. Like, maybe before the thing with the Ellis girl. Maybe that first trip to prison calmed him down. But, he killed Mr. Ellis in 1975, so I guess he hadn't calmed down entirely. Maybe he just bottled it all up. I'd love to ask him, but I am terrified of the idea of speaking to him. I think Mom would deeply disapprove. Plus, she always says how manipulative he is. She says he used to get them to do all kinds of crazy shit, and even from prison for murder, he has manipulated them over the phone. I mean, just look at how Ronnie and Lucas don't get along even today. You didn't know that? Yeah. It's not like Ronnie is Team-Achiel or anything, but he and Lucas definitely don't see eye-to-eye on the whole thing.

Well, it's because Lucas told the truth in the trial, and Ronnie lied. Look, Ronnie was ten, and he had to testify because he was there when Grandpa killed Mr. Ellis. Grandpa told both boys to lie. Ronnie did what his dad told him to. When he got up on the stand, he promised to tell the truth, and then gave the court the version of the truth that Grandpa had fed him. *It was an accident. Mr. Ellis had a knife. Grandpa tried to talk him down, but Mr. Ellis grabbed Grandpa's gun, and it went off. He fell back into the seat of his car.* When Lucas got up on the stand, he was twenty-one, not ten. He started to tell the same story as Ronnie, but then he started to cry.

The attorney asked him, "Mr. Van Slyck, what's wrong?"

And then Lucas told the court the whole truth. Exactly what happened. How Mr. Ellis came over to their property and started yelling at Grandpa. He didn't have a knife, and he didn't start to get out of his car, and he didn't grab Grandpa's gun. Mr. Ellis was just in his car, probably drunk, calling Grandpa names and accusing him of ruining his daughter's life. Which, honestly, I mean, clearly, Grandpa was guilty of contributing to that. Though, really, I'm not sure what happened to the girl. Maybe she turned out alright, but I can imagine how something like that would fuck you up for a while.

Anyway, the attorney asked Lucas why his story differed from his brother's account, and Lucas came completely clean.

"Because he told us to lie. He told us to tell that version of the story," Lucas said.

The attorney replied, "And Mr. Van Slyck, why should the court believe you? Isn't it true that you and your father don't exactly get along?"

Lucas said, "Right. He doesn't like me. But I'm telling you the truth."

Then, if there was any doubt about whether Lucas was telling the truth or not, Grandpa shouted—again, this is in the court transcripts, I can show you my printouts if you want—"When I get out, I'm gonna kill you," which, probably isn't the best thing to say in court.

Grandpa's attorney tried to smooth things over saying, "Mr. Van Slyck is obviously very upset because his oldest son has lied on the stand." From the guilty verdict that came a couple days later, it was obvious who the jury believed.

And that would be why Uncle Lucas has reason to be nervous when Grandpa gets out because he literally told him he had reason to be nervous when he got out. Mom didn't really do much during the trial, though she was called on the stand to talk about the affair Grandpa had with her friend. All that stuff was old news, so I don't think she is too concerned. Generally speaking, she isn't afraid of Grandpa. It's really just Lucas who needs to worry in three years when he gets out. Then again, Grandpa is seventy-three now. Maybe he's mellowed. I know Ronnie still talks with him sometimes, but I don't know if Lucas has visited or written. I guess we'll find out soon enough.

RONNIE (1975)

"Shouldn't we call the police?" I asked.

There was a lot of blood. If it was an accident like Dad said, then we should just call the police and let them know.

"You really think he'll get home and be alright?" I whispered.

The last time I remember seeing that much blood was when Dad hit a deer with his truck. It was just him and me in the truck, and I was seven, I think. We were coming home from the store with buns for the burgers that night. Dad was telling me how we'd go hunting soon. That was always my favorite thing to do with him. I wasn't old enough to get a license, but Dad didn't care. We'd probably just hunt on our property anyway.

I saw the deer, a buck and a doe, before Dad did. He must have been messing with the radio dial, or maybe he nodded off or something. It was dark. He might have been tired. You know how good his eyes are, so if there were deer on the road, he would have seen them if he was paying attention. The doe almost made it, but the truck clipped her backside. The buck was destroyed. The windshield was covered in blood. It was like blood had rained from the sky. Dad must have seen them at the last second because I was jerked back into my seat and the tires were squealing before we hit them. Then he swerved and steered over to the side of the road and jumped out of the truck. He ran back to where the deer were lying on the ground, and I chased after him. There wasn't much left of the buck, but I could hear the doe crying. You know that sound, it's a sort of goose honk mixed with a sheep's bah. It's such a sad sound. Dad returned to the truck and grabbed his pistol.

We had been going pretty fast. There was a dent in the driver's door where the doe's head had whipped around and smacked into it. The doe's hind end was mostly gone, but her front hooves were still pawing the ground trying to get up. Dad got up close because he didn't want to miss, and put her down. And then he fell down on his knees, on the side of the road, and cradled the doe's head and cried. I had never seen Dad cry before. Have you? I wasn't sure what to do, so I just went back to the truck and got inside and waited. After a few minutes, he came back to the truck and turned on the windshield wipers, but they just smeared the blood around for a while until he got enough wiper fluid on them. Then we went home. We didn't talk at all on the way home.

He cried for that deer, Lucas. Why didn't he cry when he shot Mr. Ellis? If it was an accident, shouldn't he have cried? And why was Mr. Ellis yelling like that? He was so angry. I've never seen anyone shout at Dad like that before.

LUCAS (1977)

Ronnie, this is a '69 Dart GTS. It's pretty much stock, but it has the 383 in it, not the standard 340, and I can pull about 300-horse from it. This is the perfect stretch of road for a quarter because there is hardly any traffic and no potholes. From here to the that green house down there, see that one? Right, with the mailbox that looks like a barn. You're going to run the stopwatch, but we should be able to get a 14.30 quarter and wind up going one hundred plus. You'll need to pay attention to the watch because the Dart is going to throw you back into your seat. This little thing is small for such a big engine, and just think, with a little work, I could always drop a 426 or 440 in it.

With Dad gone now, you know that Nova is yours, right? I figure we can work on it together. We have three years before you can drive on your own. It's just sitting there. Mom won't drive it because it reminds her of him. So, it's yours. Just start thinking about what color you want, and what kind of ride you want. The Nova is a little heavier, but it's still quick as hell. I mean, stock, you're talking 6.4-second 0-60, and 15-second quarter. We can do better.

Probably not as good as Mopar Muscle, ha! I kid, I kid. When it's all done, we'll have to drag and see who's better once and for all.

Ready? You got the watch, right? Okay.

What'd you think? We hit 110 before I eased it back. I've had it up to 140 before, and it felt like it had more left to go. It really threw you back. You should have seen yourself. It was hilarious. Did you piss yourself a little? It's alright if you did. That's why I have seat liners. Ha! Just kidding. Anyway, how are you doing with this all? You okay? Well, don't worry about it. I'll take care of you. If you need anything, just ask. I'm just down the road. No biggie. I know you don't need any help with kids at school. Ha, I've seen you take them down. I bet I can still out-bench you though. I'll drop you off, and we can see. Anywhere else you want to go while we're out? Okay.

Hey, and Ronnie, don't worry about Dad. He'll be fine. He's a tough guy. You did everything he wanted you to. You have nothing to worry about. When he gets out, don't worry about me. We'll work it all out before then. Do you want to go see him this weekend? I can take you if Mom isn't planning on going. Okay. Well, let me know. Love you, kiddo.

SOPHIE (1972)

My first concert was the Beach Boys in 1964. We couldn't get tickets to the Beatles, but Miriam got her dad to buy tickets for us to the Beach Boys. There was no way my parents were going to buy the tickets, but they said I could go if I managed to get some. We were both fourteen, back when we were still friends. It was a fun show. I always loved those surf songs, and the Beach Boys played a bunch of my favorites. They played "Fun, Fun, Fun" and "Little Deuce Coupe" and "Surfin' USA." If I remember right, they even did "Surfer Girl" and "In My Room." There were a few more that I can't remember. Maybe that goofy one, "Long Tall Texan," I think it was called. It was my first show at the IMA—I don't know what IMA even stands for, but that was a fun place to see a concert—and it was one of Brian Wilson's last shows before he stopped touring and just lived in the studio. He looked like he was having so much fun. I don't know why he'd want to give that up. I saw them again in 1967, but they just weren't the same without Brian. I think the Electric Prunes opened for them, you know that "I Had too Much to Dream Last

Night" band? That show was in East Lansing. I can't remember the name of the place. It was okay, but I liked the IMA better.

Flint is a little further away than Cobo, but I think the IMA is a better place to see shows. I used to spend all my money on records, but now I probably spend more money on concerts. I saw Jethro Tull and War last year. Hendrix in 1968. Johnny Cash in 1965 and 1967, and The Yardbirds in 1965, too. All good shows. Now that Hendrix is dead, I'm sure I'm supposed to say his was the best show. I was glad I got to see him, of course, and it was so sad that he died, but I really loved seeing Johnny Cash. He was so good. You know, it made me think of my dad. We used to listen to Cash albums together. He was one musician we could agree on. My dad would not have liked tonight's show. Ha. But I think it's going to stick with me for quite a while.

I didn't care too much for the opening acts. I know Buddy Miles was a drummer for Hendrix at one point, and I probably should have liked more of his music, but I didn't really care. He was too jazzy for me. I remember hearing "Them Changes" on the radio, but otherwise I wasn't familiar with the music. I love the drums, but I think a band really needs a lead singer that focuses on singing. And Nazareth? I'd heard "Dear John" before. It was pretty groovy. I really liked their organ. They did "Morning Dew," which I thought was a Grateful Dead song, but the lead singer said something about Bonnie-something and Neil-somebody? I'll have to ask around and see if anyone knows anything about their version. It's a cool song, but kind of creepy, and Nazareth really seemed to slow it down even more than I remember the Dead version being. It's funny what people choose to sing about. I mean, who would ever think to write and sing a song about people left over after a nuclear war?

But Deep Purple. Wow. I knew "Hush" of course. Everyone knows that one, right? Not everybody knows it isn't their song. Their version is so much groovier than the original. Joe South. In a way, his music and voice remind me of John Denver. Ugh, my dad loves him. John Denver that is. Anyway, Deep Purple. They really knocked it out of the park, and they didn't even play "Hush." They played mostly new stuff that I didn't know, but it was so interesting. And they stretched those songs out. It's exciting hearing new music like that. The lead singer said their new album just came out six days ago. That "Highway Star" song and "Smoke on the Water." How cool were they? My favorite though was "Space Truckin." I don't know what it meant at all, but it was something like twenty minutes long. They all had a solo.

Sometimes I have a hard time hearing the different instruments, even when it's live. I love when they do solos because then you can really pay attention to what each instrument is contributing to the song. When they all play together again, then I can hear each of them individually better. I loved the end, well the last six or seven minutes or so, when the guitarist was playing behind his back and playing it with his butt—that was funny—and then grinding the guitar against the amps. And the drummer kicked over the drums. It's wild to think about getting that caught up in the music. They should have saved that song for their last one, but they still played, what, four more songs? If they come to town again, we'll definitely have to see them again. Thanks for taking me. It really helped to distract me.

Oh, nothing. You don't want to hear about it again. Well, you could probably guess by now. Right. My dad. You're so lucky your dad isn't anything like mine. I'm still just trying to understand why my mom stays with him, especially after what happened last week. I mean, he literally had his hands around her neck. He was choking her, and I think he meant to kill her. How do you forgive that? I was the only one home, and I tried to stop him, but he was too big. Her face was, ugh, it makes me sick to remember it. I grabbed the phone book and tried to find the number for police—I guess we are supposed to get that new 9-1-1 thing next year or the year after—but I couldn't focus on the numbers. I just kept seeing her face. I screamed, and I guess that finally snapped him out of it. Mom was gasping and choking, and then she threw up on the floor, and he just walked out to the garage like nothing had happened.

On the way to the hospital she made me swear I wouldn't say what happened. She just kept saying, "He's my husband" over and over again. How can she stay with someone like that? Never mind all the other shit he's done, but that? That seems like it should definitely be the final straw. I just keep running over it again and again.

"Marriage is forever," she says.

"But Mom," I remind her, "you can get a divorce now. You don't need to wait until he dies."

"I'm a Catholic," she says, as if that's an answer. If there is a God, I can't imagine it wanting someone to be as unhappy as my mom is. I'm never going to let that happen to me. Sorry, I just keep going on and on. My family is so fucked up. You're probably tired of hearing about it.

I really did have a fun time tonight, and, during the show, I didn't think about my parents at all. It's just now that it's quieter, and the music isn't filling my brain, I keep trying to make sense of it all. Just take me home.

RUBY (1985)

"Somehow I never thought it would happen," I said. I wasn't sure if Kurt was listening, because he didn't respond right away. Maybe he was just waiting for me to continue? Looked like he was just looking out the window, watching the trees go by.

"What?"

When he spoke, his voice almost startled me. I had given up on him saying anything.

"The divorce," I said. "It's final today."

"Yeah," Kurt said. "I wonder why now? Shit, I would have dumped his ass immediately. Or even years ago, if half of what you told me is true."

"Why wouldn't it be?"

"What?"

I could feel him looking at me, even as I kept my gaze on the cars in front of us, picking my way through the openings.

"What do you mean, what? Of course it's all true. How could you think I would make it up? As if I could even imagine half that shit."

It was quiet for a minute. I let him sit there and I listened to the tires run over the ridges in the road. Felt the wheels grip and pull slightly left or right.

"Sorry, hon. You know I didn't mean that. I just mean, sometimes it's hard to believe."

"You didn't even have to live it. How do you think it is for me?"

"Right."

Silence again. Watching the mile markers as we pass.

"I think," I said, "it's like that boiling frog thing. You know, where the temperature rises slightly and the frog adjusts, but never jumps out of the pot. Until it's boiling and then it's too late."

"Gross."

I laughed.

"Yep," I said. "Gross."

"Do you think the divorce will change anything?" Kurt asked.

I hadn't really thought about that.

"Probably not?" I said, thinking out loud more than really offering a thoughtful response. "I mean, he's still locked up. They'll have to formally split up the finances. So, maybe that will mean something different. Probably not good. Then again, Dad kept a pretty tight rope on that, so maybe Mom will have more financial freedom?"

Kurt rubbed the stubble on the side of his face. I thought about turning on the radio. Not sure why we didn't have it on before, we almost always listened. But, now he had me thinking. Not about the divorce, but about Dad. Why he was the way he was. And how much of him was in me. Then a car cut me off and I felt that rage boil and had to laugh in spite of myself. That got Kurt's attention. I could see him turn towards me, trying to figure out what the laugh was about. Thought about letting him wonder.

He doesn't need to know every thought I have.

"You know, sometimes, when I'm in the car like this, I can't help but think about him."

"Your dad?"

I rolled my eyes. Not sure if Kurt saw me. But really, who else would I be talking about?

"If you ask anyone about him," I continued, "they'll say he was a great driver. He was really good behind the wheel. You've probably heard the story about the blowout, or him racing up the mountains, pulling trailers, backing into stupidly small spots. All that."

Kurt laughed.

"Yeah," he said.

"In the military, he drove tanks, too. Usually the family talks about his sharpshooting abilities, but they don't usually talk about his tank driving skills. I've never been in a tank, so I don't know what it's like."

"I think there are levers or something?" Kurt suggested. "At least that's what I remember from the war movies. Maybe one lever for each side?"

I nodded. That did sound familiar.

"The story I remember about Dad behind the wheel, that no one else talks about, is when we were going to grandma's for a holiday. Maybe it was Thanksgiving? Christmas? New Years? Not sure. There was snow on the ground, that's for sure. I remember. It was the kind of snow that almost blinding when you looked right into it. Kind of like that effect of going into hyperspace in space movies."

"Like *Star Wars?*" Kurt asked.

"Dad liked to go fast and he hated to be pinned in. So, you can only imagine how he felt on a day when it was snowing like that. Everyone going slow and boxing one another in. Well, he didn't like it. Ronnie and me were in the back. Not sure what he was doing, but I was just watching the snow. It had been a while since we had a storm like that. We were in the right lane and there was a car right next to us in the passing lane. I knew that was pissing Dad off. He hated when someone sat in the passing lane."

"I mean, he does have a point there. It is called a passing lane," Kurt said.

I knew he was just trying to show interest, but sometimes Kurt got on my nerves. Just let me tell my story and: Shut. Up. I debated about whether to continue or not. My silence clearly got to him.

"Sorry," he said.

"That car was along side us for a long time. I got to get a good look at the people inside. A family of four. Kids, like Ronnie and me, in the back. Parents up front. I could see them talking now and then, probably the parents yelling at the kids every now and then, because the dad would turn like he was trying to swat at them. Then I hear and feel our engine start to speed up. I look up at Dad and I see he's making a move for it. He's had enough of being boxed in. Stupid slow car in front of him, this yahoo sitting in the passing lane, and an opening."

I pause for a moment, to test the silence. Kurt passes the test, so I continue.

"Even as a kid, I can tell he doesn't have enough room. He backs off the motor a bit and the family is right next to us. I look behind us, and there's a car back there, too. Not sure what Dad's going to do, but I know he doesn't like this. You could just feel the agitation in the air. Like a vibration. No one in our car was saying anything. Then I knew what he was going to do. I don't know if Mom and Ronnie did, too, or if it was just me. But let's just say there was absolutely no surprise when dad just jerked the wheel to the left and rammed the other family car into the median.

"Oh my god," Kurt said.

I laughed, despite myself.

"That poor family had no chance, the roads were a sheet of ice and there was probably two feet of snow in the median. Maybe more. It had snowed recently and been plowed. I saw the dad look over at us, shocked, horrified, as they started to spin and then they just disappeared in a puff of snow. Dad passed the slow car in front of him, the two in front of that car, and then got over in the right lane."

"Jesus," Kurt said.

"No one said shit, but Dad whistled as he drove."

I didn't say it to Kurt, but as a kid and still now, I can't help but laugh. As much as I know I should feel bad for that family, I look at cars in my way and wonder how much of my dad is in me.

LUCIA (2001)

Thanks for driving me, Ronnie. I know you and him kept in touch. Did you know he was doing all this? All these appeals? All this paper? Looks like he was practicing his writing to make it better. Where did he get all this paper? This whole notebook is full of the letter A. Big A and little a. His writing was always better than mine, but I guess he wanted to make it look real good. Did you know about these appeals? I had no idea. I didn't know the food there made him so sick. He never did like juice. He always wanted to drink milk or water.

I remember him saying, "If I want juice, I'll eat the fruit and get the juice."

It looks like he said they made him drink juice, and it wasn't good juice. This says he was suing the prison for his cavities because they wouldn't give him floss. He always cared about his teeth. He flossed after every meal. Why wouldn't they give him floss?

This was his wedding ring. I guess he had it when he went in. Do you want it? You already have one of course, but I thought maybe you'd want something of his. I know you have his guns and things, but this was something special. You should have it. Maybe one of your boys will want it.

Look, here's another notebook full of letters. This has d and e. And this one is just f. He must have had a hard time with that one. So much paper. What am I going to do with it? Do you want it? It feels bad to burn it, but I don't know what to do with it. Do you want it? Do you want to read through and see if there's anything? I remember when we first met at the factory, and how we both didn't speak English so good. He was probably better, he always was better with languages, but we both learned a lot from the other workers. You had to, otherwise you fell behind. So, we learned, and once we decided, you know, that we wanted to spend time together, then we helped each other practice. And there was television, too. We didn't have one, either of our families, but the factory had one in the breakroom. We used to go and watch it. Of course, we listened to the radio. He used to like that *Saint* program. Did you ever hear that one? No, you wouldn't have. Sorry. It was like a Robin Hood guy, kind of like your Batman. Achiel used to love that show. Me, I liked *House Party*. There were always funny things on it. There were games and interviews and music. Linkletter, I think that was his name, was the host. Right, Art. Art Linkletter. He was a funny guy. We listened to those shows, and we learned how to speak English, and we'd laugh and laugh. The more we laughed, the more we realized we understood.

Learning to read and write was harder, and it was embarrassing to admit that you needed help. He, your dad, never wanted people to know. He would ask for help saying he didn't have his glasses. Phew. Your dad, needing glasses. Now there's a good one. At the factory he didn't have to read so much. His super told him what to weld, and your dad did it. He was so good at welding. You know he made that go-kart that you kids used to play with? And that hunting stand in the back of the property? That was him. He made those. Look, here are some letters that people wrote to him. I guess he kept all those, too. Most of these are yours. I should have written him more. And now he's gone.

Silly to worry about that when he's really been gone for most of my life. And the fight that he put up about the divorce. It was hard. I don't know if you remember that. Oh, okay. Sorry, I didn't know. You were at college and busy with your friends and work and that girl. I'm still sorry that she did what she did.

I find myself wondering what he would have been like if he got out. He only had eight months left to go. So sad. When you saw him, was he changed? Bald? Oh, that doesn't surprise me. He always had a (what do you call it?) widow's peak, even when he was young. He showed me those pictures. He was twelve and had a widow's peak. You'll probably be bald too then. Sorry. Such nice hair you always had. And him, too. Always nice and soft. Pretty color.

He always took such good care of himself. Doing those pushups and sit-ups and eating good, and walking, always walking. I guess he couldn't do much exercise in there. But I'm certain they let him go outside some. I'll say a prayer for his soul tonight. We need to start planning the funeral. A wake? How is that different? Oh. That does sound nice. We can just have people to the house. I don't know how many will come. His family is dead, I think. I only knew his dad and little Ronnie, but they both died years ago. He might still have family in Belgium, but I don't know how to find them. Will you say something at the wake? That'd be real nice. I don't know if Lucas and Sophie kept up with him like you did. I'm going to leave these papers for you to decide what to do with.

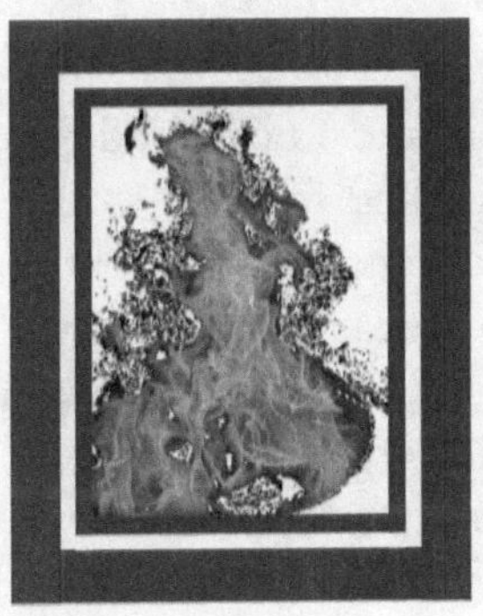

PART III: ON THE PHONE

At first, Ronnie and Lucas (and Sophie when she was visiting) actually looked forward to talking to their father. They thought he'd want to hear about how little Anton was doing, or how Lucas was liking his new job, or how Ronnie was doing in school. Maybe they would talk about how Gerry and Sophie were enjoying their first house, or how Lucas was recovering from his work-related back injury (he had a weak back just like his dad), or what Ronnie would name his new dog (spoiler alert: it would be Blackie, just like most of the dogs the family had owned, even though this one wasn't black). Maybe he'd want to hear about how the breeze in the trees sounded, or about the wildlife they had around the house. Maybe he'd want to just listen to their voices and hear them speak. Maybe he'd want to hear how his conviction had impacted them, and how they were coping with their father being in prison?

No, all he wanted was to give orders. He called to say he needed a new lawyer. He called to say he needed more money transferred into his commissary. He called to say he wanted Lucas to go to the courthouse and get copies of the transcripts. He called to tell Lucia to not pay the builders any more money until the whole ordeal with the halted-construction on the foundation was resolved. He called to tell Ronnie that he needed to keep an eye on his mother, and to report to him directly if she was seeing anyone. He called to tell Lucas to go out to the property with his Polaroid to take pictures of different landmarks and then to mail the photos to him. He called to inform them when he was transferred from Jackson to Koncheloe, from Koncheloe to Ionia, from Ionia to Coldwater, from Coldwater to Standish, and from Standish to Carson City. He would have continued to keep them up to date with his location, but after Carson City, it was obvious, even to him, that they did not care. Plus, at that point, the internet allowed for easy prisoner location. He called to complain about the food. He called to complain about The Hole— into which he went often. He called to complain about the inmates and the fighting. He called to remind them to come visit.

Because the focus was always on him, and each call typically resulted in orders and commands and sometimes yelling, cursing, and name-calling, the family became less and less interested in his calls. Sometimes when he'd call, whoever answered would hear the familiar "An inmate from …" message and drop the phone, letting it dangle by its cord and spin as it twisted and untwisted itself and holler, "Mom!" as he or she walked away from the phone. Often Lucia was left to deal with her husband and his demands and his complaints, and when he was no longer her husband, she still had to deal with this angry man who felt as though she owed him something. As time went on, she tolerated it less and less, and then one day she stopped answering, and eventually he stopped calling.

It wouldn't have come as a shock to any of them that

Achiel had found other women to call and to write, but still they were surprised to learn it when Ronnie and Lucia sifted through his trunk of papers and objects and found letters to and from women they didn't recognize.

LUCIA (1948)

Remember when in 1943 the soldiers came through our little town Licata? I loved our house there on the Gela. Every morning I'd go for a walk. I always loved that time. Usually there were some fishermen out on boats, but it was otherwise quiet. I could walk along and think and feel the heat from the sun as it came up. I remember one specific morning. I went out, and the whole gulf was full of ships. I just stood there and watched. The ships came closer and closer to shore, and then tanks appeared. And the men, oh, so many men all over. I ran back home as fast as I could to wake everyone, but the guns and bombs had already done that. It sounds silly, I knew we were at war, but I never really knew it until then. Food was rationed, and we couldn't do certain things, but when I saw our Gela full of those ships, then I really knew. That Mussolini, what a fool. Not as bad as Hitler, but those men. Why did they do it all? So many people died. Mina, do you ever think about that? Or were you too young? Achiel told me about the war where he came from. Belgium. It sounds like they had it really bad. Worse than us.

Why am I thinking about the war when my wedding is tomorrow? I'm so glad you'll be there. I don't remember if I told you, but Achiel lost his father just three weeks ago. Sixty-five. Heart attack. Pretty young. Funny. Achiel cried and cried for that man, and he hardly ever cries. That might have been the first time I saw him cry. To hear him talk about his father, it didn't sound like he loved him. It was always about how tough his father was, and how he did terrible things to him. Once, he said, he fell asleep in the barn and his father came in and found him. He had worked all day in the field and didn't mean to sleep.

"You want to sleep in the barn?" his father said. "Sleep in the barn. See if I care. But then I'm going to treat you like something that sleeps in the barn."

And his father took a pitchfork—that's the three spiked one, right?—and stuck him, right in the back. He still has scars from that. I can't imagine treating my child that way—not that I have any yet, so what do I know? But I guess that was the way with him. And the next day, of course, Achiel had to be back out to work without complaining. Terrible.

We're so lucky that our mom and dad are still with us.

If we had known his dad was sick, we would have done the wedding sooner. Of course, he always was kind of fat, and Achiel told him he should be more careful. Nothing we can do about it now. The wedding will be small. It's really just our family. Achiel doesn't have much. Two of his brothers died in the first war. He has Ronnie, and he'll be the best man. If he has family back home, I don't know about it. Huh, just listen to me. Calling over there "home" when this is our home now. I do still think of that house from before the war and our gardens. The weather was nice. Things always grew. Here, not so much. Well, you know, we have a garden, but not like over there. And here we're lucky to get six months of things growing.

Sometimes I do wonder what it would have been like if we hadn't left. I know Dad said there wasn't anything to stay for, that the city was ruined, but we didn't need much. I guess then I wouldn't have met Achiel. It's been three years now, which is how much older I am than him. Oh shush. Those have mostly been good years. I love you, Mina, and I'm so happy you'll be there tomorrow.

ACHIEL (1979)

Lucas, do you know what your mother is up to? You know what I'm talking about. Oh, shut up. Get your brother for me. Put him on the phone. I'm done with you. I already told you once. Get your brother. Of course, I remember it's his birthday. I don't want to talk to you. Get. Your. Brother.

Ronnie. Happy birthday! How's my boy? Good. Are you going to be driving my Nova? It's a good car. I know you'll love it. Wish I was there to help you fix it up. She hasn't? What about Lucas? He been driving it? No? Well, then you'll need to fix it up before you take it. Here's what you do. Go down to the shop, you know the one on Belmont and High? I don't remember its name. But you go there, and tell them you want to work there. They always need someone. Work there for a while, get a feel for those cars, and then bring my car up there. They'll help you out. Or maybe you'll learn enough to do it yourself. If no one's turned it over in a while, you might need a tow, or a jump, or a new battery. If we had more time, I would have showed you.

What is Lucas doing there anyway? I mean, is he paying rent? She'd never make him do that. He's just living there to suit himself now that I'm not around. Makes me sick. I guess if he's there, maybe he can help you with the car. I'd rather it be me, or that you learn it yourself, but maybe he can be of some use. Actually, forget about him.

Did your mom do anything special for your birthday? I know things are tight, believe me, I know, but it's your special day. When we're done talking, you put your mom on. Speaking of her, you know what she's up to? This lawyer of hers keeps showing up here and talking about assets. Pittman. I think he's one of the lawyers from the factory. I've seen him around. He says it's about the property and trying to help her out financially, but I don't like it. You know anything about him? Hmm. Okay. Well, if you hear anything, you let me know. You're the only one there that listens and cares. You were always my good boy. You were the only one who ever got me. We could sit under those trees and watch nature together, completely quiet, for hours. Everyone else got under my skin. Lucas and I used to do that some when he was younger, but not like you. You know the story about your name? How you're named after my little brother? Yeah, well you even remind me of him. Just the way he was and how he acted.

Me? I'm okay. The food is terrible, and the doctors here don't care about an old man with a back injury. Did you know they're trying to take away my disability benefits? I guess one of my COs saw me exercising and reported it to the factory. Can you believe that? We'll see how far that gets them. Right! Exercise is good for you. It helps me stretch and helps the pain. I wish you could visit more. I know you're busy, and I know your mom is picking up extra shifts, but I haven't seen anyone in months. I know, I know, you can't bring yourself. But, soon. Right? You've got to talk to your mom and tell her I'm dying in here. I need to see my boy. Maybe Sophie could bring you. I haven't seen her, or my grandson, since I got here. These animals here, they'll attack you. You have to look out for yourself. I'm doing that. So, don't worry. Alright. You have a good birthday. Put your mom on.

Lucia, you want to tell me what this Pittman is doing? He keeps coming around and asking about assets, but I want to know why. And why didn't you do nothing for our Ronnie for his birthday? He's sixteen! Oh, next year. Okay. Well, next year, I want him to have my car. You know, the Nova. He said no one's been driving it. Are you sure that Lucas hasn't been messing with it? Good. Good that he has his own car. Though, I'd like to know where he's getting the money for it. Maybe because he's not paying rent and living under my roof. He's twenty-five now. What kind of twenty-five-year-old kid lives at home? I know I wouldn't tolerate it. I guess you just run the house different now. But, Pittman. Who's that? He's from the factory, right? Well, what business does he have with you? Okay. Well, you need to watch him. You know how lawyers are. They don't listen to you, and they charge you every chance they get.

Speaking of lawyers, I need you to get me a new one. What do you mean why? Because the one I have stinks. He doesn't listen to me. He keeps going on about precedence and saying, "Oh I can't do that." What good is a lawyer if he can't do what you want him to? So I fired him. I need a new one now. What do you mean "for what?" For my appeal. What have I been telling you about all these days? My appeal? So, I can get out of here? Because I didn't do it and the courts didn't listen to me? Look, just get me a new lawyer, and pick a good one this time. Do you have any idea what I'm going through? These, these, blacks.

They tried to rape me. Four of them grabbed me and held me down, but I fought. I wouldn't let them. I can't stay here. I just can't. I need you to get me a lawyer to get me out.

And when are you going to bring Ronnie up here to see me? I haven't seen my boy in forever. I want him to know his father. You know how I feel about Lucas, but if you want to bring him, too, I'll see him. I just need to see my little boy. He's the only one who knows the truth and believes me. Can you come soon? Bring the lawyer's information with you when you do. I want to talk to him.

RUBY (1983)

Hello? Ugh.

Mom? Will we accept the charges? MOM? WILL WE ACCEPT THE CHARGES? IT'S DAD!

Ugh.

Okay. Okay. Yes. Yes. We'll accept the charges.

Hi Dad. Whoa, slow down. No, I don't have anything to write on. I don't have a pen. I thought I was just answering the phone. Just a second, let me see if I can find one. Just need to reach, a bit further. I told mom we needed a longer cord for this stupid phone. Just a sec. Be right back.

Okay. Back.

I know the call costs money. What do you want me to write down? Okay. Okay. How do you spell that? Hey, stop yelling at me. I'm doing my best. I said, stop yelling at me.

No. No. No. No. No. No. No. No. No.

You shut up.

Bye.

ACHIEL (1980)

Fat and lazy! That's how they want us. Starch and bread. Rice, bread, potatoes (mashed, boiled, and baked), pasta, biscuits, corn, grits, rolls, and more bread and more potatoes. That's all they feed us here. Sugars and starches. Where's the protein? Where's the actual fruit? There's nothing to actually keep your hunger satisfied. By the time you get your food chewed, you're already hungry again. When I tried to go in line again, they wrote me up. I was just trying to get enough to fill me and stay filled. Some days we don't even get three meals. We just get the one in the morning and one in the evening, and we're hungry in between. You really don't know how bad it is. When we get food, it's this cardboard starch, and when we don't, well then, we don't.

No milk either. Just this "fruit drink." They can't even call it juice because there's no juice in it. It's just sugar and water and food coloring. I've told the guards it hurts my stomach, but they don't care. I've written grievances, using all the forms, and they don't care. You know what one CO said?

He says, "You want good food, then stop killing people. You get good food on the outside."

Just because we're in, doesn't mean we should have to eat this trash. At first, I missed the liver and onions, and the venison. But now I just miss anything that tastes like real food. Ronnie, you make sure you tell your mother you appreciate her cooking. Ronnie?

Hello?

Hello?

You've got to be kidding me.

Ronnie!

RONNIE (1999)

Dad. Sorry it's been so long since I've been there or called. With work and the boys, I'm busy. I'll fit a visit in when I can. I'm sorry. Look, I can't talk long. I talked with one of the clerks, and I'm filing a formal grievance myself. You've done what you can from inside. I need to see if there's anything I can do to help. It's terrible what they're doing to you. They know you have diabetes, and they need to be more careful about the foods they're giving you. Yes, and your back. I know. But let's do one thing at a time. The court clerk said one grievance per form. Let's focus on the food. You need more of a high-protein diet. I doubt they'll give you liver like you used to cook, but they can do better than what they've been giving you. It's only making you sicker.

I don't want to talk about Mom or Lucas, or anyone else. I just want to focus on what we're going to do to make you more comfortable. I know. Twenty-four years. I can only imagine how terrible it's been for you. I've been to each of the prisons you've been in. I've seen the kinds of places you're living in. It's terrible. You've tried every type of appeal. I don't think there's anything else to appeal. Regardless, we can make sure they take better care of you. Better food, more preventative care. That sort of thing.

Dad, I love you, but I don't think you're ever getting out. Don't get angry at me, just look at the facts. You've appealed how many times? Right, and half of those never even got to court. I know you've learned a lot about the legal system over the years, but you're not a judge or a lawyer. They know the system better than you do. If they say—hey. Stop it. I'm trying to help you.
Look, I'll do what I can. I need to go. I'll see you on Sunday.

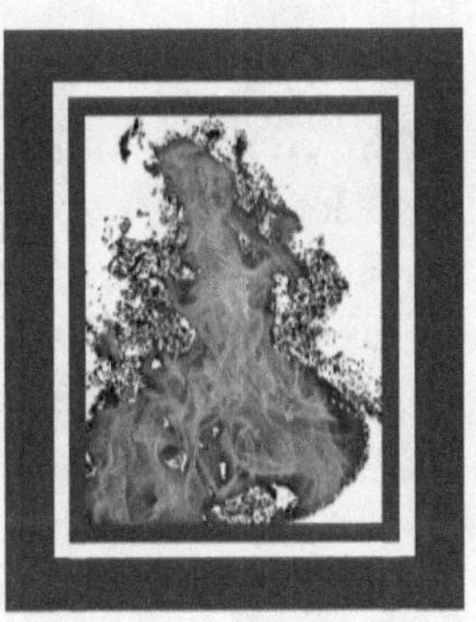

PART IV: IN THE MAIL (PART I)

Achiel was fluent in German and somewhat fluent in French, and while he learned to speak and understand English fairly quickly, he did not learn to write in English until he had been incarcerated for several years. This first proved to be a problem back when he was overseas during the wars and wanted to communicate with his wife and then later when he was in prison and he wanted to communicate with anyone. When he was in the military, he didn't have any trouble finding someone—usually Victor Mason—willing to write his letters for him, and in return Achiel graciously shared news, and sometimes cookies, from state-side when Lucia wrote. When Achiel got to prison, it was a different story. Now some kind of payment was required for the service of writing letters. Sometimes it was money, sometimes a favor, sometimes contraband, and sometimes protection.

Lucia also didn't fluently read or write in English. She spoke and read and wrote a hybrid of Sicilian and Italian, which was basically Italian with some Sicilian words tossed into the mix. It was close enough to Italian that she could communicate with Italian-only speakers, and she could read books written in Italian, but occasionally she'd stumble upon a word that stumped her. Pure Sicilian was created from the various people who controlled the island over its history, so that meant it was a language created from a mix of Arabic, Greek, French, and Italian. Because Achiel was comfortable with his French, though not fluent, and because Lucia knew some French from school, they communicated in rudimentary French until they both learned to speak English. When it came to writing letters, Lucia counted on Mina or her children to help her. Since Mina was a little younger when they moved to the States, she absorbed English quicker, and thus became Lucia's transcriptionist.

Achiel and Lucia provided the content for the letters, but the true writers were Victor and Mina. Mina knew Achiel well enough to recognize that his letters were warmer in tone and had less of an edge of coldness to them than his voice did. After a few letters, she realized it wasn't a man who was one way in text and another in person, but rather an entirely different person—which, of course, it was. In some of the letters, after she learned Victor's name, she'd leave a note saying, "Give our best to Victor." When Victor saw this, as he was reading the letter to Achiel, he didn't read that part out loud but rather kept it to himself. The first time the note was included, it caught him by surprise, and he paused over the words trying to make sense of them.

Achiel grew irritated, "What? What happened? Did you fall asleep?"

Victor looked forward to Mina's little note and often wrote her a note back in the letters Achiel asked him to write. Victor's notes changed, but Mina's did not. Her decency kept her faithful to the text that Lucia wanted transcribed other than the addition of, "Give our best to Victor."

For a while, Mina held an idea in her mind that she would one day find Victor Mason and perhaps even marry him. Victor had also had this hope, but when she failed to respond to any of his questions about her, or her family, or her well-being, he gave up on it. When American troops were withdrawn from Korea, Victor and Achiel went their separate ways. After the initial excitement of Achiel's return subsided, Mina finally asked if Achiel knew what happened to Victor.

Achiel looked surprised and asked, "You mean the weasel with the pen?"

His reaction initially surprised Mina because she assumed Victor had been a friend, but then, after she thought about it more, she was glad Achiel had so little respect for his letter-writer. It meant that Victor Mason might actually be someone who would be compatible with her, and not someone cruel and cold like Achiel. She never did see what her sister saw in that man. Still, without Achiel as a connection to Victor, she had no opportunity to find him. Mina wrote to Veterans Affairs in hopes of finding an address for him but had no luck. Again she asked Achiel, and again he proved to be of no help.

"Sure," Achiel recalled, "Victor talked all the time, but I never paid attention. His yapping was annoying. I just hoped the enemy would hit him for making all the noise and not me."

Mina had no address, no middle name, and no hope of finding Victor.

When Achiel went to Vietnam, he found another letter-writer to help him, but there was no sense of comradeship this time around. The letters were cold, short, and distinctly in Achiel's voice. It was obvious to Mina that whoever was helping him this time around was doing a literal job of transcribing without any embellishment. Mina only grew to like Achiel less and less with each passing year, and so she did little to improve on Lucia's language or sentiments in the return letters.

By the time Achiel went to prison, Lucia had learned to read and write. Unlike Achiel who was spottily employed—due to attitude and injury—Lucia's skills were always in demand, and her attitude was always positive. Her bosses made sure she had hours when she wanted them, overtime if she chose (and she almost always did), and they encouraged her to pursue self-improvement classes that the factory offered in the evenings or weekends. These were certainly for the employee's benefit, as the employer gained from having literate workers who could read instructions, doublecheck labels on parts, and leave messages to one another when necessary.

When Achiel was unemployed, he spent time in the woods, or tinkering in his shop, or teaching his boys (usually Ronnie) something that Achiel believed essential to being a man. It never occurred to him to teach himself to read or write because he didn't see the utility in it. When he needed something done, he could always find someone to do it for him. His sons read to him. When he went to war, he found other soldiers to write what he needed.

He had not anticipated going to prison. When he first arrived at Jackson State Prison, he needed someone to write for him. The natural choice would have been his cellmate, but Reed Bauer couldn't be bothered. Even after Achiel shopped around to find what the going rate was for letter-writing and came to Reed with an offer, Reed just shook his head and went back to his book. Had Reed been a weaker man, Achiel would have muscled him into it. Achiel persisted with offers, but it was evident that Reed wanted nothing to do with him, his letters, or any of his business. Achiel found another inmate, Joseph Brooks, to be more amiable. Joseph and Achiel would meet at various times to work out payment, communicate the desired message, deliver the written letter, and deliver the payment or services.

Once incarcerated, Achiel wished he had used some of his time on disability to learn to read and write and went about trying to rectify that problem immediately. However, he found the English language cumbersome and awkward, full of inconsistencies. Words he said regularly in conversation didn't look like they should when they were written, and he struggled to master them. Furthermore, because he hadn't spent much time writing much of anything (regardless of language) in the previous couple decades, his handwriting was shaky and uncertain. Since he had time on his hands, he sat with sheets of lined paper and practiced each letter hundreds of times each, upper- and lowercase. Then, when his letters were practiced, he wrote simple words over and over and over again. Finally, sentences.

While Achiel felt mostly comfortable with Victor during the war, Achiel quickly learned that anything he told Joseph could be used against him in prison, and so he had to be careful with what he dictated for his letters. It was a careful balancing act. If he said something too sensitive, he'd hear about it from other inmates. If he alluded to something he needed or wanted, someone would suddenly offer it. Sometimes this was good and worked in Achiel's favor, but particularly as a man who liked to be in control of a situation, it initially took him by surprise before he learned to use it to his benefit. He learned that he could use Joseph as a way of spreading gossip that he wanted spread around the prison, and so his letters became less for the benefit of

Lucia, his lawyers, and his children, and more for his own personal gain in prison.

Prison-business and rumor-spreading aside, Achiel's letters, via Joseph, fell into one of four categories: managing his appeals from afar, checking up on the children, asking for money or resources while incarcerated, and ensuring Lucia was still being faithful. While he was direct in asking, or more accurately demanding most things, his letters about the children and his wife's fidelity were much more discreet. They would ask questions to poke and pry, and he would draw his own conclusions from the answers he received. Of course, these letters weren't his only means of collecting information. He also had phone calls home, but the written letter allowed him to pore over the words and find meanings that he might have missed in a verbal communication.

Other prisoners might have been sensitive to embarrassing their letter-writers, or their family members, by disclosing personal information, or anything of a sexual nature, in their letters, but Achiel saw letters only as a means of communicating essential information, inquiry, and gathering information. He missed having sex, but frankly, he had more pressing matters on his mind, so it never occurred to write the kinds of letters that some prisoners wrote, and some letter-writers looked forward to writing and reading. Joseph, for the most part, found Achiel rather boring and would have moved onto another prisoner, but Achiel paid well and always paid in a timely manner. Plus, Joseph feared Achiel a little. Achiel was a little man, but Joseph could tell that he was just a degree away from unhinged.

For example, there was a period of a month, or maybe more, that he didn't hear from Achiel at all. This was unusual because Achiel almost always had something for

Joseph to read or write or teach him about the English language. Eventually, Joseph inquired about Achiel. The correctional officer said that Achiel was in solitary. He couldn't get the whole story, but the guard told Joseph, "That man is a fucking psycho," which was really saying something because that's exactly how Joseph would have described the man delivering the message.

JULY 3, 1985

Achiel,

I don't know how to say this, so I'm writing it instead. I have seen a lawyer about a divorce. If you know anything about me at all, you know how hard this is for me. We said forever, as Paul says marriage can't be "put asunder," but I can't be with you anymore. You've done too much bad and been gone too long. There are too many things. Divorce is more common now than when we were young. It's still a sin, and the Church says we should work out our differences. But, what you've done. It's just too much. My lawyer's name is John Pittman. He is going to come with forms. Please sign them. We will divide everything up. I would like to keep the house because of the kids and work. The property is already sold and that money was spent long ago trying to fight the builders. We don't have much, but we don't need much either. You've thought of divorce, too, right? How could you not? We've only gotten farther apart. It was all just too much. Please sign the forms from John. Please don't make this any more difficult than it already is.

Lucia

17 APRIL 1951

Lucia,

Is it true that Truman fired General MacArthur? Some of the men are saying so, but I don't know if it's true. He was such a great man. I don't understand why the president would do that. Where would the US be without the General? They'd still be fighting Hitler, that's where. The nerve of the president. I hope it's not true. Please tell me.

How is Sophie? I'm sorry the war came so soon after she did. I feel bad leaving you both, and of course I miss you and her. If Mina still has that camera, please send me a picture of you two. I'd love to see my girls. It's been almost a year now. I'm sure she's walking and talking. I wish I could write more, but we don't have much time, and then sometimes there's no one to take the mail. But I write whenever I can. Thank you for writing when you do. We don't get mail on the regular, so sometimes when it comes I get two or three letters all at once. The other guys are jealous because their wives and girlfriends don't write much.

I'm glad the work at the factory is still good. I know before I left, Jim said he'd have a spot for me when I come back. He's taking good care of you, too, right? How are the other ladies on interiors? Do you go out with them much after work?

There's not much I can say about the operations here. But we're safe enough. I spend most of my time in the trees or in a post somewhere anyway.

Take care of yourself and my little girl.

Achiel

11 JANUARY 1963

Lucia,

I'm on my way home. Who knows. I might even beat this letter to the States. I can finally see my little boy again. War seems to have a way of breaking out whenever we have a child. Hopefully I'll be home before his ninth birthday so we can celebrate. You've shown him pictures so he remembers who I am, right? And little Sophie. I can't wait to see her all grown up. Thirteen already? Where does the time go.

It's almost funny. I've been in three wars now, even though we aren't technically "in" this war yet, and I've had so many people shoot at me and bombs go off around me, but it's a stupid herniated disc that finally ends my war career. After enduring two tours plus being in Korea, and getting old I suppose, they're done with me. I don't mind. I'm tired of the jungle and the heat and not knowing what these people are saying. You probably won't read about it, but there was a big battle in Ap Bac that didn't go very well. We lost a helicopter and all the men on board, and a bunch of the locals died, too. I missed out on that because I was laid up. I told them they could just put me in a tree, and I'd do my thing.

Anyway, I'll see you soon.

Achiel

JUNE 25, 1964

Sophie,

Hey sis. Mom and Dad said I could write you at camp and tell you the news. First, the bad news. Uncle Ronnie died. He fell and hit his head. We're not sure how long ago, but Dad found him two days ago. He went to go check on him and there he was lying dead on the ground. I guess it's bad enough they're not going to have a viewing, which is fine with me. Who wants to look at dead people anyway? The good news is that Mom had her baby this morning. Or last night. Or, really early this morning. I'm not sure. Dad came home and told me about it this morning. Mom's going to be in the hospital for a couple days. Dad said it is because she's an old lady now, and they need to make sure she's okay. But we have a brother! I guess you always had a brother, but now I do, too. They named him Ronnie, after Uncle Ronnie. Dad is really sad about his brother, but he's happy about his new boy. Ronnie has straight, dark hair, not all curly like mine. Also, Dad's going to let me use a chainsaw to cut some trees, but probably not until you're home from camp. I'm so excited. Hope you're having fun. It's going to be different when you get home now. We'll have to get used to baby crying all the time. See you when you get home, Lucas

JUNE 23, 1964

Brother,

I'm sorry to do this to you, but I can't stand it anymore. I turned thirty-five today. Happy birthday to me, huh? Really, what have I done with my life? I don't have any kids. I don't have a wife. I can't even keep a girlfriend. I'm always alone. You've always taken care of me. You did all you could to protect me during the war, and you served your new country twice. What have I done? I just hid during the war and let you keep me alive. I'm weak. And what I remember of the war haunts me. I don't know how you could do the things you did. You needed to, but I never could. Tell Lucia I'm sorry for everything. She was always so kind to me. Tell Sophie and Lucas that I love them. Don't tell them I shot myself. Maybe tell them I fell and hit my head or something. Anything, but don't tell them I killed myself. I left whatever I had to you. Do what you want with it. There should be some money left over after my funeral. Don't do anything special for me. Buy the new baby something nice instead. Just cremate my remains and throw them to the wind. Don't worry about a headstone or a cemetery plot. Who would come anyway? I know you'll remember me, and that's all that matters. I'm sorry I wasn't a better little brother.

I love you. Ronnie.

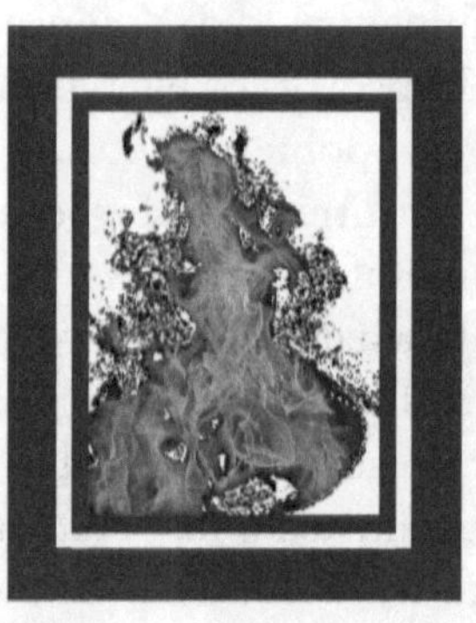

PART V: THE TRIAL (1975)

Raymond Copeland, Achiel's lawyer, was a friend of a friend. Achiel and Raymond met through the now deceased Eddie Davis one day over drinks. Raymond wasn't particularly interested in Achiel until Eddie mentioned that Achiel was a sharp-shooter and knew his way around a rifle. That piqued Raymond's interest because he had always been interested in shooting but wasn't very good. Would Achiel be interested in earning some money on the side to teach Raymond a thing or two about handling a gun? Later, when Raymond had children of his own, Achiel would teach Raymond's children their way around a gun as well, but it never extended into an exchange of cash for an education in shooting. When Achiel was arrested for statutory rape and in need of a lawyer, Raymond's name was the first one that came to mind. That's how it was Raymond who defended him and suggested the plea deal to gross indecency. Achiel served a year in prison for that, and everyone agreed it was much better that way than if they had attempted to fight the charges.

On the day following the murder of Clifford Ellis, the police came to the Van Slyck house and arrested Achiel and took Lucas into custody for questioning. They also questioned Ronnie and Lucia, but they were permitted to stay at the house. Lucia wandered the house aimlessly in shock. Police presented a search warrant and confiscated all the weapons in the house, a few pieces of clothing, two flat tires from the back of Lucas' vehicle, and various other odds and ends. Lucia wasn't paying attention. She was still trying to make sense of what had happened and kept inquiring about when her oldest son would be able to return home. The officers at the house weren't sure. They left, and Lucia continued to wander from room to room. Ronnie remained in his room, playing with his Evel Knievel stunt cycle. It was his favorite toy.

Finally Lucia came to his room and asked, "Do you know anything about your father and Lucas?"

Ronnie glanced up from his toy and said, "Dad said we had car trouble."

Lucia didn't process what the boy had told her and simply said, "Okay," before wandering into the bathroom and then her bedroom. The phone rang six times before she was able to walk from one end of the house to answer it, and when she did, it was Achiel asking her to get him a lawyer.

She should have called the local bar association for recommendations, or checked with family or friends, or even flipped through the Yellow Pages to see which lawyer had the largest advertisement, but she just went with the familiar name of someone she knew: Raymond Copeland. Had she asked around, she would have found that Mr. Copeland did not have the best reputation. Had she even asked him some basic questions, she would have learned from Copeland himself that he didn't think he was the best choice for a murder trial. But she didn't. It's not that Copeland was a dishonest man. He was just grossly underqualified. Not having any murder-trial experience should have been a strike against him from the standpoint of his client, but for Copeland it was an opportunity of a life time. A local murder would be a high-profile case. It would likely to be covered in the newspapers and maybe local news on television. This was a chance for him to make a name for himself.

Later, as Achiel sat in prison, he would construct appeal after appeal based on inadequate representation. He might have come to the conclusion to do this on his own, but it was in fact Copeland who had recommended the appeals to Achiel. Copeland felt bad about how the trial went, for both himself and his client. The trial had been covered in the news, both paper and television, but it hadn't served either of them very well. Achiel wound up sentenced to a life term. Copeland had lost, and that very public loss did not earn him respect or increase his stature in the community. In the end, Copeland never did rise above small-town lawyer status. It could have been worse, his town could have turned against him because of the loss, but Achiel was not well-liked or well-respected in the town of Lewes and no one was very surprised that he ended up in prison. Nor did they care.

Curtis Harrington, the assistant prosecuting attorney on behalf of the people, already had a name for himself, and for him the Van Slyck case was just another one on the docket. Harrington was out of Brighton. Brighton was by no means a major metropolis, but its population was nearly ten times that of Lewes. Harrington had resources and funds, while Copeland had only himself and an office secretary. It's difficult to know what "could have been" if Achiel had chosen a more experienced attorney or if his attorney had more adequate resources. When they lost, Copeland felt genuinely sorry for his client, and that's why he suggested the appeal based on inadequate representation. As was his nature, Achiel sensed weakness and pounced. Achiel took the advice offered out of kindness and self-deprecation and worked to destroy the reputation of Copeland in an attempt to free himself from prison. It never worked, but he kept trying.

One of the major failings of Copeland during the trial was his inability to establish a very basic foundation of defense: reasonable doubt. Achiel's story simply seemed too implausible for anyone to believe, and Harrington did an excellent job at exposing the ridiculousness of Achiel's claims. For one, who goes walking for eight hours with a loaded high-powered rifle with a scope, with no intention of hunting or shooting targets?

"It just felt comfortable to walk with it" wasn't a reasonable explanation.

For another, why park your vehicle in the middle of the road, blocking the only exit unless you wanted a confrontation?

"That's just where we stopped" didn't quite cut it.

Yet, that's what Copeland had to work with, and despite his coaching before the trial, that's what he got on the stand. Copeland also realized, fairly early on, that it didn't help that he believed his client was in fact guilty. This realization made his own claims and arguments ring false and hollow. He was saying the right thing for his client, but he was sure the jury could hear the lack of conviction in his voice.

The trial took four days. The timeline of the case went like this: the murder occurred Saturday night, sometime between eight and nine; the police were notified around ten; a warrant was issued overnight, and police arrived at the Van Slyck residence the next morning by nine. They took Achiel and Lucas Van Slyck back to the station for processing and questioning, seized items from the house, and questioned Ronnie and Lucia informally at the residence. Lucas Van Slyck was released around noon, but Achiel was formally charged with murder. By two in the afternoon, the autopsy of Clifford Ellis was complete. Two weeks later a preliminary examination was conducted; two weeks after the preliminary examinations, arraignment was scheduled; and finally, just over nine weeks later, the trial began.

Day one of the trial saw opening statements from both attorneys, testimony from the doctor who performed the autopsy, testimony from Mrs. Ellis, testimony from Lucas, and a discussion of whether or not the young Miriam Ellis should testify. Neither attorney wanted to put her through the stress or embarrassment of a cross examination, but Copeland wanted the option to call her as a witness if he needed her to clarify any of the details about the affair she and Achiel had. Harrington agreed, and Miriam was asked to come to court, though she wasn't required to be present in the courtroom unless she was called. The other important piece of information from the first day of testimony was that Lucas lied under oath, was caught, and then told, what he assured the court, was the truth to the best of his recollection. Sophie sat on a bench with her mother and watched everything unfold. If anyone had asked her, she would have said, "He's guilty, everyone knows it, and he's going away for a long time." Indeed, if you were keeping score, day one definitely went to the State.

Day two began with Ronnie's testimony, but it was dominated by Achiel's testimony. Achiel answered questions about the affair with Miriam and about his relationship with Clifford before and after the affair. Achiel detailed his involvement in the wars. He talked about his relationships with his sons. Most of all, he recounted and recounted and explained and reexplained the events of the day leading to the death of Clifford Ellis. He answered the question of why he carried a rifle on the property that day, and why they parked their vehicle in the middle of the road. He explained why the trigger on his .243 was altered, and how he tailored the gun to his preferred specifications. When he got to the moment of Clifford's death, he admitted he didn't know what happened. It all had happened so quickly.

His only defense for not notifying the police when he, according to him, "accidentally" killed a man, was that he panicked and didn't know what to do.

"My ears were ringing from the shot. I always wear ear protection when I shoot. My ears were ringing, my sons were crying, but I couldn't hear them. I could only see that they were distressed, and I didn't know what to do."

However, he always came short of apologizing or saying that he wished he had notified police instead of fleeing the scene. His family would look back on this moment and wonder what would have happened if he had apologized or if he'd said he wished he hadn't left Clifford to die alone in his truck.

It was obvious to everyone present that the jury, Mrs. Ellis and her daughter, and the community all wanted some acknowledgement from Achiel that he wished he had done things differently, but the thought to apologize or express remorse over his actions literally never crossed his mind. Day two closed with a brief reappearance of Mrs. Ellis and the first detective to arrive on the scene. Mrs. Ellis testified briefly that her husband drank a lot and often, but that he was a loving, goofy drunk who liked to dance and sing loudly.

Copeland asked Mrs. Ellis, "The doctor who examined your husband stated that he had a blood alcohol level of 0.22 on the night of his murder. Would you consider that common for your husband to reach that level of intoxication?"

Her response was, "I don't know about the specific level, but yes, he was as drunk as he usually was when he drank."

Then Mrs. Ellis was dismissed from the stand. Finally, the detective Alan Gil took the stand briefly to answer questions about the demeanor of Achiel, Lucas, and Ronnie when he questioned them following the murder.

"Mr. Van Slyck didn't seem disturbed at all, but Lucas was clearly very nervous."

Harrington asked, "And Ronnie?"

To which the detective answered, "Oh, he was a scared little boy."

Day three was dedicated to closing arguments. Copeland did his best, but he wasn't as practiced as Harrington was. By this time, he was utterly convinced Achiel was guilty, and it was hard to make a convincing claim otherwise before the court. It didn't help that after day two he had met with Achiel and was verbally dressed down by his client. For a man who supposedly knew little of the law, Achiel had many strong convictions about what Copeland should have, and shouldn't have done.

It was during this session that Copeland mentioned a possible appeal based on inadequate counsel.

"Appeal?" screamed Achiel, "Appeal? You've already given up? I need you to get your ass out there and fight for me. I wouldn't have to appeal if you did your job right the first time."

To say Copeland's closing argument was lackluster is

fair. Harrington, however, put on quite the performance. He went further than even Achiel had expected, and Achiel liked to think he was a good judge of human behavior. In his closing argument, Harrington put together pieces of testimony to depict Achiel as 1) a cold-blooded murderer seeking revenge for the time he spent in jail due to his affair with Miriam Ellis, who 2) blocked the road preventing Ellis from being able to leave his house, who 3) paced the property across from the Ellis residence for hours looking for an opportunity to snipe him from afar while pretending to enjoy the nature with his young son as cover, and who 4) waited until Clifford was drunk and came out to confront Achiel in person. Because Achiel knew Clifford's habits so well, Harrington went on, he knew this would happen, and when it did, Achiel shot him and made up this story of self-defense and an accidental misfiring of his rifle. Sophie didn't believe it. She knew her father to be capable of many things (bearing a grudge and enacting revenge certainly among them), but she also knew he did in fact love spending hours in nature, alone or with his children.

The jury deliberated for the rest of day three, emerging once to ask the judge for clarification between the charges of second-degree murder and manslaughter. Inside the courtroom, you could hear the jurors arguing loudly with one another. Someone was clearly yelling. They came out again, asking for another clarification of the charges against Achiel. The Van Slycks were surprised and began to wonder if their patriarch might actually not be found guilty. By nine, a juror emerged asking to call it a night. They went home. On day four, the jurors spent half the day deliberating, asked again for a clarification of the difference between the charges of second-degree murder and manslaughter, and finally emerged with their verdict of guilty. Sentencing was scheduled for a month from the day, and Copeland requested that Achiel be given credit for time served. The judge agreed, and Achiel was taken away.

Lucia, Sophie, Lucas, and Ronnie sat quietly while the courtroom emptied. Copeland collected his things and came over to them. He tried to comfort them, but he could tell comfort wasn't quite what they needed. He wasn't sure what it was, but they didn't seem disturbed or surprised. They also didn't seem to know quite how to proceed. Eventually, Sophie thanked Copeland, and the family exited the courtroom and went home.

DR. KEITH LARSON

My first name is Keith, K-E-I-T-H, last name Larson, L-A-R-S-O-N. I'm a physician licensed by the state of Michigan. I have specialties in pathology and microbiology medicine. I practice both and have for the last fifteen years. My relationship to the case? I performed the autopsy on Clifford Ellis. No, I did not know Mr. Ellis. The detective, Trooper Gil, identified the body for me. Mrs. Ellis had also identified the body, so I had no reason to question the identity. I made an official report of my findings, which I have provided to the court, each attorney, and the State Police.

Aside from the large obvious gunshot wound, there were no external injuries worthy of note. Mr. Ellis might have cut his lip shaving, but other than that, there was nothing worth reporting. That's right. The large wound was somewhere around the mid-line of the upper lip. It was consistent with gunshot wounds I've seen before. No, I did not find a bullet, but I did find fragments of what I assume to be a bullet. No, we did not find an exit wound. It's not unusual because there are lots of angles and bone that can deflect bullets. As I said, we did find lead fragments, which likely came from a bullet. I put a probe through the wound and the probe directed anteroposteriorly, somewhat superiorly towards the left—I'm sorry, upward and backward. Up and back, and to the left. Yes. That is correct. I found laceration of the tongue and fracture of the facial bones, fracture of the bones of the base of the skull, as well as some destruction of the brain stem and cerebellum, and the spinal cord was amputated completely. Correct. The spinal cord was gone. There was no connection. The metal fragments were given to Detective Gil. Yes, he was attending the autopsy, along with two other officers.

As part of a standard autopsy, we collect body fluids and perform a standard set of tests. Well, blood, bile, and urine. I gave the samples to Detective Gil to take to the State Police lab to run tests. Yes, I could have run the tests, but it's not my specialty and it's essential for the chain of evidence for it to stay with the State Police. It's standard practice. The report from Detective Gil shows that the deceased, Mr. Ellis, had a BAC of 0.22. Well, intoxication starts at 0.1. That's the limit. At 0.22, Mr. Ellis was certainly intoxicated, but no, that alcohol level would not kill him. Weight and height aren't significant because we're talking about a percentage. Yes, it can have something to do with the habitual drinking of individuals. Their consumption and well, "practice" can mean a greater tolerance to alcohol.

In my professional opinion, a gunshot caused Mr. Ellis' death. It entered his upper lip, left to the midline, and had an impact on the maxilla—sorry, the hard palate—and then destroyed the bone, sending bone fragments backward into the base of the skull, which lacerated the brain and caused the brain damage at the stem. Once that was severed, death would have occurred very quickly. Oh, the probe I inserted had a degree of, let me doublecheck on my report here, fifty degrees. So, that would be consistent with being shot from below, or at least a lower height. Thank you.

SHELLEY ELLIS

First, you need to understand. Where we live, this isn't some big road. This is a dirt road, but enough for two cars at a time, but barely more than that. Sure, we get some traffic through it now and then, but mostly just the people that live down there and others who get lost trying to find something else. The Van Slycks, they have this piece of property. It has some pretty spots. A creek, a few hilly parts, some beautiful trees. It's not big, but it's kind of a weird triangle-like slice of land. They started building a house at one point, just the foundation is there, because Mr. Van Slyck, well he has problems with everyone. That includes the builders. So of course they didn't get too far before he's yelling, telling them how to do their job, and they're saying how they're not going to come back to work until he stops and then, that's just how it stayed. They put a trailer there to live in for a time.

Now, we have a house. It's just a bit down the road from their property, or the drive to their property anyway. It's just far enough away, and there's just enough trees and hills and things, that we can't see all their business, but close enough that we know most of it.

This is how it was. We saw them come down the road. The Van Slycks. We couldn't tell who was in the van, but we could see two heads, so we knew at least two of them were in there. We figured it was Achiel and Lucas but didn't know little Ronnie was in there, too. We saw them drive by the house. Their property is just on the other side of ours, and they drove by our driveway and then turned around there at the dead end, and then stopped. I just happened to be sitting in my chair in the living room by the window and had a good view. Time? This was probably noon? I'm not sure. I didn't have a clock in the room, and I didn't think to check. So, they stop and Achiel and Ronnie get out of the van. Not for certain it was Ronnie, but I just figured he looked about the right age. I did get a good look at Lucas and could see his face in the driver's side. So, I knew it was him, and I knew Achiel because I'd recognize him anywhere. They had guns. Both of them. Ronnie had some rifle. I couldn't tell what type. Even if you handed me one, I wouldn't know. My dad shot, and so did Cliff, but I don't like guns so I stay away from them.

So, Ronnie and Achiel disappeared into their property, and I couldn't see them anymore. I didn't watch for them all day, either. I had my own things to do. I do admit that I was a little worried whenever I saw them. It's been a number of years since what happened with Achiel and my Miriam, but I still get this uneasy feeling when I see him. Anyway, I watched on and off to see if I could see them. Later, around three or so, I looked and saw the van was now parked in the middle of the road. Strange place to park, I thought. But we didn't have nowhere to go, otherwise we would have had to ask them to move it. Well, where he parked, the road is narrow. It's just one of those country roads, and it's kind of rounded and then there are deep ditches on either side. I suppose you could get around through the ditch if you really tried, but I wouldn't try it in our station wagon. If Cliff had been sober, he probably could have got around it in his truck. Like I said, we didn't have nowhere to go, so I didn't think twice.

No sir, I didn't hear any shots all day. Sometimes they'd come back to the van, and then they'd go back into the property again. Maybe they had their lunches in there. I wouldn't know. When it got to be time for Cliff to head to town, he started to get nervous about leaving us alone—especially Miriam—with Achiel around. I don't know, it's hard to say. It's just neither of us felt very comfortable around him. Cliff and I used to know the family pretty well. Cliff and Achiel would help each other with projects and stuff. We even had them over for dinner a couple of times. Friendly, but not friends. That's how I'd call them. After the thing with Miriam, well, it was never the same after that.

Cliff was pacing around wondering what to do about leaving Miriam and me alone with Achiel parked in our driveway when the van suddenly drove off a bit. We couldn't really see if they'd gone or not, so Cliff poked his head out the door and said, "I think I still hear them." He came back inside and sat down on the couch.

After a bit, Cliff started to get up. "What if something's wrong with their van? What if they need help?"

I told him not to worry about them. They'd caused enough trouble in our lives. Whatever was wrong with their van, they could take care it of themselves.

"Shel, it's been a while since what happened with Miriam. He hasn't done anything wrong to us. I need to be a good neighbor."

He made us lock up the house, just to be sure, and then he went out to see what was wrong. We could see brake lights now that it was getting darker, so we knew the van was there. Cliff took the truck and drove right up to the van.

No, I didn't see exactly where he parked on account of the trees. Later, when I went out to check on him, I saw where he had parked. Okay. So, he drove out of view, and I couldn't hear anything at first. Then I heard a shot. A single shot in the night. Yes, sir. It was the only shot I heard all day. It was loud and clear. I might not like guns, but I know what they sound like. I also knew it wasn't any .22. I just knew then. I just knew. I heard the van—sorry, I heard a vehicle drive away, but I couldn't see what it was. Miriam came to me, and she was crying.

I said, "Little girl, you come with me. We need to go see about your daddy."

I could have just called the police right then because like I said, I knew. We waited a couple of minutes because I knew that's what Cliff would have wanted us to do, just to be safe. Then we went over to see, and—I'm sorry, I'm sorry—there was a lot of blood. It was everywhere. My husband was dead. No, I'm no doctor, but I could see from the blood that no one could have survived that.

Yes, I did. I checked his pulse. There was no pulse. My little girl saw her daddy that way. No one should ever have to see that. We moved Cliff so we could drive the truck out of the road and back to the house, and we parked the truck, and then I ran in and called the police.

I didn't see who killed my husband that night, but I know who did it. It's that man right there, Achiel Van Slyck. And anyone else who ever knew him knows he did it.

LUCAS

Mom, I'm sorry. I'm sorry. I'm sorry. I couldn't do it. They asked me, and all those people were looking at me. And the judge. They were going to find out. We should have called the cops right away. Did you hear that attorney? He just kept pushing. He knew something was wrong. He knew I was lying. I could tell. Why didn't Dad call the cops right away? They would have believed it was an accident if we had called right away.

Look, again, I'm sorry. I just couldn't keep going with it. I'm an adult. I could have gone to jail as an accessory. And he did actually kill him. I mean, that's not even up for debate here. The only thing they care about is if it was an accident, on purpose, and if it was premeditated. I don't think it was premeditated. It doesn't really matter though. Michigan doesn't have the death penalty. We don't have to worry about that. Whenever you kill someone, even if it was a total accident, you're going to spend some time in jail. It's just a matter of how much time, and where, and what type of jail. Or, prison, I guess.

I don't know what Dad will do. He barely tolerated me

as it was. Oh, don't give me that. You know what he always called me. I tried. I tried everything to please that man. I did all the terrible things he asked me to. I even beat kids up at school to make him proud. I thought, maybe if I show Dad how strong I am, maybe then. But no. He just kept berating me and saying I wasn't his kid. Like you would have an affair with someone. How do you think that made me feel? Every day I woke up and wondered, will this be the day my father loves me? And every day I was disappointed. He did? When? Well, I'd like to read that letter. He certainly didn't show me he cared when he was around. And now this. Well, if there was any doubt before, my testimony sealed the deal. I mean, you heard him, right in court. They have that lady over there tapping away recording everything he said. Everyone heard him. I guess I just have to hope he gets locked up for a very long time and never gets out. Maybe he'll die in there. I know, I shouldn't say that. Jesus, it's not like he treats you well either. How can you defend him? Remember when Sophie had to stop him from choking you? That's not normal. That's not how husbands treat their wives.

No, Ronnie will be fine. He's a kid. They're not going to send him anywhere or put him in jail. They'll probably talk to him about telling the truth, but it's pretty obvious he doesn't have a wonderful role model. I can't imagine they're going to do anything to a kid who was just doing what his father told him to.

There's nothing to do now. We just wait. The jury will come back and tell the judge their decision. Then there's a sentencing hearing, or whatever, and that's when they decide how long he's going away. Well, he is. It would require a miracle for him not to. Even then, he should go away. Ma, you don't actually believe him that it was an accident, do you? I saw him. Mr. Ellis was yelling at him for what he did to Miriam, and yeah, he was drunk, but he never got out of the car. He didn't have a knife. He was just sitting in the driveway to our property, in his car, yelling at Dad. And Dad leveled that gun of his and fired. I can still see the hole in Ellis' head if I close my eyes. And the splatter in the car. There was so much blood.

Dad has been doing shit like this forever and getting away with it. It finally caught up with him. You need to accept that he's going away. The question is what are *you* going to do? And how are we going to prepare for when, if, he gets out?

SHELLEY ELLIS

Miriam, they're not going to call you to the stand. I talked to our attorney, and it's just not going to happen. You don't have anything to add that will really help, and it's only going to be hard on you. You've been through enough. We both have. What I said on the stand is all that needs to be said about what happened between you and that man. There's no reason to put you through it up there. It's hard sitting in that little box, seeing all those faces staring back at you. They're judging you when you're up there. Literally, they're judging you. Are you telling the truth? Are these real tears, or are you just putting them on? I could feel it. It was terrible. I'll go back if I need to, but I don't want you to. You don't even have to be at the trial at all. Of course, I understand. I know, he was your dad. I miss him, too.

He loved you so much. You know that, right? He might not have always shown it, but he did. If he had been more of a violent man, like Achiel, your dad would have killed him over what he did to you. But that wasn't his way. I knew your daddy since we were in sixth grade. We went to different elementary schools, but when I was in sixth grade, we were in the same school, and that's where we met. At lunch time. He was two years older, but somehow we wound up at the same table. He had that big goofy smile of his on, and seeing it made me smile, too. He always loved to have a good time, even way back then. And now, now we're going to have to learn how to move on without him. He was just forty-four. I thought I had so many more years with him. But we'll remember him, won't we? We'll keep him in our hearts, and when you see me, just know that he's there with us. I'm so thankful he got to see you graduate high school, and he got to meet Terry. He really liked Terry. It was always so nice how he would come over and help around the house. I know things haven't always been easy for you and Terry, but he's a good man. Your dad would have approved of him marrying you. I can always give you away on behalf of Dad.

First, we need to get through this though. Mr. Harrington thinks there's just one more day of testimony. He said it might go on another day after that, but otherwise it will just be up to the jury and us waiting for them to decide. I can't imagine how they can come back with anything other than guilty. Can you? I mean, you and I saw, and we know. But I can't imagine anyone else listening thinking that that man isn't guilty. I love you. You just hold onto me, and we'll get through this together.

JUDGE WILKERSON

Gentlemen, please approach. We have the matter of Ms. Miriam Ellis to speak of. Officially, she's on your witness list, but I'm concerned about her taking the stand. Mr. Copeland, I know Mr. Harrington has asked that she not be put through the rigor of a cross examination. Would you object to that? Well, object to not having her as a witness? It has been a number of years, but I can tell how visibly disturbed she is just being in the courtroom. It is important to me that Mr. Van Slyck receives a fair trial, absolutely, but it's also important to me that we don't cause any more undue harm to this young lady who has already been through a lot.

Frankly, Mr. Copeland, your client had an illicit affair with her and killed her father. He pled guilty to those charges, and he's not denying killing her father. Right. I think that sounds fair. Mr. Harrington, can you agree that we'll keep Miriam Ellis on the witness list in the event that Mr. Copeland needs to call her to clarify details of their relationship—only if that is pertinent to the case—and that she does not need to be present in the courtroom unless she is called, or unless she wishes to be present? Okay. Let's go forward with that understanding.

RONNIE

My middle name, too? Okay. My name is Ronald Hector Van Slyck. I'm ten, but I turn eleven soon. Everything went just like my dad said it did. Mr. Ellis came over, and he was so mad. He kept yelling and flashing his lights at us. All we had done all day was walk around in the woods. I caught a couple snakes and a few frogs. We saw a doe and her fawn. Lots of birds. I don't know what made Mr. Ellis so mad. He was probably drunk like he always is. No, he didn't say anything to me. He was yelling at Lucas to move the car, and yelling at Dad. Lucas tried to talk to him, but that didn't do no good. Then Dad went to help Lucas, and Mr. Ellis waved a knife around. He must have bumped Dad and the gun went off.

Me? I was in the van. Right. In those buckle seats that Lucas has. I love those. They're just like sitting up front. Not buckle seats, sorry, bucket seats. That's a funny name. Anyway, I was sitting there waiting for Dad to get done talking to Mr. Ellis so we could go home. It was dark. I was getting tired and hungry. We walked all day. Oh, I don't know, looking at this and that. Dad showed me some fox scat. You know, poop. And we found an owl pellet. But that wasn't poop, that's more like a cat's hairball. You can pull it apart and find all the little bones of whatever the owl ate. It's so cool. Usually, owls just eat mice and ground squirrels and stuff. Sometimes they get a snake, and you can tell from all the backbone bones. Vertebrae? Yeah. Vertebrae. When Lucas came back to the van, I wanted to know what Mr. Ellis wanted, and why he was so angry. Lucas was telling me when I heard the shot.

Well, it was like I said already. Mr. Ellis was waving his knife around and yelling. And Dad just used his gun to try to protect himself. Not to shoot Mr. Ellis, but like to block him. And that's when the gun went off. It was loud. And Mr. Ellis fell back. Well, Lucas and me were talking, but I could have seen it. I mean, I saw it. We were talking, but I, uh, I saw Mr. Ellis with the knife. He was waving it around, and Dad was scared. I was scared, too. No, when Lucas went to talk to Mr. Ellis, he didn't have a knife pointed at him. Right. Lucas was just saying that Mr. Ellis wanted us to move the van so he could go into town. No, he didn't have a knife. Well, I guess when Dad came over he picked up the knife. Maybe from the floor of his truck? I don't know. I couldn't see that. Like I said, I was talking to Lucas when the gun went off. Just like Dad said it did. Mr. Ellis kept waving that knife around and yelling. I can be done now? Okay.

ACHIEL

Yes, I did serve in Korea and Vietnam. Yes, technically, I fought in World War II, but I was not a soldier. It's been a long a time ago, and they are memories I'd rather not think about. It was a, uh, terrible time. For everybody. My parents had four children. Two died in the first war, and then there was me and my younger brother Ronald. He ended his own life eleven years ago. I can't say for sure, but I know Ronald always felt very alone. Of course, I stood up for him. I kept him safe during the war, and I made sure we could get to America together with our father. I loved my little brother very much. In war, you do terrible things. Whatever you need to, to survive.

We used to hunt in Belgium, and I learned to use a rifle there. A little with the bow, too, but I was never as good with that. Mostly rabbit and pheasant, but sometimes we'd get lucky with a boar or deer. My parents were very old when I was born, and they needed me. I did what I could to help. I honestly don't remember ever not being good with a rifle, but hunting meant I practiced a lot. When we got to the US, and there was a war, I enlisted. Originally, they made me a tank technician. Well, you know, I helped operate the tank and do repairs. At some point they had me be a sniper, but I don't think they ever changed my papers, so it probably still says tank technician. You'd have to check with the VA.

Three years? I'm not sure. Right, I came home, and then a year or two later, 1955 I think it was, I heard that there was a need in Vietnam, so I enlisted there. We weren't at war then, but they needed us to keep the peace. That's what they called us. Peacekeepers. There? I was a sniper. I spent a lot of time in the trees. I don't know why you'd need a sniper to keep the peace, but there I was. We were put on special duty, you know. We were within a certain company. I was assigned to the 3rd Army Division, and I would shoot for the 2nd Army on the rifle team. It was considered a sniper rifle. Yes, I received special training as a sniper. And we got nine dollars a month more for it. Well, you were considered a sniper if they put you on a sniper patrol. More specifically? As a sniper, you have to be able to pick off a target some three hundred yards, a thousand yards away. Yes, they were high-powered rifles. It would have to be to have that kind of range.

That's correct. My welding store did burn down before I left for Vietnam. It was a shame. I loved that little shop. Right, my friend Eddie's shop also burned down that night. Some crazy arsonist was going around that night I guess. I don't think they ever caught anyone for that, but whoever it was sure didn't like welding shops. No, I never filed an insurance claim because I had already enlisted. What would the point have been? The shop would have just sat empty while I was gone. As it turns out, I didn't get back until 1963, so it would have sat empty for eight years or so. Eddie? I heard he died. Got hit by a truck. His wife Valerie moved out of town shortly after all that. He was a good man. I miss him.

After the wars, I picked up welding work where I could, but I hurt my back and I went on disability. It was hard, but my wife worked at the factory, and she always had work. I earned some money here and there doing shooting. Oh, you can win a couple hundred dollars for some of the big shoots. I won quite a few times. Between the odd job when I could, and shooting, that was all I was doing to earn money. If my back had gotten better, I would have gone back to work regular. I still have the same pains.

Not so bad. I can still walk. I know guys who came home from wars who couldn't do that. I don't think I'm too unlucky. I wish I could walk better. It's one of my favorite things to do. Just go in the woods and walk. Sometimes I sit and listen and watch. I've tried to teach my children to do the same. There's a lot to see in nature if you just open your eyes and ears. When I walk in the woods? No, I don't always take a gun. Sometimes I do, just because you never know what you might see. But no, not always.

I wouldn't call myself a gun expert, but yes, I like guns. They are a hobby of mine. I have, oh, probably eighteen, I think at home now. No, no handguns. Just rifles and shotguns. I use them for hunting purposes and for professional target shooting. Well, since I injured my back, I really can't shoot for money because I really can't stand long enough to. Some events you have to shoot a hundred targets or birds, or sometimes even two hundred, and I can't stand up long enough to shoot the complete event, so I really don't participate in shooting much anymore. Yes, I do miss it. But I can still target shoot at home or on the property.

Yes, I was arrested one time before. No, not for anything to do with guns. Just the thing with the Ellis girl. Miriam. I plead guilty and served my time. Oh, just over ten years ago. Yes, that's the only offense on my record.

Well, I usually wake up early. I don't like to waste my day. On that day—Saturday, April 3rd—I slept in a little. 7:30. That's late for me. I guess I was tired. Sometimes sleep just creeps up on you. I had breakfast with my boys. Sophie's married. She moved out after getting married. Lucas moved out, too, but he was back to visit and spent the night. He wanted to talk about if I would cosign so he could buy a new car. We spent some time outside, talking and working around the yard, and then we thought it would be nice to go see the property. We didn't really have a plan. It was just a thought, like, "Oh, it's a nice day. Let's go to the property." We took some guns because we weren't sure how long we'd stay, or if we'd see something to shoot, or if we wanted to do some target shooting. You never know. So, we packed up some things to go with us. No, nothing was in season except for varmints.

My younger son and I usually go out on weekends, you know, and we walk around together. As I said, I've been teaching him to hunt. We go bird hunting and rabbit hunting quite often. Sometimes Saturday, sometimes Sunday. And sometimes I take a gun with me. Sometimes I don't take a gun. We sit down, and we talk together. Oh, about things like what to watch for, what kinds of game that you hunt at what time of the year. How to identify an animal by its signs or scat. Sometimes I tell him about hunting in Belgium or about plants and weather conditions, and how to survive.

Anyway, that's what we did. We went out to the property, and we walked around. Ronnie and me stayed together. Lucas, he went off in his own direction and did his own thing. Maybe he shot birds? I'm not sure. With Ronnie, we can just be there, quiet with no talking, and I can think. I think about all kinds of things. Sometimes I remember things, like about my brother, or the wars. You can't help where your mind goes when you let it wander.

I used to try to teach Lucas to hunt, when he was a kid, the way I teach Ronnie, and he learned some of it, but it's never the same as when I'm with Ronnie. They say sometimes people who are too much the same have a harder time, and I wonder if Lucas and me aren't too much the same. Maybe him needing his time is the same as me needing my quiet. We've always had a difficult relationship. He hasn't always liked the same things I do, but Ronnie seems like he does. He likes the quiet, and being in nature, and shooting.

On that day, Ronnie brought a .22 and I brought my .243. Why? Well, it's my favorite gun, that's why. It's light, and I use a reduced load on it. Well, this particular gun has a high velocity bullet, travels approximately thirty-four or thirty-five hundred feet a second. You can reduce the load down to about twenty-seven or twenty-eight and get less of a recoil, more accuracy and less, you know, less range. There are other modifications, too. I had it tailored so it's just right for me when I go to the range. Well, all my rifles have scopes on them. No, not the shotguns. I don't call them rifles. Just my rifles have scopes. Because, when you're shooting with a rifle you'll always want a scope. Why wouldn't you? This one, the .243, has a trigger shoe on it. Trigger. Shoe. It makes the trigger wide, so you can fit more of your finger on it. Yes, it does extend past the trigger guard some. Slightly. But that way it's easier to pull the trigger and it's steadier. That's the point of it. Less work to pull the trigger, so you don't mess up your shot. It's the same reason it has a hair trigger. Just makes it easier to pull. When you line up a shot, and then you pull the trigger, sometimes it moves the rifle and makes you miss. So, I have a trigger shoe and a hair trigger to make that not happen.

The three of us got to the property around noon, maybe a little after. Maybe one? I'm not sure. I wasn't wearing a watch. Lucas was driving. The driveway to our property was real muddy because it had rained a bunch the night before, so Lucas parked on the road, and we walked in. Yes, I already said we were carrying the rifles. Ronnie had his .22, I had my .243. and Lucas had his pellet gun. Lucas was off by himself over by the stream, and Ronnie and I went out into the field. It's mostly open, but there are some trees. There's also the foundation of where the new house is being built.

Yes, we do have some land at our place where the house is, but there's more wilderness space at the property. We didn't have anything else planned, and so we went. That's right, the property is right across from—well, kitty corner from—the Ellis house. Cliff and I used to help one another with things. When we were first planning the new house on the property, before all the delays and setbacks and the bank holding things up and then the contractors doing shit work and I couldn't find anyone to do it the way I wanted, he helped me figure some things out. He was kind of like me, in that he did a bunch of odd jobs. He knew a little of this and a little of that. I'd help him on his land, too. I'd say I knew him and his family pretty well.

Once, after I got out of prison, I went over to his house to talk to him, but he wasn't home. I had heard that him and some other people had been fishing on my property and they left a bunch of trash and bottles behind. When I got there, he wasn't home. So, no, I haven't talked to Cliff for, uh, over ten years. Sometimes we sleep in a camper on the property just to get away from the house. Sometimes I'm working on trying to move the new house-project forward, but it's slow going without the financing and being able to find reliable workers. Sometimes we go out there and walk or hunt. It's a nice break from the other place. But, no, I haven't spoken with Cliff again since that incident. Mrs. Ellis and I have talked once or twice since then. It was her I talked to about Cliff and his friends and their garbage on our property that day. And one other time, maybe, but I can't remember just what it was for. We stayed friendly enough. We didn't go out of our way to see each other.

Right. So, Ronnie and I walked for a while and when my back got tired, we'd sit and talk. Or sometimes we'd just listen and watch. No, we didn't do any shooting. We just didn't feel like it. We saw some things. Oh, rabbit, squirrels, pheasant. Well, first of all, a rifle isn't the right gun for a pheasant. You'd need a shotgun for that, and ours was back in the van. I think the shotgun was Lucas' because I don't remember putting it in the van. I don't know why he brought it. You'd have to ask him. Also saw some snakes, and the usual robins and the like. Truthfully, I wouldn't have minded getting the pheasant, that's still one of my favorite meals, but, like I said, we didn't have the right gun for it. Also, we were enjoying the quiet at that point.

Close to seven. I remember the sun was just starting to go down, and Ronnie said he was hungry. We started to walk back to the van. Close to six or seven hours sounds about right. It didn't feel that long, but it's not uncommon for us to spend afternoons that way. Like I said, we did this often. I remember the mosquitoes were getting bad as the sun went down, so we kept moving as quickly as we could. We were maybe only a mile, or maybe a half, from the road. It's real flat there, but there are cornfields on either side of the property. I could see the van. Like I said, it's real flat, and my eyes are good. As we got closer to the van, I could see Lucas was in the driver's seat.

Then, just about when Ronnie and I got to the van, a vehicle come up and stopped behind the van. At first, I didn't see who it was. Lucas got out of the van, and he went to go talk to whoever it was, and I sat down. I thought about unloading my rifle, but I was afraid of losing the bullets in the dark. Yes, I always carry my rifle loaded, because like I said, you never know. It doesn't do you any good to have a rifle and for it to not be loaded. What if I had wanted to shoot that pheasant? Then I would have had to stop, find my bullets, load them, and then get in position. If it's loaded, it's ready to go. So, I thought about unloading it, but then I was afraid I'd lose those bullets. I heard Lucas talking, and his voice got louder. Then he came back into the van. He indicated that it was Ellis in the truck behind us, but I don't remember exactly what he said. Cliff was angry about something and wanted us to move. Lucas said we weren't ready to move yet, and that he should go around. So, I went to the truck to see if I could figure out what was going on.

Yes, I took my rifle with me. I carried it like this. Kind of cradled in my arms. My left hand is wrapped around the mid-section and then my right hand is over the trigger area, but not on the trigger. It's common for someone who shoots a lot to hold a gun like this in the field. I didn't think about it being in my hands. It's kind of part of me. It's like an extension of my arm. You know, that's just how comfortable I am with it. Also, I didn't know what Clifford wanted. He sounded angry. About what, I have no idea, but he sounded mad about something. So, I went prepared to talk him down.

I walked back there and right away, he's yelling at me. Then before I even can really say anything, he's lunging at me out his truck window with this knife. Well, I didn't have time to do much more than lift my rifle up to block the knife. I didn't have time to really think or anything. I just lifted it up to block the knife because otherwise he was going to hit me in the face—or so I thought. At the same time, the truck's door hit me. I guess he opened it up into me. So, he was lunging at me with this knife and the door was hitting me, and then the gun just went off. I don't know how to explain it. Except for that trigger shoe I mentioned. Maybe that caught on one of the pockets of my jacket? I really don't know. It was so loud. Usually when I go shooting, I wear ear protection, earplugs. I didn't have any in because I didn't plan on shooting. My ears were ringing, and I didn't know what happened, or if Cliff was going to come back at me again.

I ran back to the van and said, "Let's get out of here."

They might have said something, but my ears were ringing so bad I couldn't hear anything they said. I think I just repeated, "Let's get out of here" until Lucas started driving. I really don't know if Ronnie said anything. No sir, I didn't tell my sons to lie. We didn't even talk that night, because like I said, I couldn't hear. My ears were still ringing. In the morning? We woke up early. Cleaned the guns because we got in so late the night before we didn't have a chance to do that. Yes sir, I always clean my guns. If I hadn't been so tired and out of sorts, not cleaning them probably would have kept me up all night until I did. As it was, I fell asleep right away. Yes, my wife did wake up when we got home. I don't really remember what I said, or what she said. In the morning, we cleaned the guns, and then the police came around nine. They took me and Lucas to the station, but I don't know what they did at my house because I wasn't there.

Again, I really don't know how the rifle went off without me pulling the trigger. It just did. Maybe the trigger shoe caught on something. I was wearing one of those vests with lots of pockets. It could have gotten caught in one of those. Maybe because of the hair trigger, it went off when it got bumped with the door. I really don't know. I just know I got hit with the truck door, a knife was coming at my face, and I lifted the rifle up to protect myself and it went off. That's all I know for sure.

No sir, I don't know what Lucas was talking about when he said I told him to lie. I would never do that. You'd have to ask him as to why he made that up. You heard my other boy. He told the truth. It was the same thing Lucas said until he suddenly said he was lying. I don't know why he'd change his story. Like I said, we never did get along. Maybe he wants me to go to prison. I don't know. Even if he had done it, killed that man, I would have taken the blame for him rather than have one of my sons go to prison. So, I don't know. I can only tell you the truth that I know. If I knew what caused the gun to go off, I would tell you.

Yes, I do usually wear ear protection, but I had taken it off. I wasn't expecting to be firing my gun anymore.

Look, when the gun went off, I didn't even know if Cliff was shot or not. I didn't know. I just knew he was angry, and he was waving a knife at me. So, when the gun went off, I just left. I didn't really think. Maybe when I said, "Let's get out of here," I thought that Cliff would leave us alone now that the gun went off. Maybe it scared him enough that he would leave us be. No sir, I didn't think to check because I didn't know if he had even gotten shot, and I didn't know what he would do. Also, I had my two sons, and I didn't want them to get into anything. Well, like hurt, if Cliff were to come after us. Or, trouble in case something had happened. I just didn't know. I wanted us out of there as quick as we could. No, I didn't tell my wife about what happened. I just said we spent the day at the property and had truck problems. Which was true, we did have truck problems.

Did the detective mention the tires? We had two flat tires while we were at the property. Lucas changed one before we got back to the vehicle, and then another one on the way home. I don't know what caused them, but to me, they look like bullet holes. I think Cliff might have shot at the tires while we were on the property. I don't know. He was drunk, and he does things when he's drunk. I remember one time he plugged up our toilet with newspaper to see how powerful the flush was. No, he didn't ask. If he had asked, I would have told him to go home and sleep it off. I only found out about it after the fact, when the toilet was plugged and leaking all over the place. That's how he was. Maybe he got bored. Maybe he didn't like that we were there. He's never forgiven me for what happened between me and his girl. Who knows. But I think it was him. We didn't notice the second one was flat until we were down the road.

Look, I just threw the gun across my face to protect myself when that knife was coming at me. And it just went off. If the gun is locked, you can slide the hand along the side. You wouldn't have to go just alongside it. I never put my finger on the trigger. Yes, it was by the trigger, but not on it. Or in it. Like I said, it could have went along like this, could have hit it with my hand when I swung the gun across this way as the knife was coming at my face. I'm really not sure if my hand or my clothes did it, but something hit the trigger. Well, I said, I don't really know if it hit my clothes or my hand slipped back as the door hit me and my hand slid along the side it and it went off. I don't know. The door knocked me back somewhat when it hit me.

Yes, that is correct. I went to the property, with my gun

and my sons, and we walked through the fields. I talked to Ronnie about game and birds and did not intend to hunt. That is all we did. We spent the day enjoying being outside and in each other's company. That's it. Guilty? No, I didn't do anything wrong. My actions weren't wrong, I mean. I didn't intend for Mr. Ellis to die, or to kill him. It happened. It does make me sick to think of it, but I'm not guilty because I didn't mean for that to happen. Right. I just swung the gun over towards his hand and knife to get it away from my head. No, I really don't know how it went off. My clothes, my fingers slipped, the door bumped me, maybe something hit the trigger housing. I don't know. I don't know how many times I can say that before you believe me. I don't know. I don't know. I don't know.

DETECTIVE ALAN GIL

I first interviewed Ronald Van Slyck at the picnic table in the backyard at the Van Slyck house. Because it was just an informal interview to gather some basic information, I didn't take notes. I asked him about what happened the previous day, and he said he didn't know. His condition? Oh, yes. He was nervous. A scared little boy. It didn't take much to tell he wasn't telling the truth. No, I didn't question him any further. There was no need. If I wanted to take a formal statement, I would have had Mrs. Van Slyck bring him down to the station to do that. No, Mrs. Van Slyck had no knowledge of the whereabouts of her family the previous day. She was at work until six, made dinner for everyone, and was surprised when no one was home in time for the meal. She went to bed and was sleeping when they returned. Yes sir, the two flat tires Mr. Van Slyck mentioned are in evidence.

CURTIS HARRINGTON

Thank you, Your Honor.

Ladies and gentlemen, you have been charged by the Court and instructed that you pay attention to the witnesses, observe the way they testify, the way they answer questions, and to judge whether they are telling the truth, manipulating it, or telling a version of it. This is a tall order, but that's the task put before you. Your task is to observe witnesses, hear testimony, draw your own conclusions, and to the best of your collective ability, determine if the Defendant is guilty or not, beyond a reasonable doubt, of the crimes for which he is charged. This is a serious matter, and I know you will not take lightly the obligation.

We have heard substantial testimony about the Defendant's expertise with firearms. How he was a sniper in the military. How he shot competitively. How he shot recreationally. How he hunted. How he altered his favorite rifle to fit his preferred specifications. How he packed his own bullets to control the kick from the rifle. There is no doubt he knew his way around a rifle. On the day in question, on the day Mr. Clifford Ellis was murdered, the

Defendant had his very favorite rifle with him.

However well the Defendant knows rifles in general, this particular rifle, the .243 that you see in evidence before you, is particularly well known by the Defendant. In fact, he described it in his testimony as being "like an extension of him." And yet, somehow, the Defendant lost control of this very rifle causing it to fire without his finger being on the trigger. If this rifle is indeed like an extension of the Defendant, then surely, he would have known to compensate for situations such as the one he described being in. At the very least, he would have known how to manage the wider than normal trigger to avoid catching it on a pocket or sleeve.

You have also heard from the Defendant's own testimony how far this particular rifle can shoot. It is also relevant to the case to note that this rifle fires a high velocity bullet that can travel about three times as fast as a .22, and it's carrying a lot more energy with it—probably near 15 times as much. This type of rifle and bullet are typically used for varmints (like raccoons, foxes, rodents) and for shooting coyote and hunting deer. Some people have taken down black bears with them. This is no toy, and the Defendant knows that. Getting hit by a .243 is going to do damage. He would have carried it with the respect due to a rifle capable of this kind of destruction.

And yet. And yet. When confronted with a *paring knife*, the Defendant recklessly waved this loaded rifle with its safety off, to deflect the blade. Does that sound like a thing that a trained professional would do? All this I say, and I haven't even brought up the question of whether the paring knife was an actual threat. Yes, there was a paring knife found on the floor of the truck, but according to Mrs. Ellis, that paring knife was frequently left in the truck. For all we know, it may have been there for several days or even weeks. There is no evidence that Mr. Clifford Ellis had it in his position with the intent to harm the Defendant. In fact, there is no evidence that Mr. Ellis held the knife, or waved it, or did anything to threaten the Defendant. We have only the Defendant's testimony and the testimony of his oldest son, who I remind you blatantly lied on the stand while under oath.

It's hard to know what to believe.

Additionally, the Defendant has been evasive in his answers. Remember when I asked him why he went to the truck? He didn't immediately provide an answer. I asked him again, and he mumbled something about a commotion, and then he said he just wanted to see what was going on. If he just wanted to see what was going on, then he should have said that, and it begs the question of why take the rifle with him. When I asked him to describe the commotion, he couldn't remember. But his memory becomes incredibly good when asked about Mr. Ellis attacking him with the paring knife. He's asking us to believe him. To believe him that what happened that night was an accident. That he went back to the truck to "see what was going on" and that Mr. Ellis attacked him with a paring knife—and, really, a paring knife? Is there anything less threatening to imagine than a drunk man coming at you with a paring knife?—and his truck door, and then, suddenly, mysteriously, without him having his finger near the trigger, the rifle, his favorite rifle, the one he had personally altered to fit his preferences, went off and killed a man. That's a pretty incredible story. He recalls every minute detail about the altercation and subsequent firing of the rifle.

Well, I'll tell you the truth: It wasn't an accident. The Defendant went to the property with a loaded gun. He had his son park their vehicle in the middle of the road, fully knowing that Mr. Ellis would have to leave the house at some point and not be able to get around him. Then the Defendant, a man with a bad back, walked for eight hours carrying a loaded rifle. And today he asks us to believe that this is all coincidence or accidental. I tell you, this was a premediated, intentional murder. The Defendant was there, creating the opportunity to exact his revenge.

The Ellises and Van Slycks were friendly at one time, but the affair between the Defendant and the deceased's daughter resulted in the Defendant spending time in jail for Statutory Rape. The Defendant has been waiting for a chance for revenge ever since. He's been thinking about this for a long time, and on that day he decided to take his chance. He'd drive to the property with his high-powered rifle, with a scope, and he'd wait for a chance to snipe the now deceased Mr. Ellis—as he had been trained in the military, and as he had practiced throughout his whole life—to get that revenge. He'd block the road, to ensure the Ellises couldn't go anywhere. And as the Defendant expected would happen, Mr. Clifford Ellis did try to leave his property, and he found the road blocked. The Defendant's calculated patience paid off. He didn't go back to Mr. Ellis' truck to see what was happening. There was no commotion. There was just Mr. Ellis, who had too much to drink, sitting in his truck. The Defendant killed him in cold blood.

Now, by the Defendant's own admission, he had plenty of land to walk around at home. In fact, he and his sons spent hours out there. They had land to hunt. They had room to shoot. On this day, they drove out of their way to do just that on their other property. Why? He couldn't answer that. "We just felt like it," was his answer. Well, I don't know about you, but I don't believe that. He went there to shoot and kill Mr. Clifford Ellis.

Clifford Ellis never even got out of his vehicle. The Defendant claims the door was opened into him, but there's no evidence of that. There's no dent on the door to indicate that it might have been rammed into someone. There is no evidence that Mr. Ellis had been opening, or trying to open, his door. The paring knife that the Defendant claims Mr. Ellis was waving at him was found on the floor of the truck on the passenger's side—not outside of the vehicle, the way you might assume it would be if someone had been waving it out of the window or out an open door. No one else mentioned the door being open. Only the Defendant. Only Mr. Van Slyck.

You heard the testimony of the medical examiner. He said that Mr. Ellis' death was instantaneous. The shot went into the brain stem and severed the connection between the spinal column and the brain. The bullet went through the mouth and into the spinal column. That sounds like a heck of a shot to me, not some random accidental misfiring of a rifle.

You heard his oldest son lie on the stand, and then recant his story. His second version of the story doesn't match the version his father told on the stand.

You heard the Defendant's youngest son tell a story that matches the Defendant's testimony, but the youngest son was purportedly *inside* the van and wouldn't have been able to see what was happening behind him. Additionally, he's ten, he was tired, and it had already been a long day. If you listened closely to his testimony, you can hear this is a young witness who has been coached and prepared. Not by Mr. Copeland mind you, but by Mr. Van Slyck. Little Ronnie told the version of the story that his father told him to tell.

So the question you must wrestle with, as a jury, is whether or not this was an accident. Remember, Mr. Van

Slyck told his sons "let's get out of here" instead of calling for help. It would have taken no time to go to the Ellis house and use the telephone to ask to report the accident or at the very least to alert Mrs. Ellis of the accident. Instead, the Defendant fled the scene of the crime with his boys. They drove away.

When asked about this, he said to me, "I didn't know what had happened."

Really? This is a man who's been around a rifle all his life. He's served—I mean, let's say, participated—in three wars, and he expects you to believe he shoots a man—through his mouth—and doesn't know what happened?

In sum: We have a man, the Defendant, with a grudge against another man, Mr. Clifford Ellis. The Defendant drives out of his way to be on the property closer to Mr. Ellis' house, to walk around for eight hours with a loaded sniper rifle. He shoots nothing all day. He reports no problems or concerns with the functioning of said rifle, but the minute he encounters Mr. Ellis, suddenly, boom, the rifle goes off without explanation. And then, he flees the scene of the crime.

Let me assure you, ladies and gentlemen of the jury, this was not an accident nor was this manslaughter. This was a planned, premeditated murder. When the Court charges you on the elements of murder and manslaughter, you listen very carefully because what Achiel Van Slyck did to Clifford Ellis was murder in the first degree. It was a calculated, cold-blooded, planned act to kill an unarmed, defenseless man. The Defendant wants to cast doubt on this, but the evidence is clear. This was no accident.

I understand it's not easy to say that a man is guilty of murder in the first degree, but it is your sworn duty to listen to the facts, and if you do, you will see irrefutable evidence that Mr. Van Slyck killed Mr. Ellis in a premediated act of

murder.
　　Thank you.

RAYMOND COPELAND

Ladies and gentlemen of the jury, because the burden of proof is on the prosecution, they must prove their case beyond a reasonable doubt. Remember, in this country, we are innocent until proven guilty, and I don't know about you, but after three days of listening to the prosecution's case and Mr. Harrington's closing statement, I'm not convinced.

Right from the inception of this case, it's been clear that there are holes in the prosecution's argument for murder. Keep in mind, we are not arguing whether or not the Defendant, Mr. Achiel Van Slyck killed Mr. Clifford Ellis. That is not up for debate. It happened. It was a horrible, horrible accident. While you deliberate the future of my client, remember that intent matters here, and that's where you come in. You, members of the jury, must use your best judgement, based on what you've heard these last couple days, to decide if my client *intended* to kill Mr. Ellis. Did the Defendant, sitting here before you, really go to the property on that day intending to kill Mr. Ellis? The answer is no. He did not.

Yes, the Defendant knew guns inside and out. He modified his rifle to fit his preferences. He loaded his own shells. He was a marksman. He shot competitively. He was trained as a sniper in the US Army. These are things the prosecutor has claimed as liabilities, but they are simple facts. There are lots of people who are gifted with rifles who don't commit murder. My client is one of them.

Machines aren't perfect. Sometimes you think you know a machine, and then it behaves erratically. You have a toaster that you've had for twenty years, and it has always made perfect toast, until one day the toast gets stuck, and it burns it black. You couldn't have predicted that. Maybe after that one burnt piece of toast, the toaster works fine again. It might never get stuck again, but that one day, it did. A rifle is a machine, too. You bump it just right, you nudge it, or who knows, something causes it to behave unexpectedly. It doesn't matter if you're a master over that machine or if you've seen it function properly thousands of times; sometimes things just happen. That's what happened here with the Defendant's rifle. He's shot that rifle so many times—I really wouldn't even know how to hazard a guess—but that day, on that unfortunate day, it went off without warning and killed a man.

Can you imagine being in that position? You've spent all day outside, walking in nature, talking with your children. It's been a long day, and you just want to get home. Your boys are tired. Your back is hurting. Then there's a commotion and the neighbor—who, okay, you've had run-ins with before and you're not on the best terms— is drunk and yelling at you. He waves a knife at you, and you try to deflect that knife with the rifle because it's an extension of your arm. You heard my client say that; he thought of it as an extension of his arm. Even the prosecution used that phrase. Instead of just deflecting that blade, the rifle goes off. It's deafeningly loud. Your children are saying something to you, but you can't hear them. You just hear ringing in your ears. You panic. You just killed a man. You run.

Yes, the Defendant should have done things differently. He should have stopped to see if Mr. Ellis was okay, but remember, Mr. Ellis had just threatened him with a knife. The Defendant should have gone to the Ellis house to alert Mrs. Ellis and to ask to use her phone to call for help. It hurts to hear that Mrs. Ellis had to find her husband like that, and that her daughter had to find her father that way. As a married man and a parent, I can only imagine what that was like. I can't take that harm back, and neither can my client. There was a terrible, terrible accident, and he will spend the rest of his life thinking about what he could have done differently that night. But it won't turn back the clock. It won't undo Mrs. Ellis and her daughter finding Mr. Ellis in his truck. It won't bring Mr. Ellis back to life. It can't. Sending the Defendant to prison for life won't undo any of that damage. All it will do is tear another family apart for something that was not—as the prosecutor describes it—an intentionally, cold-blooded, premeditated murder. Members of the jury, we're not here to discuss what he should have done; we're here to talk about what he did do.

The prosecutor has accused witnesses of lying on the stand—lies by this person, lies by that person. I find it hard to believe that a witness would deliberately try to mislead the court. Honestly, in all my years in a courtroom, I have never heard people deliberately lie. People see things in different ways. You've heard the story about the blind men and the elephant? Each touches a piece of the elephant— one the trunk, another the skin, and the other an ear—and they are convinced that they know what an elephant is. It's a snake; it's a tree trunk; it's a fan. To them, that is the truth. Or, forget about the elephant and blind men; just think about anything in the news, or something that happened with your family recently, something simple like a Thanksgiving dinner. Each person, each perspective, has a different idea of what happened, and for that person it's the truth.

We know Ronnie, the youngest Van Slyck, was tired that night. He was falling asleep in the van. He probably didn't know what happened, and probably didn't see what happened. Furthermore, this was something that happened in darkness; it involved a gun; and no one, aside from Mr. Van Slyck and the deceased, had a good view.

We know Ronnie respects his father and loves him very much. You can see that by how they interact in this courtroom. And remember the hours Ronnie spent with his father walking through the woods. Eight hours with no complaint. That's a boy who looks up to his father. So, if Ronnie asked his father what happened outside the van that night, he would have no reason not to believe his father's version of the accident. This is a boy who looks up to his father, and his father tells him something; he's going to take that as fact.

I don't know about you, but I have memories of things that I shouldn't have. I mean, things that happened when I was way too young to really remember. How do I remember my great-grandparents holding me when I was one? I couldn't possibly remember that. Could I? And yet I do. I can picture them clearly. My great-grandfather wore a blue suit with one of those Western-style bolo ties. He was clean-shaven. His blue eyes glimmered as he smiled at me. My great-grandmother wore a dress that almost matched the color of my great-grandfather's suit. Her hair was pulled back and done up in a bun. Her glasses slid down her nose a little, but that's where they usually sat. My great-grandfather bounced me on his knee as my great-grandmother chuckled and smiled.

If you had asked me before, I would have sworn on a Bible that this is my memory. They've done studies and shown people can't remember stuff from that young. So, how do these experts explain my so-called memory? They claim that it's based on photographs and stories and not on core memories. So guess what? I went through my photo album and found a photograph of me with my great-grandparents, dressed just as I described them. My parents probably went through these photographs with me as an older child after my great grandparents had passed and told me the story about how my great-grandfather used to like to bounce me on his knee. Somehow, my love and respect for my parents paired with those stories and photographs worked together to form a memory, and if asked, I'd swear up and down that I remember it just like the day it actually happened.

Ronnie's recollection of the events the night Mr. Ellis was killed are obviously not formed from a photograph. But it's not so different in that he has a father he loves and respects who told him what happened that night, and Ronnie believes him. So much, in fact, that it has become his memory, too. It might not be perfect, but it is what you'd expect from a ten-year-old.

Lucas is a different situation. Here's an older boy, a man in fact, who was also there that night. Why doesn't his story add up? Like Ronnie, he experienced bits and pieces of that night. It was dark, and he had just had a verbally violent confrontation with Mr. Ellis. He was a little shaken up, and he was probably nervous about Mr. Ellis getting out of his truck to approach the van, visibly drunk and angry. Even if he was looking in the rearview mirror to do his best to watch for Mr. Ellis, he really couldn't see well – again only bits and pieces of the whole.

It's natural for the brain to try to fill in the missing pieces and to make sense out of partial information. I'm sure you've played telephone before. You know, the game where you have a line of people. One whispers a phrase or sentence or a story to another one, and then each person repeats what they heard (or think they've heard) until it gets to the end of the line. Then, that final person repeats what they've been told, and it doesn't match the story, or phrase, or sentence, that the first person started out with. It's a silly little game that plays on what I'm trying to describe here. It should be easy to communicate one idea from one person to the next to the next to the next to the next and to the final person, but it doesn't work out that way. That's what's fascinating about the brain. It finds patterns where patterns might not exist. It takes gibberish and tries to make sense of it. Once it's made those connections, you believe them to be the truth until you're convinced otherwise.

In the case of the accident that night, Lucas suffered dissonance from what his brain originally tried to clarify and what he heard from his father about what happened. The two don't match up—which makes sense because Lucas didn't have all the information when he first tried to create order out of chaos, but his father did.

I don't know how many of you have ever been in that witness box. I don't remember if we asked that at jury selection, and if you answered, I don't remember who had or hadn't. I hope you never have to wind up there, because, if you have, it means something has gone awry and you're being called on to testify as to what you saw to help the Court make sense of it all. But, if you've never been there before, you don't know what it's like. If you've been there, you know it's stressful. The entire Court is looking at you. The judge, the jury, the attorneys, the court reporter, the bailiff, the defendant, and all the people sitting back there. That's a lot of eyes and ears on you, but all you have to do is put your hand on that Bible, swear to tell the truth, and then answer some questions. It shouldn't be hard. Except that it is. You start noticing all those eyes and ears on you, and you start thinking about the person who is on trial here and how what you have to say will impact the trial and whether or not that person goes to jail, or prison, or might have to pay some fine, and you start to question yourself.

Something that should be easy, suddenly is very, very hard. Now, put yourself in the position of Lucas, the oldest son of the man on trial for murder. And here he is, with his own version of what his brain put together from the pieces he saw and heard on the night in question, and the more complete version of what his father told him. Suddenly, he's not so certain of what happened that night. He tells one version, what he thinks is true. He gets tripped up by the prosecutor when he's asked some questions he can't answer, and he begins to question the truth himself. So, he tells another version that the prosecutor seems to like better. People like to please people. You can tell just from eye contact and body language whether or not someone likes you and what you're saying. The prosecutor didn't have to say, "Yes, I like this version better," but Lucas could tell from the way the prosecutor was holding himself that he did.

It wasn't that Lucas deliberately lied. It was that he wasn't sure what the truth was to begin with, and he did the best he could.

Another thing to keep in mind: The event we're talking about transpired in seconds. That's it. A lot can happen in seconds. You heard my client say "I think" and "I'm not sure" an awful lot. The prosecutor made a big deal about this and tried to suggest my client wasn't being truthful. I'd argue Mr. Van Slyck said "I think" and "I'm not sure" a lot because he was trying to be *very* truthful. When something happens that quickly, how can you be certain of anything? Mr. Van Slyck wasn't expecting the truck door to bump into him, or Mr. Ellis to be waving a knife at him, or any of that. He approached the vehicle with the intent to determine what was wrong. Everything else that happened was a surprise to him.

Let's think about that for a moment.

How many times do we hear someone say, "I don't know what happened. Suddenly I was in the ditch."

Or, "The deer came out of nowhere!"

When things surprise us, we aren't prepared to pay attention to the details. You know, my wife threw a surprise party for me a couple years ago. There was this whole group of people hiding behind couches and chairs and in the kitchen and whatnot. I had been working on a case and was late getting home. It was November, so the house was dark. I expected my wife and children were out. I walked into the living room and flipped on lights, and suddenly, everyone is leaping up from everywhere yelling surprise! They all knew I was coming, and they were watching everything I did. Afterwards, they all talked about how my face looked and how I dropped my briefcase and stumbled backwards. When you ask me about what I saw, I have almost no memory of it. I couldn't tell you who was standing there in front of me—and these are my friends and family members—because they were bombarding me from all sides. Here's the point. I wasn't expecting to be surprised like that. I wasn't ready to record detail and to pay attention. I thought no one was home and that I was going to have to warm up leftovers on my own.

Now, that was a happy occasion, but imagine Mr. Van Slyck in that moment of panic. It's dark. A man is waving a knife at him. A truck door bumps into him. His rifle goes off. He can't hear. Somewhere in that moment, he remembers his sons are waiting for him—even less sure of what's going on—in the van. And we are going to expect that he can remember, with complete and utter certainty, what happened in those mere seconds? It's a tall order for anyone. Could he have gotten some of the details wrong? Of course. Was he lying intentionally to deceive? No. Not at all. Was his saying "I think" and "I'm not sure" being dishonest? No. He was just being as honest as anyone could be in that situation.

One final point. The prosecutor wants you to believe this was premeditated murder. That my client, Mr. Van Slyck, went out of his way to orchestrate a situation to enact revenge on Mr. Ellis. If that were true, can you imagine a scenario where a man would want to bring his children to that scene? My client is, as both sides have established, gifted with a rifle. If he wanted to shoot Mr. Ellis, he could have done that from hundreds, maybe even a thousand feet away. Why would he involve his children? If this was premeditated, and my client was as devious and scheming as the prosecutor would have you believe, then why do such a terrible job of covering his tracks? My client spent almost the entire day on the property and parked in the road. The Ellis family knew he was there. You heard Mrs. Ellis say she saw them come and kept her eye on them throughout the day. Clearly my client wasn't trying to hide.

The prosecutor made a big deal about how Mr. Van Slyck could have stayed on his other property that day. That's a ludicrous argument. Mr. Van Slyck legally owns both properties. Where he chooses to hunt on any given day is irrelevant. And finally, if he was trying to be sneaky and to get away with murder, why shoot Mr. Ellis in his truck and leave him there in the middle of the road? Why not concoct a better alibi? Why not call the police and say there's been an accident? This is a man who was surprised, panicked, and ran, not a man who planned to murder somebody in cold blood.

I will conclude with this: You have all the facts before you, and it's up to you to decide if you think it adds up to premeditated murder. You aren't determining what could have or should have been done. Just the facts, and the facts clearly point to this being a terrible accident. Things happened quickly, and my client has done his best to present the truth to you.

Thank you very much.

JUDGE WILKERSON

Ladies and gentlemen, I will reread the instructions that I originally gave to you, as I am required to do. There are two kinds of murder, first degree and second degree. Murder of either degree is killing of one person by another with malice. Malice is a term with a special meaning in the law. Malice means that the defendant intended to kill and/or knowingly created a very high risk of death with knowledge that it probably would result in death and that he did so under circumstances which did not justify excuse or lessen the crime. The law that applies to this case states that all willful, deliberate, and premeditated murder shall be murder of the first degree.

The Defendant is charged with the crime of murder of the first degree and has pleaded not guilty to the charge.

First-degree murder and second-degree murder are the same crime, except that first-degree murder has the additional elements of premeditation and deliberated his intent to kill. You will first be instructed on murder of the second degree. Keep in mind that all the elements of second-degree murder are necessary to prove first degree murder. The killing of a human being by another may be entirely innocent. It is not the act of killing itself that makes it a crime, but the state of mind with which it is done. A killing is not murder if it is justified, excused, or if it occurs under circumstances that make the killing the lesser crime of manslaughter; for murder, you must find the defendant consciously and knowingly performed the act that caused death. The defendant must have either intended to kill— that is, he must have done the act intending that it result in death or in great and serious bodily injury—or he must have knowingly created a very high risk of death with the knowledge that it would cause death. The degree of risk for murder must be so reckless and wrongful as to amount to a criminal purpose aimed against a person's life and the defendant must have been conscious of that risk.

To establish second-degree murder, the prosecution must prove each of the preceding elements beyond a reasonable doubt for the Defendant before you. First, that the deceased, Mr. Clifford Ellis, died on or about April 3, 1975, within the County of Livingston; second, Mr. Clifford Ellis' death was caused by an act of the Defendant—that is, that Clifford Ellis died as a result of being shot by the rifle by the Defendant, Mr. Achiel Van Slyck; third, if you find that the death was caused by the Defendant, you must determine whether the Defendant is guilty of any crime.

Now, as I previously indicated to you, the instructions then go on as to the elements of premeditation and deliberation and willful act. If the evidence does not convince you beyond a reasonable doubt that the Defendant intended to kill, you must consider whether he acted with an unreasonable disregard for human life. It is sufficient for murder of the second degree if the Defendant consciously created the very high degree of risk of death and if he had knowledge of the probability of those consequences. However, if you find that the Defendant's acts did not amount to such a criminal purpose aimed against life, you must find the defendant not guilty of murder and consider whether or not he is instead guilty of manslaughter.

In order to establish the crime of manslaughter, the prosecution must prove each of the following elements beyond a reasonable doubt: first, that Clifford Ellis died on or about April 3, 1975, within the County of Livingston; second, that Mr. Clifford Ellis' death was caused by an act of the Defendant; third, that the Defendant caused the death of Mr. Clifford Ellis without lawful justification or excuse; fourth, that when the Defendant did the act that caused death, the Defendant must have been acting in a grossly negligent manner. Gross negligence means more than carelessness. It means willful, wanton and reckless disregard of the consequences that might follow from a failure to act and an indifference to the rights of others. In order to find the Defendant guilty of gross negligence, you must find beyond a reasonable doubt, first, that the Defendant knew of the danger to another—that is, that this was a situation requiring ordinary care and diligence to avoid injuring another; second, that the Defendant had the ability to avoid harm to another by exercise of such ordinary care; and, third, that the Defendant failed to use such care and diligence to prevent the threatened danger when, to the ordinary mind, it must have been apparent that the result was likely to cause serious harm to another.

Those are, once again, ladies and gentlemen of the jury, the instructions that I gave you. You may adjourn to the jury room.

JUROR #41

You all heard the judge. This is, what, the third time he's spelled it out for us? We have his words right here, typed out in front of us from the court lady who's typing down everything that's been said. What more do you need? Achiel did it. He meant to do it. He had motive, he had opportunity, and he had a history of exacting outrageous revenge. I really don't know what your hang up is.

Well, to that I say, listen again to what the judge said. No, no, no. Just wait. Let me find it here.

Here are the judge's words: "It is sufficient for murder of the second degree if the defendant consciously created the very high degree of risk of death and if he had knowledge of the probability of those consequences."

Blocking the road, carrying a loaded rifle, waving the rifle around, even if he was just trying to block the knife, but come on, it was a *paring* knife. You're telling me there's still some doubt in your mind about whether or not he created a, uhm, "Very high degree of risk of death"? That's second-degree murder right there. Right there. This isn't manslaughter. There's no reason to even talk about manslaughter. He killed the man. He wanted to, and he did it.

And, what's more, he doesn't seem sorry. Did any of you hear him say sorry? Or that he wished he had done something different? I know that doesn't make him guilty of murder versus manslaughter, but come on. We're done here. None of you are going to change my mind. Let's get back in there and call this a day. I never thought I'd say this before, but I want to get back to work.

RONNIE

I did what Dad told me. Am I going to get into trouble now? Lucas didn't follow the plan. Is the judge going to be mad? Is Dad going to be mad? I did what he told me to. I did it. It was Lucas who didn't listen. He started to, but then he changed his story. That lawman tricked him. Or maybe Lucas wants Dad to go away. I don't. I don't want Dad to go away. He can be mean sometimes, but he's still our dad. I like hunting with him. He always shows me how to find signs. He knows all the plants and where the deer go. I like how he fixes squirrel. My friends made fun of me when I said we eat squirrel, but I said they've just never had it the way Dad makes it. He makes it really good. George says his dad made squirrel once, but it was full of shot and he chipped his tooth. I've never chipped a tooth on the squirrel that Dad makes. He gets all the shot out of them. He's even teaching me to drive and is going to give me his Chevy Nova. I love how he builds things out of metal. He's showing me how to weld, too, so I can do that. We're working on a go-kart frame together. We just need the right lawn mower engine for it and a few more welds to finish the frame. It's going to be so fast. If Dad goes away, I don't know if I can finish it. Will you ask Dad if I can weld without him? I think I know enough now. And maybe Lucas can help me. No, don't say anything about Lucas helping. That will make Dad mad.

Do I have to come to court again? It's so boring here. I'd almost rather be at school. At least there I get recess and can see my friends. I guess you're right. I probably should be here for Dad, in case he needs me.

SOPHIE

I lost my shit. I know it's not healthy, and I know I scared the shit out of Anton, but I had just spent the whole day in court listening to my father testify about murdering his neighbor. Then, I go to pick up Anton from Matthew's house. They're in the front yard, and our little boy is standing over Matthew.

He's shouting, "You're dead! You're dead! I shot you!"

I just flipped. I jumped out of the car, didn't even close the door, and grabbed the stupid toy gun out of his hand and threw it. I let him have it. The poor thing, and then I turned on his friend.

"Do you think guns are toys? What kind of game are you playing? Shooting someone is not a game!"

Neither of them knew what to make of me. Matthew ran inside, and Anton just stood there. I waited for him to say something, and then I noticed what he was wearing. Those camouflage pants, which I think we bought him though I'm wondering why now, and this T-shirt with the words "Kill 'em all let God sort 'em out." It had a skull wearing a beret, with a lightning bolt behind it, and angel wings. I have no idea where he got that, definitely not from us. He was just swimming in the thing. It was probably three sizes too big. At this point, Anton still didn't say anything, and I had run out of steam, but I was so disgusted and angry.

I said, "Get in the car and wait for me."

As he walked toward the car, I went to the house to thank Monica for watching Anton and to apologize for yelling at Matthew. I was so distracted. It was only after I heard the crunch and snap of plastic that I realized I'd stepped on the toy gun I had thrown.

Monica wasn't mad. She understood. She said the fatigues and shirts came from her brother, and the boys were just playing guns. I haven't told many people about what's going on. Honestly, it's nice having some distance from all that now that we live here, but I figured Monica should know. So, I told her. And it felt good to get that out, to tell someone. I wasn't sure what she was going to say, but when I was done, she didn't say much of anything. She just took it in and was sympathetic. She didn't try to counter with a story of her own, and she didn't ask too many questions, which was nice. I should have told her sooner when I first asked her to watch Anton. She needed to know what was going on, and why I was going to need her to sit so many days. She doesn't seem to mind though. She said the boys always play nice and find creative things to do. She said that watching the two of them is easier than watching just one of hers. I'm glad Anton has a friend like that because usually when I get home from court, like today, I'm fried. I don't have much left in the tank for him.

Do you know what my father said today? It's so ridiculous. I can't believe he even said it. He's a smart man, but can he really believe anyone buys it?

He said, "Mr. Ellis was waving a knife around and

threatening me. I raised my rifle to block his knife, and Mr. Ellis opened the door to his vehicle. The door bumped my rifle, and it went off, shooting him in the mouth."

Can you believe that? He went on to explain how he had filed the trigger down so it was easier for him to pull it, and that's why it was so sensitive. I mean, who in their right mind uses a rifle to block a knife? And, really, how far could Mr. Ellis have leaned out of his vehicle with a knife anyway? If he was drunk, and everyone admits Ellis was drunk as a skunk, he couldn't have posed much of a threat. You know my dad. He wouldn't have had a problem handling Ellis even if Ellis had been sober. It was hilarious hearing the attorney question him back.

He kept asking, "Mr. Van Slyck, I thought you were well-trained with rifles. Weren't you a sniper? Didn't you serve in two wars? Sorry, three wars? Aren't guns your hobby? Haven't you been hunting and around guns all your life? If so, how do you explain your careless behavior with a rifle you were so familiar with? One tailored to your own preferences? And then, let's not forget, a direct shot into the deceased's mouth, severing his spinal cord and killing him almost instantly. You expect us to believe that was an accident?"

All good questions, don't you think? How on earth didn't Dad think this through a little better. Or, you know, just plead guilty and accept his punishment.

They called Lucas back to the stand today, too.

The lawyer started with, "This is going to be a tough question, but is your father a strict father, harsh, hard?"

And Lucas said, "Yes."

"Maybe a little afraid of him."

I remember those words because it was so weird. It wasn't quite a sentence or a question. The lawyer presented it more as a statement for Lucas to consider.

But Lucas answered, "Yes."

I can't help but wonder what I would have done or said if they had called me. I'm sure I would have said and done exactly the same thing. Who knows? I wasn't there, and nobody seems to want to tell me what actually happened. I know you know this, but sometimes it helps to say it out loud again. It's almost like I forget that it's real because it's so unbelievable. I only found out when Dad and Ronnie called me to say Dad was arrested. I guess it was just Ronnie and him at home, and Ronnie answered the door.

You know, it wasn't the first time police had been to our house. I mean, with a dad like mine, you can only imagine. But they didn't come often. It wasn't like we had gotten used to seeing them on our porch. Ronnie said they asked if Dad was home, and said they needed to speak with him. Next thing he knew, Dad was leaving with the officers in the squad car. Just like that. Mom was over at Mina's house, which meant now Ronnie was home alone. He called me, completely freaked out. I had Anton with me, but we went over there, and Ronnie told me what happened. I called Mom, and she said she'd be home soon. It felt like forever, and then Mom had to go to the station, too. I ended up cobbling together some dinner from odds and ends. Mom got home around eight, and Anton was already asleep by then. I brought him home, and I was just beat, and I hadn't even done anything. But, whatever we were going through, I can only imagine what Mrs. Ellis had to deal with that night.

Mrs. Ellis' testimony was today, too, and it was hard to hear. She described Mr. Ellis' relationship with Dad and how they used to work together and help one another on the property. She tried to skip over the whole thing with Miriam—Miriam was there, but I couldn't bring myself to talk to her. I hope they don't make her take the stand. I really don't know what she'd add—but the lawyer made Mrs. Ellis talk about it. Mrs. Ellis started crying when she recounted the night Mr. Ellis died. I guess they saw Dad and the boys drive by their property. Mr. Ellis assumed they were going to work on the house, or do some hunting. But then he didn't hear any hammers or saws or guns, so he wondered what was going on, and if everything was okay. Mrs. Ellis did say that Mr. Ellis had been drinking. He was laid off, and you know how he had that injury that kept him from working regular, and he was usually into quite a few drinks by four in the afternoon.

Anyway, she said that Mr. Ellis kept saying, "I wonder if they're okay. It doesn't seem right."

He wanted to go check on them, but he also didn't trust Dad, and didn't want to leave Miriam and Mrs. Ellis alone. Mrs. Ellis described how Mr. Ellis asked her to lock up the house while he checked on Achiel and the boys and to not let anyone in. He said he needed to go check things out so that he could stop worrying about it. I guess Mr. Ellis had a way of dwelling on things, and she didn't want him dwelling on this all night.

Then she started crying again because she said, "What if I had just let him dwell? Would that have been so bad? I should have just let him dwell! Then he'd still be alive."

It took her a while to settle back down, and then she said that Mr. Ellis had been gone for a while when she heard the shot. Just one. She knew he'd been shot. It was just a feeling she had, but she knew. She had promised to keep the house locked up and to keep Miriam safe, and so she waited. It didn't take long before she heard Dad and the boys drive by the house. She said they weren't speeding away, but they weren't going slow either.

As soon as Dad's truck drove away, Mrs. Ellis got Miriam in the car. She really didn't want to take Miriam because she thought Achiel might circle back around and they would be vulnerable, and so she kept worrying about what to do. Ultimately she decided she'd rather have Miriam with her than leave her alone at the house. She described how they found Mr. Ellis, sitting in his car, shot through the mouth.

She said, "There was a lot of blood, and I knew he was dead, just like I knew it before but now I could see it and knew it for sure."

Mrs. Ellis said Miriam just stood there in shock.

"She knew too, just like I did, before we left the house. We knew that gun shot was meant for Cliff."

They went back to the house and called the police.

The attorney asked her some more questions.

I can't imagine anyone on the jury not being able to connect the dots from Dad, to Dad and Miriam, to the bad blood, to Dad being on the property, a single shot, and then a dead Mr. Ellis. Even with Dad, Lucas, and Ronnie lying on the stand, there is no way someone heard what Mrs. Ellis said and doesn't know that Dad did it intentionally. He's going away, Gerry. He's going away for a long time, and I really don't care.

MINA

He's an arrogant fool. I can't believe he wanted to go on the stand, and that his fool lawyer let him. I'm sorry, but your husband thinks he can just get away with anything, and he seems to think he's walking away from this, too. I can't see any way out of this for him. And good. It's about damn time he gets what he deserves. And you can finally get yourself away from him. Wait, you're not honestly thinking about staying married to him when he's in there? That's crazy. Crazy people marry or stay married to murderers. I was reading about how that Charles Manson gets marriage proposals in the mail all the time. What's wrong with people? Hold up, Lucia. I know very well what the Bible says, but Achiel is a terrible person. I told you to get out *before* all of this. Remember when your daughter found you and had to stop him from strangling the life out of you? I don't know how you stayed married to him after that. Or when he had the affair with that girl? You know how I feel about the church, and you know I believe, but you have to also believe the Lord is sending you a sign—multiple signs—that it's okay to be done with this one. You and your kids can finally move on. He did this to himself.

Too old? At fifty-two? You still have at least thirty years maybe forty years thanks to Mom and Dad's genes. You really want to spend that time waiting for a killer to get out of prison to come back to you? Are you going to spend your retirement going to visit him in prison? Is that what you want for your life? Me, I want to go back to Sicily. I want to travel. I want to do things with you, my sister. Divorce him and come live with me. We'll travel and keep each other company. We have good schools down here. Ronnie can finish up here. If he wants to go to college, there's Wayne State or a bunch of other community colleges. Plus, it's close to Gerry and Sophie. It's almost half as far away as you are now. I know, it's your house and you worked hard to make it. But, don't you see him everywhere in that place? I know the trial isn't over yet, but you have to start thinking ahead. You know he killed that man. They're not even debating that. It's just a matter of whether it was an accident or not—and you and I both know Achiel is too good with guns to have an "accident" with one. I wasn't even there, and I can tell you what happened. That man came over, said something Achiel didn't like, and Achiel shot him right in the mouth to shut him up. He's always been a hot-tempered, cold-blooded fool, and this time he's going to pay for it.

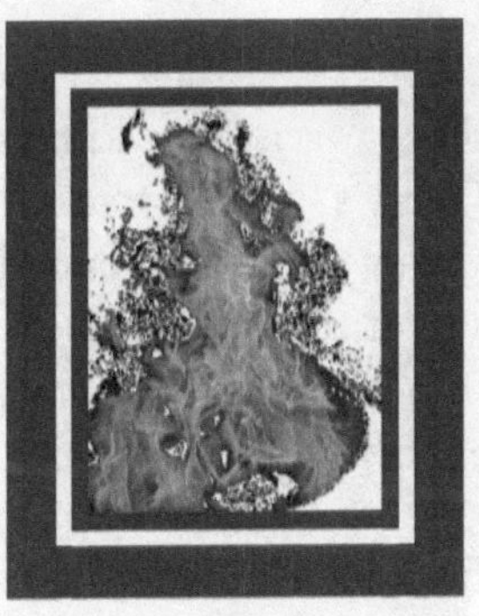

PART VI: WEDDINGS

Achiel wasn't there for many weddings, but he did make it to Sophie and Gerry's, and he walked Sophie down the aisle. That was six years after the affair with Miriam. Sophie hadn't exactly forgiven him for sleeping with her friend, but their relationship had come a long way since his year in prison paying for his crime. Sophie had always been Achiel's favorite.

Sophie is a first child, which definitely helps. She changed Achiel's life and his perspective on the world. Suddenly he had these feelings for someone that he had never had before, and he had a willingness to truly do anything to ensure her safety and happiness. As he held her early in the morning when she was first born, trying to soothe her back to sleep, he marveled at how anyone could not feel this connection to a child. This, of course, turned his thoughts toward his own parents. Their situation had been different, and difficult, but still, he couldn't help but wonder if they had ever felt this kind of love for him, too. He tried to envision his father cradling baby Achiel in his arms and trying to soothe him, but the image wouldn't come. It was incompatible with every other memory of his father.

When Lucia first told Achiel that she was pregnant, he was immediately confronted with two competing emotions: extreme joy and terror. The joy was understandable, and the terror was brought on by the fear that he would be just like his father, unable to break the cycle of abuse and emotional distance. But now, holding this little girl in his arms and almost weeping to himself as he looked into her not-tired eyes as they locked into his own eyes, he knew he had nothing to fear. He was nothing like his parents.

That all said, it was a bit of a disappointment that his firstborn wasn't a boy. He wanted a son to teach to hunt, shoot, and survive in nature. Achiel's favorite pastime was simply walking, and sometimes, even more simply, sitting in nature. He would marvel at all the things around him. He would look for signs, and track animals, not to kill, just to watch. He loved his quiet time in the woods, and he longed to share that quiet time with a son.

However, whatever disappointment he might have initially felt at Sophie being a girl was quickly dispelled as she grew up to be boyish. She wrestled with him. She loved getting dirty and playing in the mud. She tore the heads off her dolls and preferred to play with her wooden animals and toy cars. It didn't take long before Achiel realized he could do all the things he wanted to with a son, with his daughter. And so, he did.

The love and attention Achiel heaped onto Sophie was deepened by the fact that Lucas was such a disappointment to him. Here was his boy! But, Lucas was effeminate and weak and had curly hair. Achiel couldn't help but think the boy's girlishness was abetted by being named after Lucia's mother, Luciana. Worse, his skin was dark and that hair almost looked like an afro. He wasn't black-black, but definitely darker than either Lucia or Achiel. Even though Achiel knew his wife would never have cheated on him, he couldn't help but think Lucas wasn't his son. There was no way his genes could have produced a son who didn't look like him. When Lucia and he had particularly nasty arguments, he would throw that accusation at Lucia because while Sophie was definitely his favorite, Lucas was Lucia's little sweetie. She babied Lucas, which certainly didn't help the boy become any more manly in Achiel's eyes.

As Sophie got older, she became more and more like her father, which caused conflict between them but also managed to make him love and respect her all the more. She stood up to her father. When he was seething angry and out of words, he would lock eyes with his children. Lucas always looked away immediately or blinked. Ronnie rarely made him this angry, but Sophie never backed down. As comical as it seemed to an outsider, Achiel and Sophie would stare into one another's eyes until something external interrupted them. Often this was Lucia, saying "Come on, you two. Make up." And even then, with this interruption, neither would blink. They would slowly turn at the same time to look at Lucia and level their glare at her. While Sophie had grown into the person that Achiel could enjoy spending solitude with in the woods, she lost interest when she became a teenager and found boys more interesting. Then Ronnie took her place as the boy Achiel could spend hours with in the woods. Even after Ronnie replaced her on Achiel's long walks through the woods, Sophie still remained his favorite.

This is why, when she agreed to let him give her away at her wedding, he was overjoyed. He knew nothing of the arguments that Gerry and Sophie had regarding this gesture.

Gerry argued for Achiel saying, "It's just a gesture. It doesn't really mean anything to you or me, but it means a lot to him."

Sophie argued against it. "No one is giving me away. I am my own person, making my own decision."

Ultimately, what won her over was her mother, which was surprising because her mother's decision to forgive and remain married to the man who had cheated on her, and had abused her in so many ways, disgusted Sophie.

Lucia surprised Sophie one day at work and said plainly, "Please allow your father to give you away at the wedding. He loves you, even though he doesn't know how to show it. This isn't for you, or for him, it's for Gerry. It's your father's way of saying he likes Gerry and trusts him with his favorite child."

Until that moment, Sophie hadn't really given much thought to whether or not her father approved of the man she chose to marry. She hadn't, at least consciously that she could remember, ever sought her father's approval for anything she did, which is part of what earned her the most approval from her father's eyes, but hearing that she had it, that he was proud, that he was happy for her, suddenly meant the world to her and she began to cry.

So, Achiel gave her away at her wedding. He walked her down the aisle. When asked, he stood on cue and stoically said, "Her mother and I." And then he took his seat. He tolerated Lucas' somewhat drunken best-man speech, and he danced with his daughter and wife at the reception. He smiled. He was friendly. He shook hands. He didn't make a scene. This was good for everyone involved. They could all look back fondly on that night as one of the few last "good" nights for them as a family. Five years later, he would kill Clifford Ellis, and then he would never be at another wedding again. He'd miss Lucas' wedding, and both of Ronnie's weddings. He'd be dead before his oldest grandchild's wedding, and missing that one would have stung the most. He would have loved to see Anton's wedding, primarily because it would mean seeing his daughter all grown up and giving her own child away. A child he only saw a handful of times before Sophie and Gerry stopped visiting him in prison, but a child that he thought was the spitting image of himself. When he saw Anton, he saw himself reflected in a way that he never saw in Lucas or Ronnie and only to a lesser extent in Sophie.

ACHIEL AND LUCIA (1948)

Thank you. Everyone, I'm Ronnie, the younger brother. In case you didn't know. Looking around, I don't know most of you. As you probably know, our family is small and most of them have died. It's really just Achiel and me now. Our dad passed just a few weeks ago. It's still hard to believe he's gone. Anyway, I'm happy today because I can see Achiel is building a new family right here.

He's a good guy, this brother of mine. He has always had my back and kept me safe. That's what big brothers do, right? Mine even more than others. Those of you who have lived through war, you know what it can be like. Now, just imagine being ten when that war began, and having those Germans all around us. My brother did everything he could to keep us safe. He kept me safe. He got me and my dad out of there and safely here to this country. Here we are. Here we are.

This is where Achiel met this lovely lady. I've never seen anyone make him as happy as she has. They've only known each other a few years, but if you've ever seen them together, you know that's long enough to know that they're the real deal. Seeing them together makes me want what they have. I can hope to be as lucky. Let's raise a glass to the bride and groom! Love you both, many happy years!

GERRY AND SOPHIE (1970)

Brother of the bride, buddy of the groom. Haha! Right? I'm Lucas. This lady's younger brother. Thanks to Gerry for letting me be his best man. It really means a lot to me. I never had a big brother, though my sis acted a lot like one, and this man has really taken me in as a little brother. Thanks, man.

So, this kind of toast usually has a story, right? I have a couple. First, when I was in first grade, I used to get picked on. I was little then, and I remember these kids—I could probably remember their names if I thought hard enough, oh!—Charlie, Rick, and Carl. Carl was the big fat one of them. Thought he was tough because he was bigger than everyone. Truth was, he would just hold you down and hit you, and you couldn't get up because he was so fat. Anyway, they were picking on me. Called me names. I don't really remember what. Kid stuff. You know? Probably making fun of my hair. It was always so curly. That day, I had brought a stuffed animal with me. It was this little kitten that I used to carry everywhere. Mom and Dad said I couldn't bring it to school, but I snuck it in my backpack. Carl, the fat one, he dumped my bag out and found it, and started tossing it around to Charlie and then to Rick, and then Carl got it back. He grabbed my stussy—that's what I used to call it, don't ask me why, god I haven't thought about that for years—my stuffed kitten and wrapped his fat fingers around its neck.

"I'm going to rip its head off," he said.

I started crying, and then suddenly Carl was flat on his back and my stussy was being handed to me. I didn't see exactly what happened, but one of my friends said Soph decked him. Just laid fat Carl out. That's how I think of my sister. A superhero.

And Gerry. Boy, what story do I tell about you. Maybe the time we were racing down Sycamore? Nah. Or, when we found that—nah. Or when we were packing our own shells and made that—nah. Or that advice you gave me about girls and going out on dates—nah. Oh boy, just look at his face, he really doesn't want me to tell that one. Haha. The story I want to tell is a sweet one that reveals what kind of man this guy is. Sophie and him had just started dating—what was this, like four or five years ago? I was going to my first prom as a sophomore. Sorry, hon. It was with another woman. But I'd never tied a tie before, and I didn't know what to get her as far as the corsage or whatever. Gerry came over to see Soph, but she was busy doing something—I don't remember what—and I asked him. He didn't hesitate. Told me about the different kinds of corsages, I guess he'd gone to a few proms, and told me to make sure my vest was going to match the color of the corsage. You know, he's a classy guy. He also showed me the best way to tie ties, the Windsor. Right? That's a classic knot. It's no secret my dad and I haven't always gotten along the best. Tying a son's tie is one of those things that usually a dad would do. I don't want to say nothing bad about my dad. I just want to say that this man, Gerry, he was there to do it for me. Get up here man. I love you, man.

I wish nothing but happiness to my sis and my big brother, and their little one on the way. Oops. It was okay that I said that, right? Sorry. If not, the cat's out of the bag! Raise a glass to the newlyweds! Soph and Gerr!

LUCAS AND CRISTINA (1976)

When my little brother got up at Gerr and my wedding, he might have spoiled a thing or two, but he always meant well. He has the biggest heart of anyone I know, and he's been through so much lately. We all have. I'm sorry Dad's not here for you. But Mom and Ronnie and I am, and so is Gerry and little Anton. We love you.

I've only just met Cristina, but from what I can tell, you're just as kind and generous as Lucas. He needs a sweet soul like yours to keep him company. Know that if you ever need anything, you just need to ask, and we'll be there to help and support however we can. We're a small family, but we stick together.

Love and best wishes to you both.

RONNIE AND HAZEL (1981)

You're just kids, but I can tell you're in love. You have that young love stink about you. And I mean that in the best way possible. Right, Soph? Oh, don't worry, I'm not going to go on and on like I did at her wedding. Let's just say, little Ronnie and Hazel, you are a cute couple. I can tell you love one another.

Let's wish them the best and raise our glasses to the new couple. Young love!

RONNIE AND CAROLINE (1985)

Lucas got to do the toast at Ronnie's first go-a-round, so I guess it's my turn. Littlest brother, the baby, what can I say? You've always blazed your own path and found your own way. At least this time you can legally drink at your wedding. Sorry, but it's true. The fact that Ronnie was married at 17 the first time shows how passionate my kid brother is. And now he's met Caroline, and her wonderful child, Paul. They fit right into our family. I'm not really a person of faith, but I do believe sometimes things happen for a reason. Ronnie and Caroline, you both have pasts, as we all do, and with those pasts comes experience and knowledge. I know, having been married for fifteen years now, that marriage has a steep learning curve. You've both gone through that once, so it should be easier this time around. Together you'll raise Jasmine and Paul, and maybe have one or two of your own together. Then you'll have his, hers, and ours. Love to you both. Cheers!

RONNIE AND LILA (1991)

(They were married in Las Vegas and no toast was given.)

RONNIE AND LOIS (1999)

Well, they always say "third time's the charm" right? What do they say about the fourth time? Maybe something like: "I sure hope you have it figured out this time…" Which is great. You got all the practice out of the way, worked out the kinks (though, maybe you kept a couple kinks there for fun!), and now you know how to do this. Ronnie, you know Soph and I love you. It's been a tough road for all of us, but we're there for if you need us. Lois, I've never seen Ronnie happier than since he's been with you. You keep him steady. And he does the same for you. I've seen the way you two parent, and each of your kids respect you both. That takes a lot of work, even when the children come from the same set of parents. It has to be harder when you introduce step-parents and all that baggage. Sorry. What I'm saying is, you do a great job. I admire the way you parent. You set boundaries and stick to them, you show love but you're firm, and you're both someone those kids can look up to. Cheers!

ANTON AND LORRAINE (2002)

This last year has been a difficult one for everyone, and it's wonderful to see something grow out of that. I don't know if many of you know the story about how these two met, but I'm going to tell it now because it's cute, and I'm the groom's father, so I can do that. Plus, I have a microphone and everyone's attention.

So, my son was working in the basement of the university's library—at least, that's what he said he was doing, "working" on school-related projects—when the terrorist attacks happened in New York. They had TVs hanging around the library, which, if you ask me, seems counterproductive to studying, but I digress. Anton stopped what he was doing and walked closer to the television, because as we all remember, the whole thing seemed unbelievable. I remember watching it live that morning, and my brain just couldn't make sense of what was happening. Sometimes, when they show that footage now, I still feel confused by what I'm seeing. Anyway, there Anton was, standing with a small crowd of other students who had gathered around the television to see what was going on. Anton said they just stood in silence, watching and rewatching and rewatching. Eventually, he went back to the desk where he was supposed to be working, packed up his things, and headed out to his car. Unbeknownst to him, this lovely lady, Lorraine, was in that same small circle of students who had gathered to watch the television in the basement that day. She left shortly after he did and also headed to the parking lot.

They both were a little distracted by what they'd seen. We won't point fingers about who hit who, but suffice it to say, there was a little accident, and Anton's car was no longer drivable. Lori says that Anton was a complete gentleman, and that he immediately apologized. She apologized as well, and then asked him if she could take him anywhere. The only place he wanted to be was home. So, she drove him home and left Anton's car in the parking lot. His mom and I were both home. It just so happened that we had the day off. And here they come. Our son and future daughter in-law. She called her family to make sure everyone was alright, and then the four of us just settled in. We watched TV until we couldn't take it anymore. Then we made dinner and told stories. She fit right in.

Since that day, it's basically been a foregone conclusion that they'd marry. It always felt like they already were. We're lucky to have her, now a year later, officially, as a daughter. I know Sophie will enjoy having another girl around, and Minnie and Winnie will love having a big sister. Raise a glass and join me in congratulating Anton and Lori!

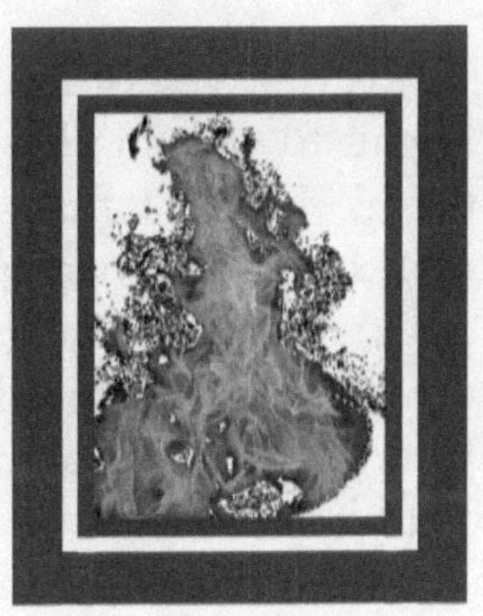

PART VII: CODED LANGUAGE

When Achiel went to prison, his name began to disappear. It happened slowly at first, but gradually, he went from being Achiel and Dad to simply "him" or "he" and things were "his" not Dad's. The grandchildren who knew about him weren't sure what to call him. Anton was the only one who had real memories of him, and the others only vaguely knew of him but had never actually met him. So, what do you call someone like that? Grandfather? Grandpa? Grandma's ex-husband? It was awkward.

When Anton wanted to interview Grandma Lucia about her husband, he stumbled trying to even begin. "When your, uh, I mean, uh." Thankfully, Lucia came to his aid.

"You mean *him*? What do you want to know?"

And then the wall was lifted, permission had been granted, the subject of the query was firmly established, and the questions could begin. "Did he ever tell you about his childhood?"

Inevitably, there was curiosity that brushed up against the crime, the trial, the murder, and whomever was asking would tentatively hedge around it, trying to figure out how to broach the subject. How do you ask a questions about something that everyone wants to pretend never happened? How do you talk about something that you're not even sure if you're supposed to know about it?

Most of the information about the crime came from the children eavesdropping when the parents, or Grandmother, were talking. Often this occurred after the children were supposed to be in bed, and then, when Anton in particular, overheard something, he felt guilty. Usually, he didn't mean to eavesdrop. Often when Anton overheard his grandmother and parents talking, or his mother talking to her brothers, it was because he had come out to ask about something to help settle his mind. Then, he'd accidentally hear a something like about how Uncle Ronnie had gone to "see Dad at the prison" and how, "Jesus, he has not changed. He's still going on about his trial." Or, if everyone had had enough to drink, Anton would overhear a retelling of the day Uncle Lucas chopped down all the trees with him, or maybe a partial retelling of the actual crime. Sometimes they walked through it again to see if they had missed something, or to convince themselves that, now, however many years later, that this was in fact something that had really, really, honestly, truly, happened to their family.

As Anton got older, he got braver and eventually he started to ask questions, but he felt like he was trespassing somewhere he wasn't meant to be. At first, he tentatively directed his questions mostly to his grandmother.

Anton might begin with, "Before the, uh. I mean, what was he like before—you know."

And Lucia might pause for a moment and then say, "Before that night?"

If Anton actually meant "before Achiel had an

extramarital affair with Miriam Ellis," then he would say, "Oh, no, that other thing."

Then Lucia would fill in, "Oh, the thing with the girl."

And the conversation would stumble along with each side slowly being clued in. There was "him" and "her" and "that girl" and "that night" and "in there"—the last meaning prison.

Anton didn't know this, but his grandmother really didn't mind talking about Achiel, or his crime, or the divorce, or his punishment. For her, they were merely things that had happened, and there was no reason to hide the past. She loved talking to her oldest grandson, and if this is what he wanted to talk about, then she was happy to have that conversation. For her, it wasn't about using a coded language out of embarrassment, it was more that she did not spend much time in that part of the past and thought of it all in the vague terms that Anton came to assume she used to soften the blow of bad memories. It was easier for her to let those memories fade because they were no longer a part of her life, and by the time Anton began asking, that time hadn't been a part of her life for decades.

Similarly, his mother Sophie had always promised herself to answer any questions she was asked. Truth be told, she was grateful that her children hadn't asked many questions because unlike her mother who saw the whole thing as a very practical matter of the past, Sophie was somewhat embarrassed about her father and his affair, and murder, and imprisonment. She was glad when no one asked her a question for several years. When Anton finally did ask her about "him," she surprised herself by how willingly she chatted and how happy she felt to unload the secrets she'd kept for so long.

This all happened shortly before Achiel died. Anton had

gone to the courthouse and made copies of the transcripts from the trial and various appeals, and then, armed with knowledge in hand, felt confident in asking questions and knowing what questions to ask. He approached his mother and grandmother on a day he was home from college and the twins were at school. His mother and grandmother answered his questions so easily that Anton was a little stunned and didn't ask follow-up questions. He didn't even realize he had follow-up questions until years later. Then, those years later, after Achiel had been dead and the threat of his being released from prison and acting on the threats he made in the courtroom were long buried, Anton found Sophie and Lucia very comfortable answering questions (follow-up or otherwise). They chatted for hours. And when he had another question, he'd call or swing by and ask. The shroud of secrecy had been lifted. Communication could occur freely, but, even then, his mother and grandmother still spoke of him, and he, and his, and Achiel's name continued to disappear from their family record even as the stories became more concrete and known and less legendary and mythical.

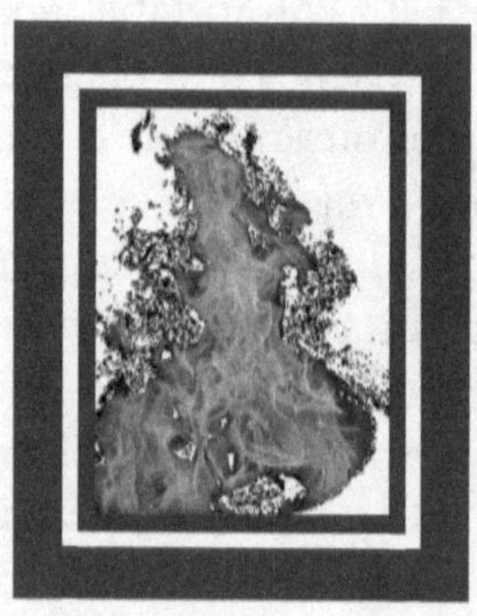

PART VIII: IN THE MAIL (PART II)

Sometimes, over the course of time, unlikely alliances form. None of the Van Slyck family could have foreseen the reconciliation of Lucas and Achiel. It would be easy to point to Lucas' recent conversion to Christianity as the impetus, but more likely it was because Lucas had been thinking about his father a lot ever since becoming a father himself in 1978. As the years went on, and Lucas had more children and watched them grow into strong-willed, independently-minded humans, he thought of his father more and more. Was it too late to do something to repair that relationship? Lucas felt like he never had a chance with the man, and the more he saw his own children slipping away from him, the more he wanted a lasting relationship with the man who had been absent from his own life.

Lucas remembered those first moments of new life when he held his children in his arms for the first time. When he held his firstborn Lucy he thought, "Wow, this is life. I'm a dad." It wasn't a profound statement that anyone was going to write down for posterity, but for him, a new dad, it was a revelation. He cried, as he figured a lot of dads did, but in part he was crying because he was pretty sure his own father had not cried at his birth. First of all, Sophie had been first. So, if Achiel was going to cry, it probably was when he held his first child for the first time. Maybe he hadn't even held him. Maybe the nurses just took him away to clean him up and Achiel went to brood in the waiting room. The baby's hair was too dark and curly. The skin was too dark. Achiel had made it very clear over the years that he believed Lucas was not his child. Every time Achiel brought it up, usually when he was yelling at Lucas, Lucia offered to pay for a paternity test to prove it once and for all. Achiel never took her up on the offer.

Work was busy for Lucas, which only made the feeling that his children were slipping away from him worse. He first felt it when Lucy went to preschool. It was only two days a week, but suddenly she was leaving the house with a little backpack on. Then, before he knew it, she was in middle school, wearing make-up and looking so mature. Lucas blinked and Lucy was graduating and going to college, and Carl and Georgie weren't far behind. By 1999, he had an empty nest, and his thoughts, more than ever, turned to his father. What was that man doing in there? How was he? Would he be up for parole? Behind all these other thoughts was the lingering question: Does he still want to kill me?

Somehow, over the years, Lucas was finally able to look beyond his fear and wonder if there wasn't some way that he could make peace with his father. Put all the questions of paternity behind him, forget about the name-calling, and start over. Any father would like that, wouldn't he?

Lucas toyed with writing a letter or suddenly visiting, but every time he almost convinced himself to reach out, the old memories caused him to chicken out. Finally, he decided to rip the bandage off in a single pull. He told

Cristina what he was going to do, and then he did it. He showed up at the prison and was almost turned away because he wasn't on the list and hadn't filled out proper paperwork. Fortunately, he showed up early enough in the day to get all the paperwork completed, and his father was now in a minimum-security facility, which required less paperwork.

He had no idea what he was going to say to his father, but when the bloated, old man appeared in front of him, Lucas no longer had to wonder what to say.

He simply asked, "What happened to you?"

His father had more than doubled in size. Unlike that sled hill that you remember being a mountain as a child, Achiel had become larger than Lucas' memory recalled. The man's once-sharp blue eyes were now foggy and dim. His perpetually short-cropped, military grade haircut was gone and he was entirely bald. The man who always wore a small and only on occasion a medium, now had a body straining against an extra-extra-large prison outfit.

His dad sneered a little, laughed, and then said, "You don't look so great yourself."

The two wasted no time on the past and instead dove into the various health-related appeals that Achiel had made over the years.

"I'm going to help with this, Dad," Lucas said.

It was difficult to know whether Achiel believed him or not or felt any remorse about how he'd treated Lucas, but he was more than happy to entertain more frequent visits and interruptions of his routine. At seven-four, Achiel knew it was too late to really do much to improve his health, but the fight was still in him, and the prison had done him wrong. He could fight the prison because he was bored and had nothing better to do but also out of principal. He was indeed a man of principals, even if they were very different principals from the average man.

Had he forgotten about the promise to "fucking kill" Lucas when he got out? No, he had not. Was he still planning to follow through on that promise? It was tough to say. On one hand, he was a man of his word. He didn't like to have outstanding debts, and taking his son's life was a debt that had been outstanding for twenty-five years. It was beginning to collect interest. On the other hand, if Lucas was able to ease some of Achiel's loneliness and suffering as he served out the rest of his term, maybe he could reconcile that good will against his outstanding debt. Maybe he even considered trying to convince Lucas to be a character witness for his next parole hearing instead of standing on the side of the rest of the family who showed up to argue against early release. Achiel figured he had nothing to lose. His son hadn't asked about his intentions upon release, and so Achiel had the luxury of waiting to make a decision until that moment presented itself.

LETTER FROM ACHIEL TO COPELAND

1977

You're a fool. My wife should have never hired you. Because of you, I went to prison two times. First for that girl—why did I ever listen to you with the plan you had for gross indecency?—and then now, look at me here, in this place. I'm disgusted. To think I wasted my time teaching your children to shoot, and how did you repay me? You never even tried a murder case before! But did you tell Lucia that? Did you warn me? No. How was I supposed to know? You can be sure that I'll bring that up in my appeal. That, in addition to not providing adequate counsel, you also lied to me. Misled me. Whatever word you want to use.

You were more than happy to take our money, weren't you? And when I saw you were going to be no good, and I told her to find me a new lawyer, she said you wouldn't give that money back. Just wait until I tell the judge and see what he says about that.

You didn't talk to me before my trial, not until the very day of it.

You didn't answer my calls.

You just showed up at that hearing before the trial. That's the first day I saw you, and all you wanted to talk about was poaching deer and how to load reduced bullets. How was that going to save me from prison? I didn't ask because I'm no lawyer. I figured you had some kind of plan. But, you had no plan.

"Tell them you were poaching deer with your rifle," you said.

What good would that have done? That would just gotten me into more trouble than I already was.

You didn't tell me I could have had a bench trial with just the judge. I didn't know about those until I was talking to one of the guys in here. A bench trial would have been better because a judge knows how things work, and people, those jurors, were soft and easily influenced by that prosecutor.

You didn't talk to me about what witnesses I should have for my trial.

You didn't meet me after the trial each day to talk about how it went and what we should do the next day. I never knew what you were doing, or what your plan was, or why you were doing it. If we had talked, I would have realized you didn't have a plan.

You didn't ask anything about the rifle or about the modifications to it. I could tell you were surprised when I brought it up at the trial. Even worse was you asked me about what happened that night and I told you, and I could tell you didn't believe me. That's why you didn't ask me any other questions.

You didn't bring in a gun expert to talk about whether or not the rifle could have fired without my finger being on the trigger. I told you to bring Red Hill in because he is an expert. He could have demonstrated what could have happened. He would have shown the jury. He knows about trigger shoes. And reasonable doubt.

That lawyer made such a big deal about my comment about my rifle being an extension of my arm, and you didn't stop him. I was just saying, I don't know, I was just talking. I mean, it is an extension of me, but not in the way he twisted my words to make it sound. Then you had to go and say it in the closing statement, too, and you basically said the same thing.

You didn't ask if I wanted to testify. I didn't even know I had a choice. I would have wanted to, but still, you should have asked. We were supposed to be a team, but you didn't bother to include me in any of it. You just made your own calls and decisions. I'm learning so much in here about what I should have done, and what a real lawyer should have done.

You didn't talk to me about the types of people who were on the jury, and who I would have wanted there. I never would have chosen those people. I could tell they were all soft and easy to convince.

You didn't ask me for character witnesses, or people who could have backed up what I said about spending hours with my sons in nature. That man, Harrington, he made me look like a fool when I said I would spend hours in nature. I could have had people on the stand who would have said they saw me, or knew that I did that.

You didn't even talk to me about my military service.

Instead, you talked to me about your children, and how their shooting was coming along, didn't you?

You didn't talk to me about no plea deal. Not like last time. Instead, here I am serving for the full time.

You didn't ask about the flat tires, or how I thought the tires went flat. I would have told you that Ellis probably shot, or stabbed, our tires. He was up to no good. I know he was. I could see him watching us and moving around. I wonder what that jury would have thought of that? But we'll never know now, will we?

Remember when you said, "Oh we'll be having steak dinners" when the trial is over, and how you'd buy us a dinner at my favorite place? I thought you knew what you were doing. I thought you had a plan. Well, I'm still waiting for my steak dinner.

You never objected to anything. Harrington objected all the time, but you never objected to anything. You never objected when people made statements or said things that I knew weren't true. And I told you. I told you, and you just said for me to remain quiet. To be polite and quiet. Well, I was, and where did that get me?

I was counting on you to get me a fair and just trial. You were supposed to help me.

And it was you who told Lucas to lie because you thought it was a better story than the truth. You put that idea in his head, and look what it did. That's why that jury said what they said. That's why I'm in here.

Don't even get me started on your closing statement. I mean, what does the game of telephone have to do with a murder trial? What does a photograph and memories of your great-grandparents have to do with me and whether I go to prison for life? What was that all about? No wonder that jury went back to their room scratching their heads about what to do. If someone came to me and talked about photographs and games and all that when we were supposed to be thinking about a murder trial and a man's life, I would have been confused, too.

Harrington rebutted your closing statement and made it all sound like flowery gobbly-gook, which it was. I know it was, and they knew it was. Even with your goofy story about your great-grandparents and all that, the jury still came back and asked about manslaughter and how it was different from murder. They had reasonable doubt. Just imagine if I had a real lawyer who knew how to make a real closing statement.

I kept thinking, "Oh Lord, there's a chance here. Even with this lawyer and his sentimental stories and all that."

Remember what you said on that final day? When you said I was a killer? Don't think I will forget that. I'll remember when I get out. I'll find you then, and we'll have a conversation.

LETTER FROM LUCAS TO COPELAND

May 17, 2000

Mr. Copeland,

I am Lucas Van Slyck, the son of Achiel Van Slyck. You represented my father in his 1975 murder trial, and I'm his oldest son. It has taken time, but he and I have begun to repair our relationship, and I'm trying to help him with some difficulties he's been having in prison. I don't know if you've followed him or not, but he's recently been relocated to Ypsilanti in a lower security prison. In part, this is because of his advanced age, he turns seventy-four this year, but also because of his good behavior. I know he wasn't always a model prisoner and that he spent a lot of time in solitary confinement, but in the last ten years or so he's turned that all around. However, now, he is finding that he's struggling with dietary needs and health concerns in general. I was hoping you might be able to help with that.

From my visits and his letters, I gather that my father has attempted to reach out to the warden through the proper channels to request a healthier, more balanced diet, more exercise opportunities, and better medical care. The prison diet has long been a concern of his, and he has written several letters (in addition to the CSJ-247A grievance form), but now, again in his advanced age, it is even more of a concern. The prison provides sugary beverages, while my father would prefer water and milk. He has never been one to drink juice, even if it was 100% juice. The "juice" provided to prisoners is sugar water with food coloring, not to mention the fact that it's unconscionable to provide sugary drinks to a man with diabetes. On a similar note, he has requested a higher protein and lower carbohydrate-based diet. These two simple changes would help keep his diabetes in check. However, despite these fairly simple requests, his letters are not answered and his grievance forms (CSJ-247A) are denied for unspecified reasons. I have seen some of his grievance forms, and they are returned with single word, or short phrases in response to his detailed requests. Often they say "vague" or "duplicative" or "multiple unrelated issues" without further response or explanation.

The longer this goes unchecked, the more likely his health issues will increase. For example, he has always had perfect vision throughout his life and did so until ten years after his incarceration. He never had diabetes nor any kind of weight problem until he had been in prison for five (or so) years. He now has hypertension and cardiac concerns that were never an issue before incarceration. Furthermore, he has no family history of diabetes, cardiac issues, hypertension, or obesity. Prison has done this to him by providing him an inadequate diet and restricting his exercise. Additionally, his conditions are worsened because of the slow response to his complaints by prison administration. We don't know what caused his vision to deteriorate so suddenly, but he complained of reduced vision years before a prison staff member took him seriously and he was given an eye exam. Similarly, it's unknown how long he suffered from diabetes before the prison personnel acknowledged his condition and began to provide insulin.

I write to you because you're a lawyer, and you're familiar with his original case. I know my father and you have had your differences and difficulties, and, frankly, I'm not sure what he would think about me reaching out to you for help, but I hope you can see past that to help him. He's an old man now and he needs our help. It is very likely he's going to die in prison, but I'm trying to do my best to ensure he doesn't suffer more than he already has. If he's going to die there, I hope it will be because of old age and not because of some condition imposed upon him by his incarceration. That would feel like he was paying twice for the same crime.

I have already tried petitioning the warden and written letters, but I don't seem to be able to make any headway. I was hoping that maybe you, even if you're retired now, might be able to have better luck. Perhaps you even know someone who might be able to help. In the end, I hope you can find it in your heart to forgive my father and to help me improve his situation.

God bless,

Lucas Van Slyck

Even if they sin against you seven times in a day and seven times come back to you saying, "I repent," you must forgive them. (Luke 17:4)

Get rid of all bitterness, passion, and anger. No more shouting or insults, no more hateful feelings of any sort. Instead, be kind and tender-hearted to one another, and forgive one another, as God has forgiven you through Christ. (Ephesians 4:31-32)

LETTER FROM LUCAS TO ACHIEL

May 25, 2000

Dad,

First, let me assure you that I'm doing the best I can about your diet and exercise concerns. It disgusts me that they don't take your health seriously and that they disregard your complaints. I've written more letters and have reached out to other people who might be able to help our cause. So, you know where we stand there, and I'll let you know if anything comes up. I'll do all I can to help.

The last time I visited, I started to tell you about my conversion, but I got interrupted, so I'm going to finish that here. It's one of my favorite things about writing letters to you. I can pick up stories here and there and write when I have a chance and actually think it all through.

I know you weren't ever a man of faith. I know you were dealt a difficult hand in life, and the wars you lived through were terrible. I was never much into faith either, probably because you raised me and I took on your beliefs as my own. Why would a kid want to go to church if he didn't have to? So, of course I didn't.

When Cristina and I married, she wanted to get married in a church. I didn't much care, but it mattered to her, so I figured it wouldn't hurt me. At the time, I didn't think much of it, but now that I look back, I remember feeling a strange power around me in that church. I think He was trying to reach out to me and show me the way, but I wasn't ready yet. I know, it sounds hokey to someone who doesn't believe. At the time, I also thought it was just the pressure of getting married and being in front of all these people I didn't know—most of them were her family since our family is so small.

After that, sometimes I went to church with Cristina. She always liked it when I went, and when we had the kids, then she wanted me to show support for bringing them up Christian. I still wasn't Christian then, at least I wouldn't call myself Christian. You know how Jews say they're "culturally Jewish?" Well, I guess I always felt "culturally Christian" because that was what everyone else around me was. Of course, Mom has always been Catholic, but she never made us go to church with her, even though I think she wanted us to. Anyway, as my kids got older I went less and less. They started doing their own thing, and I started doing mine.

Did you worry about Y2K in prison or hear about all those people worried about the end of the world? I never know what news reaches you and how current it is. There were people buying water bottles and stockpiling ammunition and canned goods to prepare for Y2K. That was Cristina's family. She insisted we stock up as well. At first I resisted, but Cristina was insistent. We bought a bunch of non-perishable stuff and kept it in our basement. Just in case.

On the night of the predicted Y2K disaster, New Year's

Eve, our family sat in the basement and prayed and prayed, and then we went to sleep in our sleeping bags. Well, they prayed, and they slept. I closed my eyes at first while they were praying, and then I opened them to see what they did when they prayed. They all kept their eyes closed and looked down at their interlocked fingers, until Cristina said, "Amen," and then everyone opened their eyes after saying it, too. Then they all went to sleep.

I laid there for hours and watched them. Nothing happened. Finally I got up. If the world was going to end, I wanted to hear it. I wanted to see it. I wanted to be there. I didn't want to sleep through it. I got up and went upstairs and looked around. I stepped outside and walked around the house. I'm not sure what I expected to see, but there was nothing. You would have liked it though because it was so quiet. I heard an owl and a coyote in the corn field next to us. He'd stop now and then and yip, and then I'd hear the crunch of the snow. It was the kind of snow that had that crispy edge to it but was soft inside.

It was cold, but not in that bone-chilling kind of way. It was more refreshing than anything else. It made me think of you, and how we'd go into the woods when I was young. I don't know if you know this or not, but even when you stopped taking me into the woods, I still went by myself. I still listened and watched. I loved those times when we were together, even if we weren't speaking or doing anything. There was something peaceful about it. When I went by myself, I liked it, but not as much. It was lonelier. Plus, I couldn't focus as much on nature because the thoughts in my mind got in the way. It was almost like you somehow helped block those out because I don't remember that being a problem when we went in the woods together.

Anyway, on that night, the new year, for the first time

my brain wasn't spinning. I was just listening and watching. I was waiting for some kind of sign that the world was ending, or that something new or different was happening, but nothing came. Nothing happened. It was just another day.

I can't remember if you told me this, or if it was someone else, but there are three dawns: astronomical dawn, nautical dawn, and civil dawn. The astronomical dawn is the one where it's barely, just a hair, light. Usually you can't tell the difference, but if you're far enough away from light, if there's no light pollution, if you're far enough away from the cities, then you can see it. Then there's the nautical dawn, which the sailors could use to tell the difference between the sky and the sea, but on land it doesn't look much different from astronomical dawn. And finally, civil dawn, which is just before proper sunrise. This, this was astronomical dawn. The faintest of light in the darkness, but I knew the new day was beginning. It wasn't going to end, like everyone said. No, it was just going to be another day.

For everyone back inside, and all of Cristina's family, this was a disappointment. They had prepared for the worst, and now they had to live with the disappointment of it not arriving. We had these stockpiles, like I said they weren't perishables, but Cristina's family had serious, serious stockpiles. They'd spent all kinds of money on things. People had laughed at them when they were stocking up, and now, now they'd have to suffer even more humiliation. Some of them actually lost their faith over it and stopped going to church.

I didn't know this until I looked it up, but people have been predicting the world to end for a long, long, long time. Even in my life time it's happened numerous times. There were predictions that the world would end in 1975,

1976, 1977, 1980, 1981, heck, almost every year up to 2000. People seem to like years that have sixes in them, or round numbers especially, because with 2000, large numbers of people were convinced it was End Times.

Ironically, they lost their faith, but I found mine. Where they all saw disappointment, I saw a new hope. A new opportunity. The world wasn't going to end because someone didn't have enough digits to allow the date to roll over to 2000. That night, when I sat out there in the snow listening to nature and watching the dim, distant glow of the sun coming up, I found God. Not in the traditional sense of some being with tablets and a burning bush, but more of feeling part of a bigger idea, or greater sense of being. I imagine it's what you felt when you were in the woods, though you would never have connected it to God. I'm not saying I'm going whole hog and reciting verses and going to church multiple times a week, but I do feel connected in a way I never have before. If they want to say that the bread and grape juice (we don't have wine) are the blood and body of Christ and call that communion, that's fine, but for me the communion is being part of the community and sharing belief in being kind, and valuing life. Those ideas, really the teachings of Jesus and the scriptures of the New Testament, are things that I can get behind.

So, yes, now I call myself a Christian. I go to the church. I forgive the sins of others because no one is perfect, and we're all sinners, and I hope others will forgive my sins. And that is a long way to get to the point which is this: I love you, Dad, and I forgive you for all you've done. You're not being treated fairly where you are, and I want to do everything I can to help make your situation better. I'll do all I can. And when my family is ready, I'll bring everyone out to see you. Cristina isn't quite ready yet. I've started

talking to the kids about you, and I want you to meet them.
I want them to know their grandfather. I love you.

God bless,
Lucas

LETTER FROM LUCAS TO ACHIEL

June 19, 2000

I haven't given up yet, but I am getting frustrated. I don't even know how many letters I've written or how many calls I've made, but no one is interested in our case. Sometimes they don't even call or write back, and so I don't know if they've read the letters or listened to my messages. You'd think they would want the work, but I can't find a single lawyer to help us.

Don't be mad, but I even called and wrote Raymond Copeland. I figured that it's been long enough, that maybe he'd moved on and forgotten some of the bad stuff. I guess he's all but retired now. That, and he hasn't forgotten the bad. I called several times before he finally answered one of my calls. I started to say who it was, and he said, "Oh, I know who it is, Lucas. Stop calling me. The answer is no." Then he hung up. I know at work the phones have that little screen where we can see who's calling, but I wouldn't have thought a lawyer in Lewes would have had one. Anyway, I don't know where to go from here.

Have you had any luck? You mentioned a jailhouse

lawyer named Sven, I think? Can he actually fight your case or help with the paperwork?

You asked about the kids. Lucy is 22 now, Carl is 20, and Georgie turns 19 in December. Georgie is going to stay at home and commute to the local community college. It will save him some money, and frankly, Cristina and I aren't ready to have an empty house yet. It's bad enough having Carl living two hours away, doing who knows what, and Lucy spending all our money at Michigan State. She's doing fine, but she's having a hard time deciding on a major. Lately she says she wants to be an engineer, and it seems to have stuck. We'll see. As for Carl, I worry about him sometimes. He's drinking a lot and going through that phase. I hope it passes quickly, but I also know it won't do any good to step in and try to stop him. He needs to get it out of his system.

Ronnie just got remarried again last year to a woman named Lois. Sophie and I are hoping the fourth time is the charm. Somehow, Ronnie is always falling in love, but he just has a hard time staying in it. I really do hope this one works because Lois seems really nice and like she has her head square on her shoulders. Of course, I also liked Lila, so what do I know. Then again, if they had been able to have children, maybe they would have stayed together. Anyway, Lois has two kids from her first husband, named Julie and Leslie. They seem like good kids. Of course, Jasmine is right between Carl and Georgie. She just turned 19. Randy is 14 and Noah turns 12 this year. Then there's Paul, but I can't remember how old he is. We don't see them as much as I'd like, so I don't know too much about how they're doing. Last I saw them, probably Easter, everyone seemed good. I know Ronnie is still in touch with you, so maybe you already know all this.

Let's see. Anton has to be getting close to 30 now, and

he's engaged to a woman named Lorraine. They're talking about a wedding next year but haven't set a date yet. She seems real nice. The twins are 21, and they're both going to the U of M. Unlike Lucy, they seem pretty focused. Winnie is going into psychology and Minnie is going into law. They're both in for plenty more school than just the four years—I hope Gerry and Sophie have saved their pennies. If we can't figure something out to help our case, then maybe Minnie can help the cause when she's done.

All your grandchildren are growing up and moving on.

I've talked to Cristina, and I think she's almost ready for me to bring her and the kids in to see you. She wants to come with me first before we bring them. I'm hoping we'll come this Saturday.

God bless,

Lucas

LETTER FROM LUCAS TO ACHIEL

October 27, 2000

Dad,

It's taken a while, and I think we both lost hope for a while there, but I found someone willing to consider our case. She was a little discouraged by the number of appeal attempts, but I reminded her that this is not an appeal. This is us demanding better treatment while you're incarcerated. The lawyer's name is Brandi Owens. She's been practicing for five years, and she works for a firm out of Ann Arbor. It's not a huge firm, but big enough. Definitely bigger than Copeland's office in Lewes. She requested a bunch of paperwork, which I sent her, but she also needs copies of your grievance forms. Can you send them to her or have copies made to send her? She needs to construct a timeline of your complaints. Also, she'll need copies of your medical records. She said if you have them, you can save her the time of requesting them by sending them over.

She'd also like to meet you. Do you have any objections?

I'm sorry I wasn't able to bring the kids like I had hoped to. I know they're adults, and they're my kids, but it's important to me that Cristina is alright with it. Frankly, right now, she's just not. It would have helped if you had been a little nicer when we came to see you. It's frustrating because I know a whole other side of you, but you don't let her see it.

I was surprised to hear that Ronnie hasn't come to see you in a while. What's going on with you two? I thought you were always close with him and that he was coming to see you regularly. What happened? He hasn't said anything to me.

Honestly, I haven't said anything to anyone outside of Christina about me visiting you, or writing to you, or helping you with this case. I don't know why. I'm not ashamed or trying to hide it. I just don't know what they would say or what they would think. You know how you always were with me. I just don't know that Sophie and Ronnie would understand. Neither of them is big on forgiveness or religion for that matter.

Soph and I got in a big fight about two weekends ago. Soph and Gerry came over for dinner. Cristina made this wonderful roasted chicken, and I made some ribs. It was so good. The night was going along fine, and then it was like Sophie wanted to pick a fight with me. I don't know why. She'd find little things to nag me about or to make fun of me about this or that.

She said, "Lucas, the heat on the ribs is too high."

Then she'd say, "You only have whole milk?"

Then she snorted when we prayed before dinner. It was rude. She knows Cristina and I pray. We didn't make her do it. We just wanted her to respect our home and our rules. All she had to do was sit there, be quiet for a minute or two, and then go about her business. But she had to snort, and then it was like she had the giggles or something. I couldn't believe it.

So, after dinner, when Gerry was helping Cristina with the dishes, I asked her, "What's your problem?"

And she started in on me and my religion. "How can you believe in all that stuff? I thought if there was one thing that Dad taught us properly, it was that there is no God."

I know that this has been a relatively new thing for her to see me this way, but it's not like Cristina hasn't been praying with our children all these years. I couldn't understand why, suddenly, it bothered Sophie so much. So, she yelled a bit and made fun of me, and then grabbed Gerry and said they had to go. I haven't spoken to her since, and I'm really not sure how to go about talking to her again. She owes me and Cristina an apology. It was so unprovoked and unlike her to behave that way.

Does she ever call or write or visit you? I was just wondering. You know, we never talk about you as a family. You're like this secret that we all keep, and I'm tired of it. I want you to be a part of our family again. I mean, despite your flaws, you are our father, and we are all flawed. You did teach us a lot, and you helped make us who we are today. I don't know if it was different for Sophie because she had already moved out of the house when the thing with Ellis happened, but I'm sorry for all the years that I didn't reach out, or call, or write, or visit. I wish I had done more of the last twenty-five years.

Please let me know about if you want me to proceed with Brandi, and if you can send her the documents she needs.

God bless, Lucas

LETTER FROM LUCAS TO MICHIGAN DEPARTMENT OF CORRECTIONS

September 30, 2001

Michigan Department of Corrections
206 E. Michigan Ave
Grandview Plaza
PO Box 30003
Lansing, MI 48909

To Whom It May Concern,

I'm sorry if this isn't the proper form or method for this. I'm not a lawyer, but I represent the estate of my deceased father Achiel Van Slyck, and I wish to file a wrongful death suit against the Michigan State Corrections Department. Over the course of this last year, I've been working with a lawyer, Brandi Owens, to improve the conditions in the prison where my father was incarcerated. He had filed several grievances regarding lack of health care and poor dietary nutrition, and Brandi and I have been working to ensure that his concerns are being addressed. His earliest complaints began near the time he was initially incarcerated in Jackson State Prison, and they continued up until his death on September 12, 2001. Now, because of his death, I would like to lodge a complaint of wrongful death. If necessary, Ms. Owens can help me with that, but I thought I would start with my own complaint first.

Claims:

As we were attempting to show before he died, my father has suffered for years in the prison system due to a lack of proper dietary nutrition, exercise, and health care. Though he was in prison, and not always the model prisoner, that does not excuse the Michigan Department of Corrections from the type of treatment he received. When my father entered prison, in 1975, he was a healthy 49-year-old man. After one year in Jackson State Prison, he gained 25 lbs. from the starchy diet given to him and the lack of exercise. He made it known, immediately, that he preferred a high-protein diet, and that starches, particularly, were tough for his body to process. Those concerns went unheeded. He repeated those complaints all throughout the rest of his life. You will find copies of all the grievances he filed, and some my mother filed on his behalf, enclosed with this letter. Over the course of twenty-six years, he filed 158 grievances. Most of these complain about the diet and his weight gain as a result of it. That is roughly six grievances each year. Initially, he filed more grievances annually than he did later in his life because when he first arrived he was so shocked at the treatment he received. You have to remember, he is an immigrant and this country took some getting used to, but he did it. The prison system was harder for him to adapt to. As he got older and he adjusted, his grievances decreased. My father was not a tall man. His driver's license says that he is five foot six, and I believe that is accurate. At the time he entered Jackson State Prison, he weighed 139 pounds. At the time of his death, he weighed more than twice that: 283 pounds.

Along with his weight gain, my father also became diabetic. My family does not have a history of diabetes. If my father had remained on a diet consistent with what he had been accustomed to before incarceration, there is no reason to believe he would have become diabetic.

Similarly, there is no family history of hypertension or cardiac disease, and yet, when my father died, he died of cardiac arrest. Furthermore, according to the few medical reports I was able to obtain, my father also was suffering from high blood pressure and had "several cardiac events" prior to his death.

Even if we assume that these are natural conditions that he would suffered from outside of prison, or on a familiar diet with regular exercise, his conditions in prison were exacerbated by the lack of medical attention. My father made the correctional officers aware of his increased thirst, dizziness, fatigue, frequent headaches, and blurred vision, and requested a visit to medical. These requests were denied. He brought these concerns up during his annual physical, but the medical professional refused to acknowledge his concerns. It was only five years later, when a new medical professional began working at the prison that my father's health concerns were taken seriously and a diagnosis of type 2 diabetes was confirmed. A similar situation occurred when he again complained of vision problems, chest pain, difficulty breathing, and headaches, and it was only several years later that a medical professional diagnosed him with high blood pressure. Again, he complained of symptoms consistent with cardiovascular disease.

My father did everything in his power to alert medical professionals and correctional officers that he was suffering from grave physical ailments, and those concerns were disregarded and ignored. It is because of these delays in medical care that he died at the relatively young age of 75.

Achiel Van Slyck also lived through the riot of 1981 at Jackson State Prison, which occurred due to negligence on behalf of the correctional officers, and resulted in my father being terrorized by the fires and inmates running wild through the prison. Several of the men enjoying freedom during the riot were men who had cornered my father and beaten him during opportune moments when correctional officers weren't paying attention. Though my father complained about these incidents and reported the men who abused him, nothing was done to prevent future occurrences or to penalize the men who had abused my father. These abuses, the 1981 riot, and the continued neglect for my father's grievances demonstrate a consistent pattern of negligence within the Michigan Department of Corrections. While the riot was unique to Jackson State Prison, my father continued to face similar abuses from other inmates and to have his health and dietary concerns ignored wherever he was incarcerated in the State of Michigan, including: Jackson State Prison, Chippewa Correctional Facility, Bellamy Creek Correctional Facility, Iona Correctional Facility, and Huron Valley Men's Complex. It is possible that I missed one of the facilities that he was housed at because he and I lost touch for a period of time. I was able to reconstruct the list of facilities from the various notes, grievances, and letters I found in the personal property returned to me after his death.

Finally, the prison did not conduct an autopsy, which was one final show of disrespect and neglect.

Damages include:
- My father's suffering, over the course of his twenty-six years of incarceration, and his death as a result of the conditions created by the Michigan Department of Corrections.
- The loss of enjoyment and life.
- The loss of enjoyment, loss of society, and loss companionship of his children and grandchildren.
- His children and grandchildren's loss of enjoyment, loss of society, and loss of companionship of Achiel Van Slyck.

If possible, I would like a jury trial for this case.

Thank you and God bless,

Lucas Van Slyck

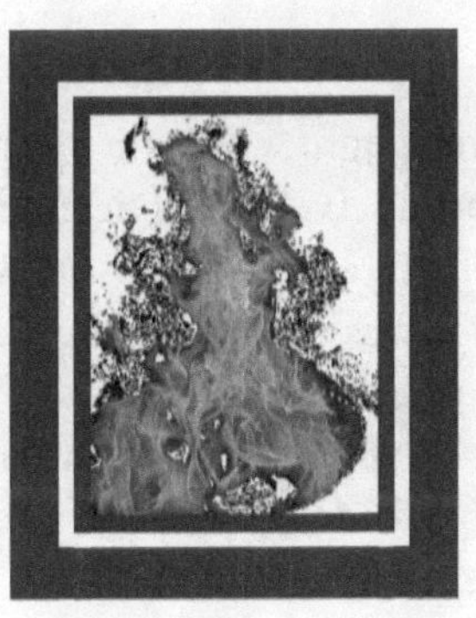

PART IX: OVER DINNER

We ate what he caught, shot, or trapped, but that's not all we ate. We had an IGA, and sometimes Mom would bring something from a place near her work or along the way home. When it was something he caught, it was often squirrel, rabbit, pheasant, or deer. Pheasant was his favorite. He used to talk about how amazing the pheasant was that his mother used to prepare back in Belgium. He always tried to replicate it but couldn't get it quite right. Mina, on occasion before her hatred of him fully set in, could get pretty close. Mom never knew where Mina learned to cook pheasant, it wasn't like it was readily available in Sicily, or that Mina had many occasions to shoot pheasant and prepare it once they had moved to the States. Yet, somehow, Mina had a knack for it. While Ronnie definitely took to the game-meat that Dad brought home, I never really cared for much of what he caught or shot. Whenever Mom tried to prepare it, she overcooked it, or over-seasoned it, or did something to make it inedible. The roasted stuffed pheasant that Mina made though – wow that was something else.

Dad's favorite dish was liver and onions. It was something Mom made as a treat to him, and he loved the way she prepared it. It wasn't, however, a treat for us kids. Each of us took our turns refusing to eat dinner and then spending the rest of the night at the table because Mom and Dad wouldn't excuse us until our plates were clean. Lucas learned the lesson on the first try, but I took a couple times before it set in, and Ronnie wasn't a quick study. He fought eating liver and spent the night at the table at least a half dozen times. In fact, I'm pretty sure he ended up feeding the meat to the dogs after everyone went to sleep.

We didn't have a local butcher, so Mom always got the liver from the IGA. Before it was an IGA, it was a Wrigley's, and then a Richie's for a short time, but it was an IGA for most of my life. Might still be one for all I know. Funny how things get renamed but basically remain the same. They had a decent selection of groceries. Mom never complained about it anyway.

She would usually pick up the liver on her way home, but sometimes she'd swing by home and take me to the store with her, and I'd have to stand there, watching her ask for liver, and then watch the person behind the meat counter slap the weirdly colored meat onto paper and wrap it. As much as I liked going into town and shopping with Mom, seeing the liver and knowing what was to come was terrible. I always hoped that the price per pound would be too much for her to justify. If it was on sale, then it was usually under 79 cents a pound, and that almost always meant we were having liver for dinner.

On most nights, because Mom worked so much overtime, we had quick and easy meals. It was only on special occasions that we came to dread dinner. My favorite meal was always kielbasa and peppers, or hotdogs. Those were things any one of us kids could fry up in a pan and aside from cutting the peppers or onions or opening a can there wasn't anything dangerous about preparing that meal.

Dad didn't respect state-determined hunting seasons, so we ate wild game whenever he happened to kill something. Anything smaller than a deer, he considered varmints and claimed you could dispose of them whenever you wished. Once in third grade during reading-out-loud, a teacher stopped me from reading and asked the class, "What's a varmint?" She did this periodically to check if we were paying attention to what we were reading and that we weren't just glossing over vocabulary. Usually, if I didn't know what the word was, I could figure it out from the context. When she asked about varmint, I didn't have to think about it. I had heard this word my whole life.

I immediately said, "An animal smaller than a deer."

She nodded and then said, "Anything else to help us narrow it down?"

I wasn't sure what else she was looking for, but did add, "A wild animal? Like one that isn't a pet or on a farm?"

She nodded again, and then said, "Usually varmints are destructive, or troublesome. For example, a woodchuck."

I immediately wondered if I had ever eaten a woodchuck. I didn't think so.

Then Ms. Doddson went on, "Because woodchucks destroy barns and dig under buildings."

That was the day I learned Dad had a very broad definition of varmints because the "varmints" he shot included a whole range of animals I'd later learn there were specific hunting seasons for.

The dinner table in our house was also a place for communication. It was one of the few times everyone was in the same place at the same time. If Mom and Dad had something they wanted to talk about, it usually happened there. Announcements about family trips were made at the dining room table. Everyone took turns talking about their day. Dad would lay out whatever chores needed to be done. Mom would talk about the schedule and calendar.

The table was also a place to dispense punishment. When someone got in trouble, Mom and Dad rarely dealt with it individually. Instead, they preferred to bring everyone to the table and then deal with it as a family. The idea, I think, was that whichever kids were not involved in the trouble would learn from the mistakes of the one who was. If we were caught not paying attention while the other was being scolded, we'd get yelled at too.

Dad always liked the phrase, "This could be you next!" and frequently used it to remind us that it was only a matter of time before we found ourselves in the same, or similar, predicament.

INTERVENTION, LUCAS (2001)

Lucas, look, I've talked with Mom and Ronnie, and we're not okay with this. You need to stop. Dad is dead. His story is over. Yes, it was sad that he suffered while in prison and that he died before he was released. But he was a prisoner. He made choices that got him there, and those choices have consequences. When you're in prison, you don't get to dictate what you want for dinner. You don't get to complain about the kind of juice you're given. You lose rights and freedoms. That's kind of the whole point of prison.

I don't know what's come over you lately, with this whole come-to-Jesus thing you have going on and this whole reconciliation with Dad, but let me remind you: He was not a good person. He did terrible things. Hell, during his trial, in open court, he threatened to kill you. Have you forgotten about how we all showed up at parole hearings and begged the state not to release him? We all feared for our lives. Him dying in prison, honestly, was the best possible outcome for all of us. It really was. And for you to fight this now and drag all this shit back up again and pull our family through this drama, after he's dead and gone, it's offensive and painful. You need to let it go.

Is this some kind of money-grab? I mean, what's your end-game? A wrongful death suit isn't going to bring Dad back, and him being in prison didn't cost us any money. The only money we gave him in over twenty five years was for his burial. And honestly, I'm happy to part with that three grand if it means not having to think about him and all the shit he did again. I don't want to step foot into another court. I don't want to have stand in front of a judge, or magistrate, or a jury and talk about Dad. I just don't. I'm done. Mom's done. Ronnie's done. You should be done, too.

Should I remind you how he talked about you when you when he was alive? How he claimed you weren't his kid because your skin was darker and you had frizzy hair? Do you remember when he strangled Mom? Or any number of the times the police came to our house? What about when he burned down Eddie's welding shop and then burned down his own welding shop? How about when he caught you with that girl in your room, and he threw her out of the house, beat you, and then kicked you out of the house for the night? Or when he told everyone how Ronnie was his favorite and that you were a loser that he was ashamed of? How about when he had that affair with that girl? Or when he killed her father? And he tried to get you to take the blame for it, even though you were an adult and would have gone away for life? Or, again, when he yelled, "I'm going to fucking kill you when I get out of here!" in open court? How about when he told Mom that he didn't you want you coming to see him in prison? Maybe you've forgotten how manipulative he was, and he was only talking to you in his final days because everyone else had gotten sick of him, and he was just using you because he wanted something. He manipulated you into fighting his fight.

I know you want to believe people can change, and to forgive and all that, but Dad wasn't like other people. Normal people don't do the shit he did. He was a psychopath who only cared about himself. He was going to get out and the shit would all start again.

He got fat. He was being fed crap food and was locked in a cage. It doesn't take a rocket scientist to figure that out. It's called being in prison. Frankly, it's a miracle he didn't get caught sooner for the other shit he did. He should have been in prison long before that poor man had to die to finally get Dad locked up for longer than a year. What you're trying to do now, it just diminishes Clifford Ellis' life. If he had to die to get a psychopath locked up and keep us safe and the rest of the community safe, then at least some good came from that family's loss. You trying to sue MDOC is just sad. We'll have no part of it. Seriously, we beg you to please drop the case. It's not worth it. It's going to rip us further apart.

If you want to pursue this for some greater good, like improving conditions for prisoners in general, then fine. But don't do it for Dad. He wouldn't have done shit for you. In fact, you buddying up to him a year or two from his release date would have just made it easier for him to meet and kill you like he promised when he went in. Dad was always very good at keeping his promises, and you better believe that was one that he would have kept.

INTERVENTION, RONNIE (1996)

Three kids. Three failed marriages. And look at you, you're a stumbling drunk. Ronnie, you're so much better than this. When are you going to get your shit together? Seriously. I understand why things might not have worked out with Hazel because you guys were so young, and even Caroline because you wanted different things, but Lila? She seemed perfect for you. Why did you have to go and fuck that up? If you didn't want to have any more kids, just tell her that. Don't go and get vasectomy and not tell her about it. Did you think she wouldn't figure it out? How far would you have gone if she wanted to pursue fertility testing before you came clean? Look, little brother, I'm not saying I'm some kind of pinnacle of virtue, because I'm not, but come on.

Forget about love and what you're going to do to your children, just think about it from a very basic economic level. Each time you get divorced you're giving away half your shit. Not to mention alimony and however that works. I don't know, I've never been divorced, but you should have it all figured out by now.

He always said you were the most like him. Not that you're killing dogs or cutting trees or having sex with teenagers—at least I don't think you are, are you?—but you definitely have the selfish, self-serving, bull-headed thing down. You even look like him. No, he didn't drink as much as you do, but when he did, this is what he looked like. Maybe that will wake you up. Go look at yourself in the mirror and see what you've become. Remember how he was always unemployed and riding disability? It looks like you were paying attention then to see how it was done. Good thing you took notes, I guess.

If you need a place to stay while you sober up, of course you're always welcome at the house. Cristina and I will take care of you. But you have to be serious about getting your shit together. It's disgusting watching you throw your life away.

You're lucky that Lila is such a good person. Of course, I talked to her, how do you think I found out? She doesn't want the house. She doesn't want much of anything. She just wants a clean break. Stay with us for a bit, let her clean her stuff out, and you two can go your separate ways. But when you do sober up, you're going to realize how big of a mistake you're making with her. She was a good one.

INTERVENTION, CARL (2003)

You're twenty-three and living at home. Which is fine but come on. If you're going to live under this roof, it should be common sense that you can't steal from us. We need you to be honest with us. Your mom and I don't expect you to be perfect, and we don't expect you to have all the answers, but we do expect honesty. It might take you a while to figure out what you want to do with your life. You have a long life in front of you, and there's a lot of time to figure it out. You may even change your mind along the way. A business degree will be good for something, you just need to figure out what. If you need to go back to school, to get a MBA or whatever, then that's fine. We'll help you.

But don't steal. Just ask. We'll give.

Don't lie. Be honest. We'll help.

Things are just things, but when you steal from us, it breaks that trust. You're old enough you should know better by now. That trust gets broken even more when you lie. I'm not going to make you go to church, but I think you might find some answers there. I know, I was skeptical

most my life, but look at me now. I'm a church-going kind
of guy. Anyway, you know your mom and I love you, your
whole family loves and supports you, you can lean on us
and expect us to help you. We'll do that. We just ask for
some very basic things in exchange. Can you do that?

INTERVENTION, GEORGIE (1995)

I won't lie to you, I had my first drink when I was twelve. Who knows, you might have started drinking then, too, but don't tell me. I don't want to know. It doesn't matter. You're just fourteen, and you'll have a lot of time to drink, but school, or at a school-related event, is a terrible place to do it. If you want to drink, your mom and I would much rather have you drink at home. It's safe, and we can help you if you get sick. This is not a trick, or a trap. It's just an honest offer. Have your friends over if you want, that's fine with me. The only requirements is that they have to be honest with their parents about what they're doing. I'm not going to keep any secrets from anyone.

Did I ever tell you about what my dad did when he caught me drinking? Well, he had a very small bar in the basement. Dad didn't drink much. When he did, he drank hard liquor. A lot of times it was this stuff he called Jenever, which to me tastes like terrible gin. Do you know what gin tastes like? Never mind, don't answer that. It tastes like Pine-sol. Anyway, he said Jenever reminded him of growing up in Belgium. He had a bottle of that stuff, another of vodka, and one of rum at his bar. There might have been a few others, but that's all I really remember. My friends and I were mixing the vodka into different juices. Making screwdrivers and cape cods, and whatever else we could come up with. Dad was out of the house somewhere, I don't remember where now. All my friends left and I took the bottle upstairs to fill it back up with water, you know, so he wouldn't notice how much we drank.

No idea when he got home. Either he was intentionally sneaking around the house, or I was buzzed enough not to notice him. But I was concentrating on getting water in the bottle and not all around it, which was hard because I was a little drunk, when over the sound of running water, I hear him laugh from behind me. I turned off the water and turned around. He was smiling.

He said something like, "Today my boy becomes a man."

He took the bottle from my hands and poured it into the sink.

"Don't waste good liquor by watering it down."

Then he gave me this weird little smile and told me to come downstairs.

He got out shot glasses and filled them with that Jenever stuff, and then handed me one.

"To the old country," he said, and then tossed it back.

I had never done a shot before, but I tried to do what he had done. I was drunk enough that my aim wasn't so good, and I managed to splash liquor in my eye and choke on the stuff as it hit the back of my throat. He laughed and poured us another shot. I tried to wipe the liquor out of my eye, but it just burned and I managed to rub it deeper into my eye. I knew better than to complain though, so I just kept that eye closed and sucked it up. He poured more shots. The stuff was terrible. Remember, think Pine-sol. After five or six shots, I was wobbly and starting to feel sick. He was still smiling. In that moment, drunk as I was, it was clear to me that this was not an invitation to drink his liquor again. This was a punishment.

I woke up later on the floor in the basement, crawled up the stairs, and went to bed. The whole way the walls and floor spun. I had to crawl or I would have fallen, but eventually I got to my bed. The next morning, I felt like shit, but Dad wanted to spend the day in the woods, and I was going along. He woke me up early enough that I think I was still drunk. He didn't say anything at all that day, and I wasn't sure if I was supposed to say anything, or acknowledge what had happened, or what. I kept waiting for some kind of punishment, or beating, or anything. But he never said anything about it. It was almost like it never happened. We spent the day in silence, walking, then sitting, then watching. Midday, he pulled some wax-paper wrapped sandwiches from one of his pockets and gave me one. We ate in silence. It was just bread and bologna, which was always one of his favorites, but I never cared for it. That day though, that shit was glorious. It was heavenly. Then it was back to silently sitting and observing. When the sun started to go down, he got up and walked back to the house. He didn't tell me it was time to go home or indicate he was leaving. He just got up and left. I followed him home, we had dinner, and nothing was ever said about what had happened. I'm not even sure he told my mom. He was like that.

Your mom, of course, knows. We don't keep secrets like that, and we don't expect you to keep secrets from us. Don't sneak around. Don't lie to us. Don't lie by omission. Just talk to us. We were kids once, even though it might seem impossible to you. We made mistakes. Sometimes we got caught, sometimes we got in trouble, and sometimes we even got away with things we shouldn't have. I'll tell you, with my dad, I never knew if I actually got away with something or if he was just waiting for the right minute to bust me on it. I'll never do that to you. I want you to know where we stand, and that you can always come to us with things. Always.

RUBY (1981)

I got home the usual time. Connie gave me a ride after volleyball practice. There was still some light in the sky, so the house wasn't fully dark yet. Went about my usual routine, going through my bag. Looking at the homework I should be doing, but not doing it. It's my senior year. What are they going do? Not let me graduate? Grades are good enough, I can afford to coast. Plus, when am I ever going to care about social studies again after this year?

Long day, but nothing that a little Juice Newton won't solve. I know most people think about "Angel of the Morning" or "Queen of Hearts," of course those are the big hits off *Juice*, but the whole album is perfect. I listen to it from start to finish and start all over again. There's something about her voice and her sense of melody.

When I went to flip the record again, I heard the door close. Probably Mom, I thought. I assumed it was. But, living out here, so far from anyone else, I can't help but wonder. My mind wanders. It probably doesn't help that Kurt and I had seen *In Cold Blood* when they reran it at the theatre a few towns over.

"Mom?" I called.

No answer. But now, I'm not sure if I turn on the light. If I do, and it is someone else, it will call attention to where I am. Plus, I'll lose my low-light vision. That's something Dad told me about pirates. He said the whole reason they wore eye patches, was to make sure one eye was always used to the dark. Then, when they went into the hull, they'd switch the patch to the other eye. I'm not sure if it's true, but leave it to dad to know something about how to hunt and take advantage of something others might assume to be a weakness.

There weren't any other sounds, like if they were stealing things or something. But I also didn't hear Mom's keys hit the countertop or her starting to make dinner. You can only stand still for so long before the curiosity gets the better of you. At least, for me that is.

So, I start a slow walk out of my room and down the hall with the lights off. I've walked the whole house in the dark before, I don't even know how many times. Sometimes I even close my eyes when I walk at night, just to remain half asleep and to see if I can do it without stubbing my toes or smacking into a wall.

When I get to the kitchen, I see something on the floor. It's big—like a big black Hefty bag—but it's not moving. Or at least, if it is, I can't see it in the dark. It doesn't look threatening, but it definitely wasn't there when I got home. The knives are on the counter, but on the other side of where the form is. Just as I'm reaching for a pan, the thing on the floor makes a moaning sound. That's not quite right, but it's the closest I can think of to describe it.

"Mom?" I asked again.

"Ruby?" she said.

"Do you want the lights on? I can—" but she stopped me, by reaching out an arm.

"Here, just come here."

She pulls me in close and holds me. I can smell her. Sweat from the workday, the salty brine of tears on her face, and whatever perfume she put on this morning. It's strange. Not the smell, but the closeness. I know she loves me, loves all us kids, but this isn't something that happens often. She's not the kind of mother who says she loves you, or thank you, or shows emotion like this.

"Are you—?"

"Hush, hush."

I don't know how long we stay like that, but eventually it's kind of uncomfortable. I mean, my back was bent weird and I was kind of hunched to keep all my weight from being on her. She must have sensed it, too, because she finally let go. She brushed my hair with her hands and in the dusk I could see her smiling. I could see the tear-streaked cheeks. She reached and wiped her cheeks with the palms of her hands.

"I'm sorry," she said. "You don't need that."

"Need what?" I asked.

"Shhh," she said. "Never you mind."

"Work?" I asked.

"All of it," she said, looking around in the darkness. "What do you want for dinner?"

"No, Mom, what's going on?" I asked.

"You know," she said. "It's him. It's all so much."

"Dad?"

"When I growed up, my parents, they had fights, but they were married, how long?" She sputtered. "Me? My husband? He does that with a girl, and the war, and that man. And so many other things."

I really didn't know what to say. She'd never really talked about dad before, at least not like this.

"My friend, Sandy, she says I'm grieving. But who died,

I asked. Who died? Other than that man. It's been, what? Six years now? Why grieving now? Today, it was just like a, boom, I felt it. Knowing, this was it. This was my life. My husband, locked away. Me, a single parent. You kids, from a broken home. And him, ugh, him still taking and taking and taking, even though he's away. Sandy said it was healthy to grieve, to cry, to let it out. But I can't at work. The line keeps going, there's no time to cry there. When I got home and saw it dark, I thought maybe you stayed late or went with that girl. Connie."

"Did it help?" I asked.

"Help?" Mom shook her head. "Help? Now I just feel stupid *and* sad."

As she got up, pulling herself up by the countertop, I couldn't help but see how old she seemed. The veins were visible on the tops of her hands and she seemed unstable, wobbly even on her knees.

She let out a big breath of air.

"Dinner. Spaghet? Soup? What do you want?" she asked.

"Here, let me help," I said, knowing she'd want soup, and getting soup bowls down.

INFORMATION (2000)

Look, just because you went to the courthouse and the police department and you got all this paperwork, it doesn't mean it's the full story. It's part of the story. Maybe even a good chunk of the story, but it's not the final word. Don't get me wrong, your grandfather was a terrible person, and he did horrible things. The trees? Absolutely. Killed some pets? Yep. Cheated on his wife with a fourteen-year-old? Yep. Killed a man? No question. But, some of these transcripts are just one person's distorted opinion and thoughts.

Like here, when Shelley is being interviewed by the police the night of the murder. I can only imagine how much stress she was under and how terrible she must have felt. She just found her husband dead in his truck, and then she has to stay up all night answering questions at the police department. It was ten at night before they got to the scene, so her interview probably went past midnight. Tired, exhausted, sad, and probably worried about Miriam too, for that matter.

But here she says, "Achiel terrorized our family. He

killed family pets, he ran Clifford off the road when Clifford was on his tractor, he chased Miriam into a ditch with his car, and he stalked by the house late at night. Once, he drove by our house real slow-like, rolled down his window, and threw one of our cats into our yard that he had killed."

Now, obviously, I don't know everything my dad did, but I can tell you a few things. Him chasing you off the road? That was his sense of humor. He thought it was funny. He didn't mean any harm, and he wouldn't have actually run them down. He liked to give people a good scare, and he thought it was funny to chase like that. The thing with Clifford in the tractor, well, Clifford's tractor took up the whole damn road. Dad was just trying to get passed him. Dad was a very good driver, and I don't think a lot of people knew that. He could fit into the tightest parking spots and manage his way up narrow mountain paths. So, what Clifford might have thought was Dad trying to drive him off the road was just Dad fitting tightly by him. It might have made Clifford uncomfortable, but it wasn't Dad's intention. I'm sure of it.

Again, I don't mean to defend him, but some of this just isn't true. The thing about the cat, that might be true. He didn't like it when other people's pets were on his land. He really, really, didn't like cats because they killed birds, and Dad loved bird-watching. He even got mad at us when we shot them with bb-guns. So, it's possible he killed their cat and threw it in their yard to send them a message. The message wasn't, "I'm coming for you next," like she says here, but more like, "Keep your pets under control." Most of the dogs he killed were because they kept coming over to his yard and shitting or pissing on it.

She says, "He said that he was gonna 'get us all' because of him going to prison."

I'm sure he probably did say something like that. He didn't like when people got one over on him, and he probably was angry. Dad definitely could keep a grudge, but he didn't act on it until he was good and ready. And he wouldn't mess around with getting revenge on something like a pet for something like him going to prison. If he wanted revenge for going to prison, it would have been something big. Like, you know, killing Clifford. I think when the lawyer said that in court, that was pretty close to the truth.

Shelley also said that Dad loosened lug-nuts or did something to their cars. Where was that? Oh, here.

"He shot at us before, he shot over our heads, he cut our tires on three cars, and he loosened something at least one time because the wheels damn near came off."

That does sound like something he would have done. The shooting over their heads, yes. That's classic Dad. He did that to us all the time. You have to remember, he was a marksman. If he wanted to hit someone, he would have hit them. When he wanted to miss, he missed.

When he did it to us, he used to say, "Just keeping you on your toes. Never know where the enemy is."

Which would have been helpful if any of us had any plans of going into the military, but we didn't, so it just scared us more than anything. Dad might have done the lug-nuts thing. It's tough to say. He definitely knew his way around cars. But again, if he wanted revenge, he'd want someone to know it was him. Tinkering with a car seems a little too passive. He'd want to be in their face and let them know who did it, like when he burned down Eddie's welding shop. He called Eddie and told him over the phone. He wanted him to know, "I burned your shit down. What are you going to do about it?" That was how he rolled. Tinkering with cars that may or may not cause an accident? That's not really like him. He'd want it to be for certain and for them to know it was him.

It is very interesting to see all this paperwork after all these years. I mean, we were all there in the courtroom, we heard it live, and yet reading it again is very, very enlightening. Seeing the police report is interesting, too. I had no idea they interviewed so many people. Interesting that so many of the neighbors didn't hear or see anything. I never knew what Mom said when the police talked to her. She really didn't know much of anything. Dad never told her anything. In a way, it protected her, though I don't understand his motivation. It was probably more along the lines of wanting fewer people to keep their stories straight. Also, kind of weird seeing the polygraph results and questions they asked. It all seems like so long ago.

I never knew they gave Lucas a lie-detector. Never knew what he said or how worried he was. You hear about this stuff second-hand from them, but it's a whole other thing to read their actual words. That said, like I said earlier, it's not the whole story. You put someone under the stress of a police interrogation, you put them in that position of being the son of a man who just shot someone, a son whose father claimed wasn't his because of skin color and curly hair, and what do you expect? He might say things that his dad wanted him to say. He might say things the police wanted him to say. Some of those might be true, and some might be just because he was under pressure to say something. Maybe he really didn't know it.

This part, where Shelley says, "He was supposed to go for psychiatric help, but it didn't do him too much good," is interesting. Pretty sure that never happened. Maybe it was court mandated, but I can't imagine Dad going to a psychiatrist. It doesn't strike me as something he'd be willing to do. Even if he did go, because it was court mandated, I can't imagine it would have changed him at all. It's not like he came out of prison—the first time around— any different than he went in. There's all this talk about him holding a grudge because of the affair, but I didn't personally notice any difference from before he went in and after. He was the same guy. I do wonder how prison has changed him this time around because he's been in so long. I don't wonder enough to go see him and find out. I've heard enough from Ronnie about what he's like. Doesn't seem like he's changed much.

You have to remember, I wasn't living at home when this all happened. Your dad and I had moved out. I got a phone call from Mom saying that Dad was in jail. When she said it was for murder, I immediately knew it was Clifford. Dad had a temper, but he'd never killed anyone before. Despite that, if there was anyone who he would have killed, after years of simmering over perceived wrongs and slights against him, it was Clifford. When Mom finally said who it was, I wasn't surprised. I guess it really says something about the character of my father that I wasn't surprised he murdered someone.

Who knows how many people he's killed over the years. He fought in three wars. He killed people while serving his country. I mean, you're not trained as a sniper to not pull the trigger. If he was a mechanic, or even an Army welder, I could imagine him getting through Korea and Vietnam without killing anyone. But as a sniper? And given his temperament? I'm guessing he killed a few people in his time. Anyway, I was so removed from all of this and heard everything second-hand. It is really interesting to read it now and see what was said, or, at least, what was recorded as being said.

Little Ronnie's statement is heart-breaking. You can hear the love he felt for *him* right there on the page. Word for word, it's what *he* wanted him to say. Even though Ronnie was in the vehicle on that night, and even though he heard the whole thing, here he is, ten years old, lying to the police because his father told him to. He was a little trooper.

I suppose if you take these papers and you take our stories, and you add them up and divide down the middle, you'll find the truth somewhere in there.

REFLECTIONS OF HIM (2015)

Sometimes, I see things in you that remind me of him, and it scares me. Not that I think you're going to kill someone or something, but there are other things you do that cause me to remember him. Like, the other day when we were driving downtown, and we stopped at that light downtown, and people were crossing the crosswalk. Remember that?

You said, "Watch this," and you revved your engine.

There was a flicker of my father on your face as you grinned when they jumped. Or, when you see a sign that says not to do something, something you probably wouldn't have done anyway but because there's a sign telling you not to, you do it. Sometimes it's funny. The photos you share of you swimming next to the sign that says "no swimming" or standing next to the sign that says "no standing" or talking on your cell phone at the gas station where it says not to—all kind of funny, but sometimes you go too far. For instance, the photograph your friend took of you taking a picture at a border crossing, where photography was prohibited. That could have gotten you in serious trouble. You walk that line between funny and antisocial behavior and don't always seem to know which side of the line you're on.

Dad always parked wherever he felt like it, regardless of the signage or where the lines were, and I guess that just reminds me of him when I see you do things like that.

Your temper is worrying also. I know, I know you're well aware and that you've been working on it, but still. You need to watch it. I don't mean this as an insult, but you're not physical like Dad was. It's not like you go around beating people up, but I've seen the way you hold a grudge, and that does worry me. You're creative and inventive, and you know other ways of getting back at people. Remember that moving company that you got angry at? They broke some of your things and lost one or two items. You were mad, and I get that, but you went above and beyond what a normal person would do. How many times did you call the Better Business Bureau? And then you created that webpage and used your connections with whoever you know at those internet places to make that webpage come up whenever anyone searched for the company or the people associated with your move. That was devious. On one hand it was admirable that you had that kind of dedication to what you felt was justice. On the other, I can't help but see my father doing something like that. In the end, you got what you wanted. They replaced the broken and missing items, but the part that worries me is that even when they had done all that, you didn't remove the webpage. I saw that it's still there today. I know you want other people to be warned about what to expect from them, but maybe they were just having a bad day? Maybe they usually do exceptional work, and this was the exception, not the rule?

Unlike Dad, this doesn't seem to affect your personal

relationships, which is good, but I can't help but think that your temper is part of the problem you've had with keeping a job. I don't mean to nag you about this, but how many jobs have you had since you graduated? I know you're still trying to find your way and figure out what you want to do, but you're forty-four now. Most people have figured it out by now, or at least found something that doesn't make them miserable. Every time you get fired from a job, that's one less reference you have for the next one. I know you know this, but the point is, that's something that Dad would do. He'd pick fights with his boss, he'd complain that a coworker wasn't working as hard as he was, or he'd find some way to work the system.

Did you know he was on disability but kept working part time under the table? And then he continued to collect disability in prison, until he pissed off the wrong person? It started when he refused to sign his checks for Mom. She needed the money to pay the bills and feed us kids. Their arrangement was that he'd sign the checks, and Mom would get half for the family and put the other half into his commissary. But Mom did something to piss him off, and so he stopped signing the checks. Someone told her she could sign for him, as long as they were still married, and so she did. He was so mad when he found out, but there wasn't much he could do. Eventually one of the guards heard him grumbling about the whole thing. That guard passed the information up the chain of command until someone, who knew someone at the factory, informed the factory that Achiel was clearly no longer suffering from a physical disability. The factory representative sent a letter to Achiel informing his disability had been terminated, and as part of the evidence they provided Achiel's own complaints demanding more time for exercise. He screwed himself because of his anger and temper.

I worry you could do the same. I love you. I just worry. Be careful, okay? You digging into this thing about Dad has been great because as a family we've been able to open up and talk about things I never thought we'd talk about. Sometimes I worry you're like an emotional sponge, soaking up all his bitterness. Reading that stuff over and over again, the way you have, can't be good for your mental health. And studying Clifford Ellis' autopsy and crime photos. I think you just need a new hobby. Or maybe a sport?

Now that we've aired the dirty family laundry, can you let it go? I think it would be good for you. Your sisters seem to have taken it in stride. Though, in truth, they never really seemed very interested in him. Your cousins enjoyed hearing about it, but I think even they're tired of hearing whatever new nugget you've found, or think you've found. I'm sure MDOC and the various Federal agencies you've contacted would appreciate a break from your inquiries. It might just be time to let it go, and to move onto something new.

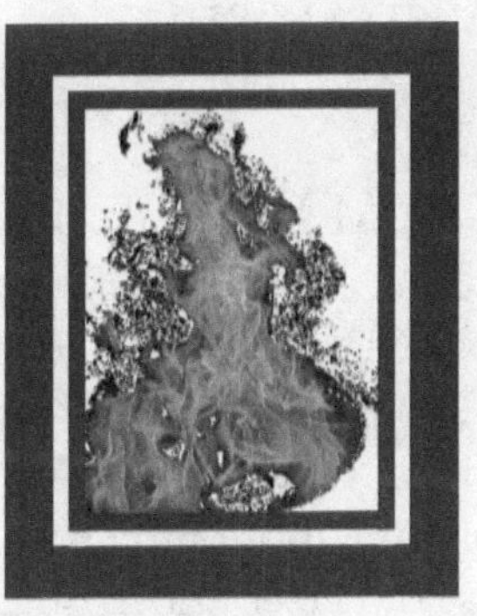

PART X: THE DIVORCES OF RONNIE VAN SLYCK

FROM HAZEL, 1983

I really didn't think I'd even have to see her. I thought you said I wasn't going to have to see her. She can have half of whatever I've got, which isn't much, but that little girl is mine. I'll fight for whatever I've got to make sure Jazzy doesn't spent any more time with that woman than she absolutely has to. Hazel is a terrible wife and an even worse mother. I want full custody. A pack of wolves would raise her better than she ever could. Come on, honey, even you'd admit that. Right?

Seriously, Judge? Magistrate? Well, whatever, you know what I mean. This woman, my wife. She's looney. I'm sure you've heard it all before, but this is the real deal. I grew up in a fucked-up family (pardon the language), but she really takes the prize. I know I'm not perfect, but if that woman raises my little girl, she's going to grow up a crackwhore, and I won't stand by and let that happen.

My name is Hazel Brewer Van Slyck, and I am the

plaintiff in this case. I married the Defendant on March 21, 1981 at the Livingston County courthouse. I filed a complaint for divorce on May 11, 1983. I lived in Michigan for my whole life, and have not left the state since filing. When I filed my complaint for divorce all the statements were true. All the statements in my complaint for divorce are still true today. There has been a breakdown of the marriage relationship such that the objects of matrimony have been destroyed and there remains no reasonable likelihood that the marriage can be preserved. I do not believe there is any possibility of reconciliation. I am not currently pregnant. The Defendant and I have one minor child together. Her name is Jasmine, and she was born January 19, 1981. She is three years old. I have read all of the terms of the proposed Judgement of Divorce and am in agreement with them. I would like to change my surname back to my maiden name, which was Snyder. I ask that this Court grant an absolute judgment of divorce. Thank you.

FROM CAROLINE, 1989

Your honor, I don't know how to put this any more plainly. I can't live with this man anymore. We have two children together, Randy and Noah, and the kids and I regularly fear for our lives. We're never sure which Ronnie is going to show up when he comes home from work. Sometimes he's loving and wonderful, and other times, most times, he's drunk and angry. When he doesn't have work, it's even worse. Not because he drinks any more than he does after work, but because he's angry about not having work, and he takes that anger out on us. We don't feel safe in our home. He needs help. I've asked and tried to help, but he won't listen. I'm happy to share custody of our children with him eventually—they are 3 and nearly 1—but he needs to sober up and get treatment first. No, I have no desire to change my name at this time. Thank you.

FROM LILA, 1996

I'd just like to say, Lila, I'm sorry. I should have been more straightforward and honest with you. I enjoyed our almost-five years of marriage more than any other time in my life, and I know my children will always think of you as their mother. They respect and cherish you. I'm sorry I couldn't give you children of your own. It was selfish of me to withhold that I was incapable of having children, and I'm sorry that you had to find out the way you did. I hope, with time, you'll understand that when I had my vasectomy I was in a different place than I was when I was with you. And when I met you, and we were such a good match and you made me so happy, I couldn't bring myself to disappoint you. And then, time goes by and how could I bring that up? Be honest. Anyway, I fully accept responsibility for this divorce, and hope you find the happiness I couldn't bring you. I agree to whatever terms she believes is fair, your Honor.

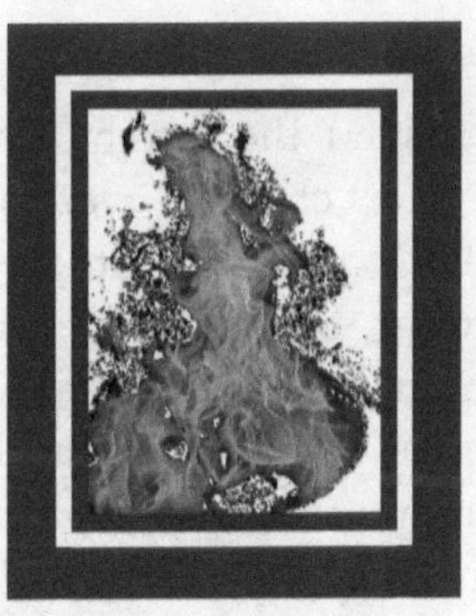

PART XI: PRAYERS

Until Cristina joined the family, only Lucia went to church regularly. Her children were discouraged from going by their father's negative attitude to religion so they never, or rarely, went, but when Cristina married Lucas, Lucia wasn't alone in her faith. Lucia was delighted that Cristina wanted to say grace before meals. She was equally excited to see family gatherings organized around faith-related holidays in a way they never had been before. The family had always celebrated Easter and Christmas, but it had been in the more commercial way of giving gifts, eating candy, and watching television.

When Achiel was a part of the household, the only way to differentiate a holiday from an ordinary day was that, if the factory was closed because of the holiday, he was home when he normally wasn't. Of course, that's assuming he wasn't overseas fighting a war, or unemployed, or on disability due to an "injury." In those cases, there was no way to differentiate a holiday from an ordinary day. Achiel was a practical man, and for him holidays served no practical purpose. The family spent enough time together and didn't have extra money to waste on gifts and treats. If the kids needed something, he could make it, or buy it if necessary when the need arose—he didn't see a reason to wait until a birthday or a holiday. He also looked upon most toys as frivolous. Why waste money on junk when you're surrounded by the playground of nature? He could occupy himself for hours just watching and listening to nature, and he wanted his children to be able to do the same. If they were spoiled with crap like Mr. Potato Head, Matchbox Cars, Pogo Sticks, and whatever the heck a Gumby was, they'd fail to see the beauty around them and find their own entertainment.

Church fell into a similarly practical category for Achiel. He had never believed in a God, because he wasn't raised to, and ever since, he had no reason to change. Early in their marriage, Lucia would beg him to go to church with her, and he'd refuse. She would typically retort that she was going to pray for his soul and then go to church on her own or with her sister Mina.

When she pushed more than usual, Achiel would counter with comments like, "Why does it matter where someone prays? Can't I pray at home?" and "Can't you believe in God without going to some building to surround yourself with people? If you need companionship, stay home. That's where your family is. God didn't do nothing for me. Why should I go to his house? He don't need to come to mine."

Lucia used to try to take the children, but Achiel put his foot down.

"No brainwashing. Let them become adults and then decide if they want to go. They ain't smart enough to know now."

Lucia fretted over her children, and because Achiel wouldn't allow them to be baptized, she secreted holy water from the church and did her best home-baptism when he wasn't looking.

Now, with Achiel in prison, she had no resistance from her husband, and with Lucas' marriage, she had a powerful ally in Cristina. There was a problem though. Lucia was Catholic, and Cristina was a Christian Scientist. Lucia knew what a scientist was and what a Christian was, but she'd never heard the two words put together in that manner.

So, she asked, "What's that?"

Cristina paused because in Lucia she saw an opportunity. In the past, when she tried to explain Christian Science to other people, they were baffled and ended up thinking she was part of some weird cult. So, rather than launch into all that, she simply said, "It's not so different from Catholicism." This wasn't exactly true, and in fact most Catholics think Christian Scientists are neither Christian nor scientific, but Lucia didn't know better and she didn't care. She just wanted a fellow-believer.

This was fine with Cristina because it was becoming harder and harder to find Christian Scientists like her family. The churches were closing, and even in 1976, membership was down. Plus, she was only a Christian Scientist because that was how she had been raised. While she was technically deceiving Lucia, her intention was not to trick her. It was to take advantage of this opportunity to actually become more like her. If Lucia was Catholic and went to church regularly, then maybe Cristina could become Catholic as well. How would they ever know if she just started showing up at her new mother-in-law's church with her and taking communion there? Cristina doubted anyone would ask for her baptismal records. They might ask what church she came from, but she could in fact tell them the truth: It was a small church in Washington.

This was the church she always thought of as "her

church" because it was the one she was raised in. Even though she hadn't lived in Washington for almost fifteen years by 1976, when she thought of a church where she felt at home, where she felt connected to the community, where she felt truly at peace, it was her church in Bothell, Washington. The church was one of the few things Cristina truly missed when her parents divorced and she moved with her mother across the country to Michigan. She'd tried a number of Christian Science churches in Michigan, but none of them fit quite the same.

So now, in Lucia and her church, Cristina saw an opportunity to find a sense of community and "home" that she'd been missing all these years. She knew that Lucas wasn't a man of faith. Early on, Cristina had held out hope that she could change him, but as she'd come to learn from Lucia, the Van Slyck men didn't seem to take to faith very easily. Lucia told Cristina how she had tried to take Ronnie to church with her after Achiel "went away," but it was too late for Ronnie. He went because she made him. When he was in church, he sat there and read the Bible. He didn't stand to sing or participate in any of the church traditions. He refused to be properly baptized and didn't want to become confirmed, so he couldn't take communion. It was a disaster. Lucia gave up trying to force it, so Ronnie stayed home on Sundays to get drunk and watch whatever was on TV while she went to mass and prayed for his soul.

Lucia had tried with each of Ronnie's wives, hoping to encourage them and their children to go to church, but each of Ronnie's wives had slightly different relationships with religion. Lila was intensely religious, but she was private about it. She prayed by herself, didn't go to church, but kept each of the religious holidays. She was delighted to hear that Lucia and Sophie "took back" Easter and Christmas and was happily on board to celebrate in a way that focused attention on religion and not on gifts and candy.

Caroline was the opposite. She was not religious and openly made fun of the church and faith in general. This particularly disturbed Lucia because it meant that Randy and Noah were being raised, not just by someone who didn't attend church, but by someone who mocked the Lord, his house, and the scriptures. When Noah came out to the family, Lucia didn't openly say anything, but she was pretty sure his "gayness" was a result of not going to church, well, that and bad parenting.

Lucia would have found a kindred Catholic with Hazel because the girl held deep belief and faith, but at the point Hazel entered the family she was too young and preoccupied with being a teen mother to engage Lucia's interest in church. By the time Lois came into Ronnie's life, Lucia and Cristina had solidified traditions. They were happy to take on another like-minded individual, but they had no patience for anyone offering an alternative opinion.

"What about Sophie?" asked Cristina, hoping that the Van Slyck women could bond together in faith and plan Easter suppers and the like. Lucia had to inform Cristina that Sophie was too much like her father in that way, and that she wouldn't step foot in a church, not to get married, not for rummage sales, not for nothing. When she was invited to weddings, she went to the reception only. It was just how she was. And now Ronnie was taking after her and their father as well.

It would just be the two of them then, but maybe if they worked really hard, they could convince Sophie and Ronnie that the children should be exposed to church. To see what it was like, so they could make their own decisions. Yes, Cristina and Lucia would work to try to make that happen.

AT CHURCH (1991)

Let us pray.

Heavenly father, giver of life and health, we ask you to provide comfort and relieve the pain and suffering for your servants who are ill and need your love. Your power of healing is needed among so many, we pray together hoping that you can aid Reginald Hodges, who is recovering from cancer; Gretchen Salazar, who has been hospitalized for her heart; Sharon Rice, who is so near to joining you in heaven, please ease her pain; Danny Herrera, who fell yesterday; Ella Berry, who needs your comfort as her father has recently passed; Laura Stone, whose son recently was deployed, please watch over him; Kurt Chandler, who just lost his daughter; and so many others who need your comfort. Please watch over them.

Please care for those less fortunate than us. Those who find themselves in need. Our recent discovery of men, like Achiel Van Slyck, who are incarcerated and are in need of companionship during dark times. As your servants, we will do our part to offer our love in the form of prayers and letters, but only you can offer the promise of eternal life

and guidance.
  We pray in Jesus' name, Amen.

SELECTIONS FROM THE COLLECTED PERSONAL PRAYERS OF LUCIA VAN SLYCK (1943-2015)

1943. Dear Heavenly Father, please protect my family and our neighbors. I'm scared. The soldiers have taken over, and I don't know what will happen to us. Please, Lord, please save us. Please let this war end soon. Please, please, please, please. Amen.

1948. Blessed Mother. Hail Mary, full of grace, the Lord is with thee. Blessed are thou among women, and blessed is the fruit of thy womb, Jesus. Holy Mary, Mother of God, pray for us sinners, now and at the hour of our death. Amen. Today's my wedding, and I should be happy. I worry that my sister doesn't approve of Achiel, and that I'm not seeing something she is. Please bless our marriage and keep my sister safe and in my life. She means so much to me. Thank you Mother, Amen.

1950. Heavenly Father, my husband has gone to war. I thought he would have had enough of war after the first one, but we saw him off this morning, and he goes to fight again. Please keep him and all our soldiers safe. Please let this war end soon and bring everyone home safe. Please don't let there be another Hitler or Mussolini or Hirohito. End this war before it can spread. Please, Lord. Amen.

1955. Lord Jesus, my husband is going to another country to fight another war. I don't even know where Vietnam is. Please keep him safe.

1964. Blessed Mother. Hail Mary, full of grace, the Lord is with thee. Blessed are thou among women, and blessed is the fruit of thy womb, Jesus. Holy Mary, Mother of God, pray for us sinners, now and at the hour of our death. Amen. Please forgive my husband Achiel. And please forgive that girl, Miriam. She was young and didn't know better, I'm sure. Please forgive the awful things I said to her and to her parents. I shouldn't have blamed it on them, or her, because it wasn't their fault. I was wrong to place blame. Please Mary, guide that young girl. She needs you. I need your guidance, too, about what to do with Achiel now. How can I stay together with him after this? How can I be with him? I know I am supposed to forgive, but I'm having a hard time. He went against God and our marriage. I need your strength. Please show me my path. Give me a sign. Amen.

1975. Holy Father, I pray for the souls of Clifford, Shelley, Miriam, and Achiel. The Ellis family has gone through a tragedy, and they need your help to get through it. If it wasn't enough what my husband put them through with their daughter, now this. I fear it might be too much for Shelley and Miriam. Please be with them. As terrible as it is to take another's life, please forgive my husband. I have forgiven him for so much, and with your help I will forgive him again. But I won't stay with him. Father, I need your guidance. I know divorce is a sin, but how can I remain married to this man? He already broke our marriage vows, and now he has taken another life. Yes, I can forgive him, but I can't love him. I can't be with him, and I don't want my children to be tainted by him. Please, Lord. Please guide me. Amen.

1985. Holy Father, please forgive me, Father. I am getting a divorce. I tried. I forgave him for all the horrible things he's done. I've waited, ten long years since he went away, and almost twenty from when he first ruined our marriage. But I can't wait any longer. I know it goes against you and the vow I swore, but he brings out the worst in everyone around him. When I visit him, I'm so angry. The kids and I fight and argue. I can only imagine our lives will be better without him in it. I don't care how much it costs me. I just want to be done. So, forgive me Father. I've waited for your guidance, and I've given him as much of my life as I'm willing. Now I need to move on without him. He will find his way if he accepts you into his life. Amen.

1987. Holy Father, I know I should be saying a Hail Mary, or one of the Creeds, but I am praying today for a selfish thing. We need something to help us with the bills. With the divorce, and all it cost us, I need help with the bills. Or, maybe this is my punishment for the divorce? I'm sorry, but I couldn't see another way around it. Work at the factory has slowed down, and the boys have long moved out. It's just me in this big house, and I guess I never realized how much we counted on the extra money from the disability checks or for the boys to pitch in to help. They're not offering overtime like they used. It might be time to sell this place. Maybe that's what I need to do. I should be thinking about retiring, but I don't know how I can retire at this rate. Please, Lord. I need you. Amen.

1990. Lord Jesus, he is up for parole again. You know what kind of man he is. The children and I will be there to speak out against it, but we need you to help make sure he doesn't get paroled. I ask for me, and the children, but also for the rest of the world. The world is a safer place when he isn't walking in it. Please, for the sake of all God's children, please keep him in prison. I know it's terrible to ask that for someone who I used to love, and who gave me these beautiful children. But you heard him in court. If he gets out, he's going to kill someone. Probably Lucas. But he might not stop there. Please, Lord. Amen.

1996. Lord Jesus, I pray for my son Ronnie. This is his third divorce now. Please show him the way. There was nothing wrong with his wives, not that I could tell. Not like in my marriage where one had done something horrible. Did I give Ronnie the idea to divorce Hazel when I was talking to him about divorcing his father? Maybe if I had stayed married, maybe Ronnie would have stayed with Hazel. I feel such a heavy burden for his divorces. But then I would never have my grandsons Randy and Noah, and I love them so much. Jesus, I'm afraid Ronnie doesn't take marriage seriously. He's the only one of my children who has had a divorce, and now he's had three. His drinking certainly doesn't help. Thank you for helping him get that under control. He says that's not you, but I know it is. He can't see your work like I can. Amen.

2001. Dear Heavenly Father, thank you for taking him. I hope his soul is at peace now. Amen.

2015. Lord Jesus, I'm ready. I've enjoyed seeing my children and grandchildren grow. They are such gifts. I am so blessed to have lived all these years, and to be in good health so I can truly enjoy every year of my life. I thank you, my Lord. Thank you for all you've given me. Please watch over my children, as I know you will, and keep them safe. I know they'll make mistakes, like we all do, but please help them find the way and keep them safe. Please let them know peace and happiness as I have. Thank you. Amen.

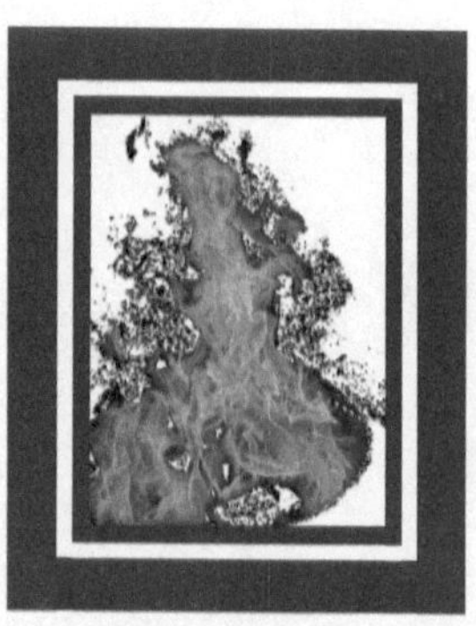

PART XII: THE OUTLAWS

An outlaw was anyone who married into the Van Slyck family. On paper, they were treated like blood relatives and their opinions were valued just as highly as Lucia, Sophie, Lucas, and Ronnie, but in practice, it was more lip-service than anything. The longer someone was an outlaw, the more their opinion held weight, but the less that outlaw expected their opinion to matter due to years of experience to the contrary. For example, when Gerry first suggested a family reunion in 1990, the core Van Slycks responded favorably to it. They liked the idea. Gerry pitched it as, "A time for us to get together, all of us, when there was no other holiday to distract us from spending time together."

Gerry was right. It had become increasingly difficult to get everyone together, even at holiday times. When the family gathered for a holiday, there was usually a short window to gather and mingle before somebody had to leave to spend time with their other families. This meant they saw each other briefly for Easter, Fourth of July, Labor Day, Thanksgiving, Christmas, and sometimes New Years Eve, but they really never spent much quality time together because everyone was on a tight schedule, and sometimes those schedules didn't overlap. Gerry brought the reunion idea up at a rare moment when everyone was gathered on Labor Day, and he pointed out that he hadn't spent more than ten minutes with Ronnie in the last year. It wasn't anyone's fault, they were all busy with children and their lives, but Gerry felt like he was losing touch with his in-laws, and he missed them.

Gerry proposed an annual weekend set aside entirely for family time. Each year, the family would take turns planning the event (selecting the venue, making reservations, etc.), and it would rotate from eldest to youngest. This meant Gerry and Sophie would plan the first one. Everyone agreed that the idea sounded great. But then Lucas pointed out that adding yet another weekend to gather would make it harder to make it to the already established traditions of the five or six family gathering times. Gerry countered that rather than make it more difficult, it would actually take the pressure off making all of those other times. Instead of spreading themselves so thin, they could concentrate on making the family-prioritized-weekend Gerry was proposing (since that was dedicated to family time without other obligations), and if people could make it to the other gatherings, then great, but it was not expected. By way of example, Gerry offered that while he thought the Fourth of July gathering was great, he really didn't give two shits about fireworks or the independence. Cristina piped up that she agreed. Also, she didn't like Easter because she thought the Easter bunny was creepy and hated lying to her children. Ronnie, who was a year into his second divorce and had just started dating Lila, commented that it would help him navigate holidays with his ex-wives because they could have the kids for more of the holidays instead of trying to split time with him. Everyone seemed on board, and so Gerry began to plan and organize the first ever Van Slyck family weekend outing.

Gerry chose the weekend of May 11-12, 1991. The hope was that it was early enough in the season that any place they reserved wouldn't be overrun with vacationers. It wasn't a traditional time for vacation because Memorial Day was only two weekends away and would still be warm enough that they wouldn't have to worry about being snowed in or treacherous driving conditions. In fact, if they had actually gone that weekend, it would have been a gorgeous day. The small campground Gerry found recorded near-record temperatures of 82 degrees in mid-May. It was almost unheard of. But they didn't go. The family valued Gerry's input and thought his idea was great, but none of the original four came up with the idea, and none of them had spear-headed the project. Despite Sophie's support of her husband, it wasn't enough for her to be able to sway her mother and brothers. Gerry kept anxiously trying to get everyone to commit so he could reserve the cabins, but as the winter of 1990 arrived, no one had responded. In January, Ronnie proposed to Lila, and they began to plan a June wedding. No, they couldn't imagine having time to get away in May. Sorry, Gerry, it's a great idea, just bad timing. You couldn't have predicted this. Message loud and clear sent to all outlaws: thanks, but no thanks.

In the seniority ranking of outlaws, Gerry was at the top of the line. By 1990, Gerry had been part of the family for two decades. If he couldn't get the family to do something, what hope did any outlaw have of being taken seriously? Yet, each did try, and each learned the lesson like Gerry did. Some, like Hazel and Caroline who were barely blips on the radar still tried to leave their mark. When Lila, Lois,

Lorraine, and Ken joined the family, they wouldn't initially believe the stories they'd heard about the way outlaws were treated. In time, they'd learn, and then the outlaw label became a sort of badge of honor, something they could rally around with the other outlaws.

The only outlaw to find an inroad with Lucia was Cristina, and it was because she gained the ear of the matriarch and leaned heavily on something near and dear to her heart: religion. The thing was, the way Cristina went about it, none of the family knew Cristina had anything to do with the changes. They just observed that she was a champion and in favor of the changes. When Lucia brought forward a price-cap on Christmas presents and insisted on attending Mass on Christmas Eve, the rest of the family just assumed it was something the matriarch had come up with on her own. They didn't know that the price-cap in particular was an idea that Cristina inserted into a conversation she was having with Lucia about financial struggles. She didn't so much say, "We should put a limit on spending on Christmas presents," but that's what Lucia walked away from the conversation thinking about. Now that she had several grandchildren and non-blood family members to buy presents for, it was getting a little out of control. Also, wasn't Christmas really about the religious holiday and not about commercial gift-giving in the first place?

Lucia posed this question to Cristina, who all but Amen'ed in response. Lucia, empowered by Cristina's affirmation, said that it was a shame that her children and their families were being raised outside of the church. She wanted to bring them back into the fold, if even just for one holiday. After the success of Christmas, Cristina and Lucia put an end to talk about Easter bunnies and candy, and refocused the Easter celebration on sacrifice and rebirth. Though they attempted to curtail the candy-gathering and mask-wearing associated with Halloween, there they failed. This was Sophie's favorite holiday, and while she saw the wisdom of not overspending on Christmas and was willing to step into a church at least twice a year to appease her mother, she was not willing to give up the joy she felt at doling out candy and seeing her children dressed up like monsters. Plus, it was an occasion for her to make chili, and she loved making chili.

To be fair, Cristina's successes as an outlaw were limited to Easter and Christmas. When she attempted to use the same techniques to inspire change in other matters, she was shutdown and faced the same result as Gerry had with his failed family reunion.

Hazel argued that the family should go in together on a time-share, but she was too young and naïve to make the argument go anywhere. The idea died before it ever took off.

Caroline wanted her children to receive "experiences" (like passes to museums or zoos) instead of presents, but her kids continued to receive whatever was being advertised as the hot new toys from their aunts and uncles.

Lila thought the Van Slyck family property should be partially used to raise farm animals. It would be good for the kids, she argued. They'd have a summer job and then could enter the animals into the fair. There was even a precedence for this because the Van Slycks had raised pigs and chickens at one time. Just when Lila was ready to bust out her numbers and figures, the family nixed the plan. They'd rather let it grow over and eventually sell it.

Lois heard Ronnie mention Hazel's original idea of the time-share once, though he was making fun of it, and that became her pet project for a while. Look, we could go different times of the year and each only pay a fraction of the cost. It would be great! The kids could make lasting memories by going back there again and again, but the idea barely was out of her mouth before Lucas said, "Haven't we already talked about a time-share?" Everyone nodded and the matter was closed.

Lorraine wanted to start an oral history project, so family stories could be recorded for future generations before they were forgotten. Anton had warned her this would be a bit dicey, given how little family members wanted to talk about Achiel, but Lorraine brought it up at Easter. There was some interest, but ultimately Lucia didn't like the idea of being on camera and didn't like the sound of her voice.

Lorraine approached Mina about doing it, but Mina predictably replied, "What did Lucia say?"

Discouraged for sure, Lorraine didn't quite give up. She asked Sophie and Lucas if they still wanted to do it. Lucas flat-out wasn't interested in any kind of "permanent record," and Sophie was afraid of going against her mother's wishes. Lorraine did score a small victory because Sophie caught her arm and whispered, "Maybe when Mom is gone?"

Ken had only been dating Noah for a year before Lucia died, so he was the first outlaw to bring an idea to the table without the oldest and longest-serving member of the Van Slyck original-4 counsel. In fact, he proposed to Noah on the very day Lucia died, though neither knew she had passed at the time. They were just about to call to share their good news, when the phone preempted that, and they decided it was best to wait until after a little time had passed to make an official announcement. Ken's idea came up during a rare Fourth of July gathering when everyone was present. Everyone was there because they were discussing what to do with Lucia's estate. She had a will that had been executed, but there was the matter of the house and property to decide. Up to this point, Sophie, Lucas, and Ronnie were splitting the taxes and insurance, but they didn't want this to be a permanent arrangement. The whole family enjoyed the property, and did make use of it, but not enough to justify the expense. They had decided to sell it. The current debate was over how much to list it for and how much to put into renovating it before listing it.

Ken, who really liked the idea of the property attached to the house, posed the possibility of him and Noah buying it from the family. This idea was considered longer than most outlaw proposals, but ultimately Sophie snuffed it without room for further comment.

"I think it's a bad idea to mix family and business. I love you and Noah too much to put you in the middle."

Ken argued they'd be willing to match whatever other offer the family received, and that they wouldn't need to renovate at all, but Lucas reiterated Sophie's point and patted Ken on the shoulder. The house and property were sold and the money was divided equally between all living Van Slycks—grandchildren included—because that's what they thought Lucia would have wanted.

Ronnie delivered the check to Ken and Noah after the sale and said, "It's not much, but it will help with a downpayment."

They hugged, but Ken continued to carry a grudge that no one took his offer seriously.

In other families, outlaws might have been able to influence their spouses to push an agenda that wasn't initially their own, but that didn't work with the Van Slycks. So, after each outlaw had his or her shot at pitching an idea to the family, and it was summarily shot down, they stopped offering comment and just let the counsel of 3 make decisions with regard to the greater family matters.

This shortcoming was compensated by the fact that in their own houses, the outlaws held sway and control over of their own family matters and the "true" Van Slycks found themselves powerless without their mother or siblings.

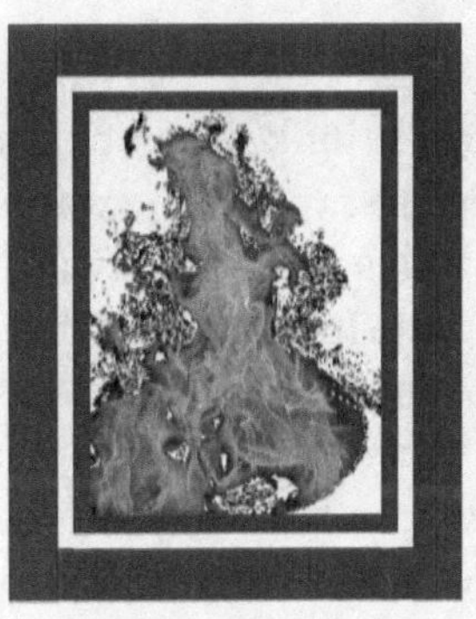

PART XIII: MIRIAM (2015)

That boy, Anton I think his name was, called me once. He didn't even need to say what he wanted because I knew. The minute I heard his voice on my answering machine, I knew. I hit play on the message and that voice came out of the speaker. He sounded just like his grandfather. It made my skin crawl. I wasn't home when he called, but sometimes, even if I am home, I just let the phone ring and go to the message. I wonder what I would have said, if I had been home and had answered it, and I heard that voice talking to me. Who knows.

I thought about calling him back a couple times, but I could never wrap my mind around how that conversation would go. What would I say to him? What did he want? In his message, he said he just wanted to talk. Why does he have to go digging the past up?

I heard the old man finally passed. I won't lie, it felt good to hear it. I shouldn't wish ill upon anyone, but after all he did, he overstayed his welcome. It was past time for him. Frankly, his whole family should be glad he's dead. What good could that man have brought to anyone? He threatened his own son in court. He said he was going to "fucking kill" him. Right there. The judge and everyone heard. I don't know how Lucia stayed with him for so long, even after all of that. I remember her talking to Mom about the divorce and telling her it was final. Good for her. I hope she found someone else and made peace with all that.

Mom's been gone two years now. She was the last Ellis. When I got married I took Terry's name, Guzman. Dad never had any brothers or sisters. I might have some cousins out there, but none I know how to find. Once, I did try that ancestry.com website, but it was expensive. I just did the free month trial and meant to cancel it right away, but forgot. Man, did I ever hear about that from Terry. I had written a reminder on the calendar, but then I forgot to look at the calendar. Viola, that's our girl, is always getting on me to use the reminders on my phone, but I forget. In that month, well really two months that I had an account, I found a lot of Ellises, but I couldn't quite figure out which I was related to and which I wasn't. There was almost too much information for me to make sense of, and I gave up. I should have given up before I got charged. That's the real sad part of the whole thing. I didn't even need the extra month that I ended up paying for, but I guess that's how they make their money.

Terry and me are coming up on thirty-eight years now, in just a month. We've known each other longer than that, but after what happened with Dad, we waited a little while to get married, out of respect to Mom. Wow, we're almost to forty. Hadn't thought about that. I wonder sometimes how long Mom and Dad would have made it. They always seemed so in love, but I know Dad's drinking made it hard sometimes. Who knows.

We just have the one girl, Viola. She's thirty-five. Married only a couple of years ago to a sweet man. She's not a Guzman anymore, but there are plenty of Guzmans out there—Terry has a huge family, and we get together a number of times a year. It's a lot of fun, so many characters there. She married Lyle King. Four years, I think? No, six. Wow, that many. Their little Andrew just turned three. I never thought I'd look forward to becoming a grandparent, but it really is the best thing that ever happened to me. Terry and me spoil that kid. We spend every extra minute we have with them. I take Andrew three days a week to help out with daycare. I'd take him more, but Viola said she couldn't take advantage of me that way. Take advantage? That's what grandparents are for. She's a good girl, and I know she means best. I try to respect what she wants for him and them, even if it isn't what I would do or want. It's their life and their rules. I just want to be there and with them as much as I can.

No, I never told her about what happened to her grandpa, and she never asked. I don't know what I would have said. There were times, of course, when she saw a photo of Dad and asked, "Who's this?" And I'd just say, "Oh, that's my dad." She never knew him and has never been curious to know more. He was dead five years before she was born. When she asked what happened to him, it was just as easy to say he died as it was to say he was murdered. Both are true, and a lot less baggage comes with the latter. We did give her the middle name Clifton, as a tribute to my dad. He was a Clifford, but that sounded too much like a boy name, so we went with Clifton. She's never asked about that either. I suppose kids fill in the gaps with their own ideas. I imagine she thinks it's my maiden name, or a family name or something. It's funny what people overlook, and what others latch onto. If it were me, I don't know if I'd ask either. It's like her grandad. He was just never in the picture so why would you ask? And Clifton was just always her middle name. It just was, so why ask?

Here I thought I didn't have anything to say about all this, and now I've been chatting for this long. Maybe I should call that Anton boy, though he's probably not a boy anymore. I wonder if I even have his number still. I kept that number hanging on the board for the longest time. You know, the one by where the old phone used to hang on the wall? Old habits. If I think of it later, I might get up and try it.

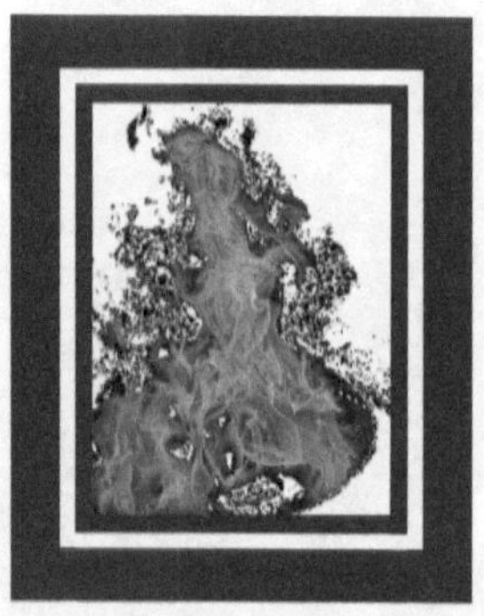

PART XIV: A PRISON STORY (1991)

You wanna hear about prison? You wanna hear a prison story? You wanna hear about doing pushups in your cell because there's nothing else to do? You wanna hear about the gang of men cornering people and having their way with them? You wanna hear about waiting for a phone call, or a visitor, or a letter, or something from the outside? We had a library, but what good is a library when you can't read? I had to teach myself to read before I could escape into books. I had to do favors for terrible men, more terrible than me, so I could get taught whatever I couldn't teach myself.

Do you know what solitary is like? It's nothing. It's like sitting in the woods, without the woods. It's getting lost in your mind. I could close my eyes and imagine the woods around. The sound of the owls, the crickets, and the wind blowing the grass. I spent so much time in the woods. I could see it without being there. Solitary is blocking everything else out and just focusing inward. Some guys went crazy in solitary. Sometimes they'd break me out of my trance with their screams and fits. Me, I didn't mind it so much. Going to solitary made my case for parole harder, but it also meant gaining the respect of the men who would have attacked me otherwise. Being small in prison is dangerous. They think you're weak until you show them otherwise. Surviving solitary and coming back sane was one way to show them I wasn't weak.

I was only inside a couple years when the Jackson riot started. That's a story for you. Your mom always loved to go to the movies. I went because she liked them. She especially loved those Elvis movies. Well I can tell you for certain, when the riot broke out in 1981, it was no Jailhouse Rock, though some of those inmates who rioted might have gotten whipped by the warden, like Vince was in that film. None of those movies we saw got it right. Not *Riot in Cell Block 11*, not *Riot*, not *Criminal Code*, not *Caged*, not *Cool Hand Luke*, not *The Great Escape*, and not *The Hill*. Funny how many prison movies she used to take me to. Maybe she knew something that I didn't. Of them, it probably was *Riot in Cell Block 11*—did you know that was based on an earlier riot at Jackson prison, from 1952?—that got closest to what the riot really looked like. Not everyone was rioting. Maybe only like five hundred? Others, like me, were trying to keep out of it. We didn't want any more time added. Those prison movies had some ridiculous happy ending that just aren't gonna happen in real life.

Did you know, at the time of our riot, Jackson was the largest walled prison in the world? It held something like 6,000 people. It was huge. Easy to get lost in. Our riot was in Cell Block 4 and didn't even last a whole day. Maybe six hundred people rioted. I read the papers, and they said, "nearly 1,000," but there's no way that was true. It seemed like a lot, but when you knew how many thousands of prisoners there were, it seemed like a small group was actually doing the rioting. They threw a fit, and burned some stuff, and ruined some things. More law enforcement officers came to patrol the outside of the prison. They cut the power, so we didn't have lights at night. No one died or was seriously hurt. But when the rioters were done, everyone was punished. We all had to deal with the smoke and the stuff they ruined. So much was wet because of the firehoses spraying everything down. All for what? They had a couple of hours to feel big and powerful and in charge, and then they went right back to being caged up again. A couple officers and deputy wardens were fired, but do you think the ones they replaced them with were any better?

It was a huge waste of time. No one got away. It wasn't like anyone was free because of the whole thing. It would have been something if we had at least gotten out and gone to a McDonald's—which I hate, so you know how prison has ruined me that I would be so desperate for anything from McDonald's—or some burger joint to get some real food for a day before they put us back in our cells. No, the prisoners that rioted just made their quarters worse than they already were, and then we all had to suffer with it being worse while the prison took its sweet time fixing things up again. After that we were on lockdown for two months because they thought we'd do it again. There was no consideration for the people who weren't involved. When I complained, they said I should have told them there was a riot planned. I didn't know. And even if I did know, I wouldn't have told them. That's the kind of thing that gets you killed inside. More than anything, talking isn't my kind of thing. I just wanted to do my time and get out of here. They didn't care about that. To them, all of us are the same.

There, that's the riot story. Is that what you wanted? I mean, I stayed in my cell and did my own thing, probably reading or practicing my alphabet. I don't really remember. That was a while ago now. Something like ten years? The whole thing was because some inmates didn't like that the guards were going to perform an unauthorized weapons search. I kept saying, "What's the big deal? We don't have any rights, and we're not supposed to have no weapons." Of course we all did have weapons. You need to protect yourself from those animals.

You don't really want to hear about prison. Your old man has been here long enough now to know that you only ask because you want to pretend you care. People always ask, "What's it like?" I tell you, you want to find out so bad, there are lots of ways to get yourself in here to find out. Even if the movies don't get it all right, you get the picture. It isn't fun. That's really all you need to know. I didn't mean you don't really care, maybe you do. I just mean, the average day in prison is boring. Nothing happens. If you want excitement, you have to make it yourself. That's how so many guys get in trouble. Me, my day is full of reading, writing, and doing pushups. When I can get outside, I walk. That's about it. Day in and day out. The only thing that changes is when I have a visitor, and as you know, those have tapered off considerably. Though I'm working on that.

There are lots of people who want to write to prisoners and visit them. Who knows why, but I figure I may as well let them. It will give me something to do with my day if nothing else. I get some letters here and there. Most want to hear about prison, like what you're asking. They want to hear about the drama and the violence and all that. But the truth is, that stuff doesn't happen often. Sometimes inmates kill themselves. We have gangs, and they fight sometimes. However, if you're like me and you're unaffiliated, then they leave you alone for the most part.

The neo-Nazis wanted me to join them when I first came in, but I lived through the real Nazis and didn't have any interest in that. I'd rather do my own thing. The one big guy with the shaved head tried to push me around, but you find they're all more bark and less bite. They want to seem tough to protect themselves, but they're not. None of them have carried bodies like I did and buried them or burned them. None of these tough guys have had to fight and steal food to survive.

I see one of those guys eying me, and I know he's going to come and try something. So I keep my distance, pretend I'm avoiding him because I'm scared. Finally, I let him corner me and he starts in. He's laughing and taunting me with his big dumb mouth. When he's close enough, I grab his cheek from the inside and tear through it with the fingernails I've grown and sharpened. Then he's not laughing, but I am. Some guys go out of their way to send a message, but I would have left this guy alone if he had done the same. Now all I have to do is stare at anyone and they think twice about messing with me.

When you see prisons on movies and television, they amp up the drama and make it seem like we're always fighting one another and whatever is going on in the bathrooms or when someone is alone, but that's just to sell tickets to theaters and products during the commercials. Prison is about puffing up your chest, surrounding yourself with people with puffed up chests, and then doing everything you can to avoid confrontation. Some of those guys, with their big act and puffed up chests, go off and read poetry to themselves in their cells.

You know what I miss most? Well, besides the obvious. The food is shit, of course. More than anything, I guess what I mean is, I miss little things like being able to turn on and off a light switch. That's something you lose control of in here. I miss being barefoot in the carpet. Privacy, fresh air, freedom, and being outside, of course. One thing you don't think about, until it's gone, is how nice it is to be able to set your own schedule instead of having it set for you. I used to work at factories, so I know about routine and monotony, but it wasn't until I was in here that I really appreciated how boring a set routine is. Every day the same thing. This is why visits and letters are so nice, they break up the monotony.

There are all kinds of women eager to have some kind of jailhouse boyfriend. One of the guys said it's because they know where we are and don't have to wonder if we're telling the truth. From what I've heard, everyone in here lies in their letters. Whatever rep they have in the prison, it is greatly exaggerated in the letters. That's because, like people paying to see a prison film, readers want drama, too. I learned that with you kids and your mom. After a while, you get tired of hearing the same crap. Me going over my trial again and again. All I think about is how I'm going to get out of here, but I suppose with a pen pal you need to temper that. You need to give them a little story here and there to keep them on the hook. Maybe they write because they've lost someone, or because they're all alone. One guy I used to bunk with gets letters from his victim's wife. At first, I guess the letters were angry and were asking all these questions, but then, over time, the letters turned into some kind of friendship, and now they're talking about getting married. Keep in mind, he killed this lady's husband. In cold blood. And he's serving double life. He'll never see the light of day. What's the point of a marriage like that? Control? Maybe she feels like she was powerless before, and now she can be in control of him because he's in prison?

My cellmate subscribes to all these magazines. Some are

music ones like *Metal Edge*, *Circus*, and *Hit Parader*. I've never heard any of the music that's in there, but he tells me that there are classifieds in the back where you can post your information for someone to write to you. I guess women who read these things like men who live dangerously, and what's more dangerous than prison? Plus, rock stars have tattoos and so do a lot of prisoners. Then there are all these car magazines. Most guys get them because they're the closest thing we can get to pornography in here. The women on the cars and trucks show some skin, but not enough to be contraband. You know, titles like *Hot Rod*, *Custom Car*, and *Autobuff*. When they come, I like to read those because the articles talk about rebuilding engines and customizing vehicles. It gives me ideas for what I can do with my welder when I get out. There are also classifieds in the back of those, but I imagine most of the readers are men, and I don't really need any male pen pals.

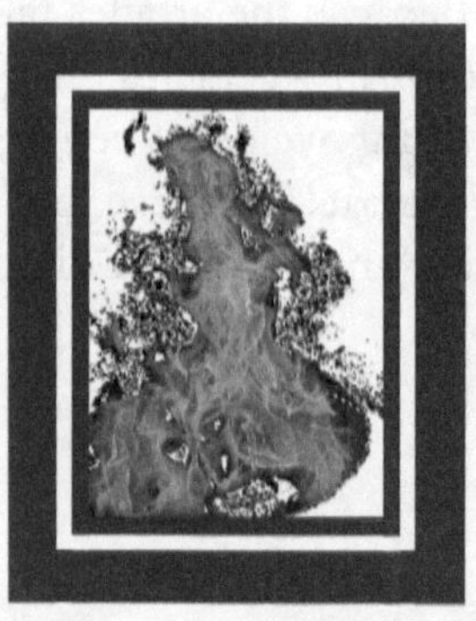

PART XV: DEATHBED REFLECTIONS

I feel sincere guilt for the animals that I killed. Not the ones I ate, but the ones that belonged to people as pets. I never received any joy from killing the dogs and cats, and especially the horse. The killing was just a means to an end. It was the people I wanted to teach a lesson, and their pet was just the vehicle to drive home the point. I never really cared for cats. They're sneaky little bastards, but I do respect their hunting ability. Respect only goes so far though. In the wild, animals respect one another's territory, and I was just making sure their owners respected mine. So, maybe I killed twenty or thirty cats. I don't think that's unusual. My mother used to drown kittens and puppies when she found them. Couldn't have extra mouths to feed. Who knows how many she killed. Probably hundreds. Those things were crawling all over our town back in the war. The neighbors in Lewes, they thought they could just let their animals run wild. They talked about having "barn cats," but the cats didn't stay in the barn. They ended up in my yard, killing my birds and rabbits. I gave the neighbors one warning, and then I'd just take care of their pet the next time I saw it. We only had a couple neighbors, and people didn't move so much back then. So, I'd warn them once about a cat, and once about a dog, and then I didn't bother warning anyone anymore after that.

The horse was a one-time thing. To hear my kids tell that story, I was some kind of serial horse killer.

I've heard them, "Remember the time Dad killed that horse?"

You kill one horse, and no one lets you live it down. What they don't remember is that the horse scared the shit out of their mother. She was leaving early, like she always did. Opened the garage door, and bam, there's a horse standing there right behind her car. She freaked out. I guess they didn't have horses in Sicily, or not many. Either way, if you imagine it being four o'clock in the morning and the fog was still hanging in the air, and you're half asleep, open the garage door and see a horse staring at you, I think you'd be afraid, too. She says she tried to shoo it away, but it just looked at her. Finally, after I don't know how long, she came in to get me.

"There's a horse, there's a horse!" she was saying, waking everyone in the house up.

I'm thinking there's no way there's a horse on our property. There were horses at the farms nearby, but who lets a horse run lose? Those are worth good money. I grabbed my shotgun, and I went out there. Your mother followed closely behind me, and as I looked, I didn't see anything. Your mother started crying. I'm not sure if she was relieved, or afraid of the horse, or afraid of what I might do for her waking me up, but she stood there bawling these big tears.

"Hail Mary full of grace," and all that.

I started to turn around to shush her, and holy shit something big started coming out of the fog. I lowered my gun and shot. The thing reared back and it made this terrible noise. I shot it again, and it fell over.

Lucia was crying and the kids were screaming, and I just needed everyone to shut their fucking mouths. I couldn't think. She got the kids back to their rooms and went off to work, and I was left to figure out what to do with this thing. Suddenly, I knew exactly whose horse it was. That asshole with the trees. So, I figured I could teach him a lesson and get him to shut his mouth once and for all. I got Lucas, and we dragged that dead horse to the barn. We field dressed it as quick as we could. I had him bury the entrails, and then I took the horse head and left a gift for Harper in the middle of his driveway. He couldn't help but see that thing. I knew I wouldn't have to say anything at all, and if he asked, I would never answer him. But, there it was.

Prison is a big rumor mill. Inmates trade in it. Somehow, someone heard the horse story and asked me about it.

"Did you get the idea from *The Godfather?*" they asked.

I had never heard of the movie, so I didn't know what they were talking about. The thing with the horse happened in 1966, shortly after I got out for doing time because of that girl. The movie didn't come out for another six years, so maybe that filmmaker stole the idea from me. Who knows. All I know is we ate all the meat from that thing. Saved on the grocery bill for almost two months. Rumors in prison are a funny thing, and you need to be careful about which ones you let fly about the place. There was no harm in the horse story spreading, so I told the story to whomever asked. I made it a little more dramatic each time, and made it like I wanted to kill the horse instead of it just being an accident. Of course, even if it hadn't surprised me like that, coming out of the fog, I probably still would have shot it for scaring my wife.

Lucia really is the one person I care about in this world. I know the kids say I treated her really bad, but I did the best I could. She was the only person I never wanted anything from. There was no angle with her. There was just some kind of pull. Some say true love, but I don't buy that. I think there was just something more animal-like that pulled me to her. When my dad didn't like her, it did make me want her even more, but that wasn't the only reason. There's just something about her. Everyone else, you could say I used them. That's what they'd tell you. Lucas, Ronnie. Maybe not Sophie. She was always the one with the backbone, and the one who would stand up to me or anyone else who picked a fight with her. I think there's something special about your first kid. At least there was with mine. I tried with Lucas, but I just couldn't be in the same room with him without wanting to smack that child. All his whimpering and blabbering and this and that. It just drove me nuts. I tried hard with Ronnie, hell I gave him my brother's name, but he disappointed me, too. Neither one of them have the guts that Sophie does.

Other than the animals, I can't say as though I'm sorry for much. And even with them, I'm not really sorry. I served both of my countries, which is more than I can say for either of my sons. I watched those planes crash into the buildings in New York. We watched the attacks all day in the prison, they kept playing them over and over. The first time I was surprised, because it was so genius. I didn't know of anyone who had ever thought to use a plane like that. Everyone around me was shocked and some were even crying.

My cellmate kept saying, "I know people in New York!"

Jesus Christ, keep your shit together. It's a big city! It'd be surprising if you didn't know someone from New York. So two thousand people died. It's a drop in the bucket.

How many died in Korea? Or Vietnam? Or either of the World Wars? And even then, America has never seen the kind of loss that the rest of the world has. They were acting like the deaths of these people up in their fancy offices was the end of the world. These generations have been here long enough that they forget what it's like when someone attacks you. Everyone here thinks they're so safe and protected. They forget that their grandparents, or great-grandparents, or relatives who once lived in Germany, or England, or France, or Spain, or Belgium, and then enemy soldiers walked the borders, and dropped bombs on them, and invaded their countries and took over. Did they really think that traveling across an ocean would save them from that? Everyone here has gotten soft. I couldn't help but laugh when I looked around and saw all these prisoners, who put on this tough front, crying. Of course, neither of my sons volunteered to do anything about the attack. It's a shame.

At that time, my cellmate was Jackson. What kind of name is that? Seems like a last name to me, not a first. He didn't bother me much, but that night, after watching the planes, he was bawling in his bunk. I told him to shut up. He said he just couldn't stop thinking about it all, and he went on about how it's so hard in prison because there's no comfort or hugging. I asked him if he wanted me to hug him. I thought he knew I was making fun of him, but he asked, "Would you?" I didn't answer. He crawled down from the top bunk and looked at me with those stupid eyes of his. He came closer and I reached out with my arms, and then stabbed him in the side of the neck. He gurgled a little and then was quiet. It was the best night of sleep I'd had in a long time. In the morning, the guards asked what happened. I told them how upset Jackson was about the attacks and left it at that.

Joan, one of the women who wrote me, asked about the wars I was in. People like her want to know things that they don't think they should ask, so they ask these ridiculous questions. I mean, when I tell you I was a sniper, it's pretty safe to assume I killed a few people.

She'd ask things like, "Did you ever see combat?"

Of course I saw combat.

Then, "Did you ever shoot anyone?"

Yes.

Then, finally, "How many people did you kill?"

That's what they want to know. How many, and what was it like? They want to know because they don't have what it takes to kill someone, so they want to hear about it, or read about it, or see it on TV. The truth is, I don't remember how many I killed. When you're in war, things just happen. You shoot things, they stop shooting at you. You're ordered to fire this way or that, and you do what you're told. Did I kill everyone I shot? Maybe. There are probably a couple where I miscalculated the wind, or the distance, or the angle, and they might have gotten away. But they don't promote snipers who can't hit a target. I couldn't tell Joan the whole story though. I didn't tell her about the people I killed in Belgium. She paid for transcripts of my court hearings, and paid for a copy of the police report, so she knew about Cliff. She just didn't know what happened in between. Usually, when people like Joan write, they want to hear about your crime. They want to know about whether or not you really did it, or if you're guilty, or what your version of the story is. But she already knew. She wanted to hear about things that weren't in the reports and transcripts. In a way, it was kind of a relief. No one ever asked me about Korea or Vietnam. Not even my wife or kids.

You're trained to kill, given a license to do it overseas,

but when you come home you're suddenly supposed to obey all the rules again. If you want to set fires and get revenge state-side, you need to be careful and think it through. So many people I served with rushed into things and got caught right away. Me, I took my time. I thought it out. I waited for the right moment. I could be impulsive, but when I had something big to do, even when I really, really wanted to do it right away, I held it in check. Like the trees, I waited and planned that out for months. I remember Lucas asking me why we were cutting down Harper's trees. I thought it was plain and clear, but that boy never was very bright. Harper liked to hunt. He'd wander wherever he saw game. When he came on my land, I'd shoot at him to let him know I knew what he was doing. Nothing big, just the bb-gun or pellets. Enough to let him know. He never quite learned. When he shot Blackie, that was the last straw. First, trees are expensive. Especially all those pines he had planted. More than that, trees provide cover for game and animals. Harper liked to hunt. Without trees, he wouldn't have anything to hunt. I made it plain to him that if he came on my land again, I'd shoot him dead. He'd have to go find somewhere else to hunt. After he came over that day and I laughed at him through the screen door, I expected to see him on my land again. I kept waiting for him to try it. There were days where I'd sit in the woods, or in the dining room with the screen pulled out of the window, with my 0.243 and watch him in the scope. He wandered around his land, and once I think he was tempted to cross over. I had my finger ready, but he turned back around and stayed on his own property. I could have had him if he had taken three or four more steps, but I'm a man of my word. As long as he stayed on his land, I had no problems with him.

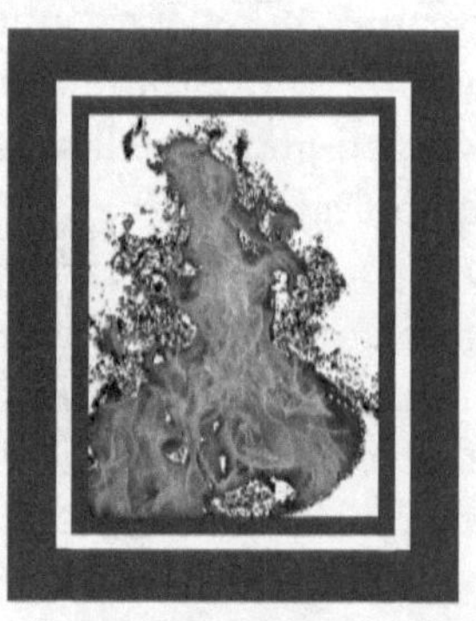

PART XVI: GENERATIONS X & Y
(SEPTEMBER 2015)

All the Baby Boomers and Silent Generation members who came to Anton and Lorraine's housewarming had gone to bed. Only the next generation of Van Slycks remained. As far as any of them knew, this might have been the very first time they had all been under one roof without adult supervision. Generation X only had two representative members: the hosts of the party, Anton and Lorraine. Otherwise, in age order, Lucy, Minerva, Winifred, Carl, Jasmine, Georgie, Randy, Noah, Paul, Julie, and Leslie represented the Millennials. Though Leslie was close to the cut-off for Generation Z, or iGen, or Centennials, or whatever that generation would ultimately formally be called, she missed the 1996 mark by a year and a half. So, here gathered Generation X and Y.

The new house was more than big enough for them all. It was Anton and Lorraine's third home, and this was really less "housewarming" and more "open house" because they didn't need anything new for it. That didn't stop anyone from bringing something. Most brought alcohol, which was consumed during the party. What hadn't been consumed already was being worked on by the remaining guests. Leslie, a freshly-minted twenty-one-year-old, was enjoying the freedom of having drinks without having to hide it. The group sat in clumps around the living room, holding drinks, and chatting.

"Too bad Grandma didn't make it to see your new place," Carl said in the direction of Anton and Lorraine. "I think she would have liked that you have a garden."

"She could still make it to ninety-two this year," said Anton. "She might bounce back again." But even he didn't sound convinced. "I'll take her photos when I go and see her tomorrow."

"In, October?" asked Jasmine.

The rest looked at her puzzled.

"Ninety-two, in October, right?" Jasmine said.

"Right," said Lorraine. "October 10th. Ten, ten, twenty-three."

This generation of Van Slycks didn't know it, but 10:10 was a special time for Achiel and Lucia throughout their relationship together. Achiel liked numbers, and 10/10 struck him as important and special. To show Lucia that he was thinking of her, he'd always try to time his phone calls around 10:10. When he was overseas, he timed the writing of his notes so he concluded at 10:10. Of course, for Lucia's birthday he always made the day special, but he also did something extra special at the two 10:10s of 10/10. Sometimes it meant finding her at work and surprising her with a kiss or flowers. Other times, it was something as simple as massaging her feet if she was home or writing her a note about what he loved most about her. When Achiel went to Korea, he left his favorite wristwatch with her. He waited until it wound down, and then set the time to 10:10, so she'd know he was always thinking of her.

As if compelled by Lucia from her hospital bed, in an attempt to fill in the knowledge gap for this new generation, Jasmine looked up at the clock.

"Huh, 10:10," she said.

"Spooooooky," said Paul and everyone laughed. He drank from his beer. Even though Paul was Caroline's child from a marriage previous to hers with Ronnie, he fit in well with this group, even after the divorce.

"Maybe we're surrounded by ghosts right now," said Randy. "You know, earlier generations. Maybe they're swirling around us. Listening in."

"Pretty sure Grandpa would be in quite a different place from the rest of our family," said Winnie, "or at least I'd like to hope so. If I believed in such things, that is."

"Is that how you think of him?" asked Carl curiously.

"As burning in hell?" asked Winnie.

"No, as grandpa," said Carl. "I'm never sure what to call him."

"Well, he is your grandfather," said Winnie.

"Biologically, sure," said Minnie. "I'm with Carl. I tend to think of a grandpa as some loving person, like Grandpa Carpenter."

"I just mean," said Carl, "I really don't know anything about him. My dad never talks about him."

"There's a good reason for that," said Anton.

And then Anton told them what he knew. About Achiel's involvement in World War II, his service in Korea and Vietnam, about the "girl," about the murder about the trial, about his time in prison, and about the various other stories he'd collected.

"He burned down his own welding shop?" asked Julie. She only entered the family in 1999, and then it was through her mother's marriage to Ronnie. While her mother Lois complained about Julie's father, Julie was now wondering what kind of family she had acquired in trade.

"Why did he kill that guy's dog?" asked Georgie. Though Georgie had heard some of the stories before, the ones about animal cruelty were new to him and particularly hit him hard. He'd had no idea the list of dead animals included several dogs, several cats, a horse, pet rabbit, two cows, and a number of chickens sniped from afar.

"Was he a war hero? I mean, was he decorated?" asked Randy. He had considered enlisting, but in 2001 he was too young, and in 2004, when he finally turned eighteen in August of that year, his excitement for the war had soured. Popular opinion in the US was that America had marched into war under false assumptions, and troop morale was low because of vulnerabilities of Humvees, lack of body armor, and the number of physically and mentally injured troops coming home. Still, as a bank teller, Randy looked back on the previous eleven years and wondered, "What if?"

"Could he really shoot bats from the sky? They fly so erratically." Winnie had heard the claim about her grandfather before, and it was one of her favorites. Occasionally, when she needed a mental break, she'd search for videos to see if anyone could actually shoot bats. Many of the videos were disappointing and borderline cruel. People shot at bats that were motionless, hanging from a ceiling trapped in a house, or in caves. But some, believe it or not, had managed to capture footage of someone shooting a bat mid-flight. One video, cleverly titled "How to Shoot Flying Bats," was not, as Winnie had hoped, instructional, but rather just a herky-jerky video of a man shooting a bat as it flew across a pond. Winnie must have watched the video twenty times. Even though she knew there should be a bat there, skimming the water eating bugs, she couldn't see it. Either the man with the camera, and the man with the rifle, had better eyes than she did, or they posted a crappy video claiming to have shot a bat mid-flight and assumed no one would question it. Winnie imagined someone might get lucky once, but the story she had always heard was that her grandfather could shoot several bats from the sky.

Winnie's training and education taught her better than to diagnose people without having met them, but as a psychologist, she was pretty convinced her grandfather must have been a psychopath, even if only half the stories were true. Like Georgie, Winnie was also affected by the stories of animal cruelty. She wasn't sure if shooting bats fit into that category because so many people thought of them as pests and vermin, but Winnie hated mosquitos, and so she tended to think bats served a rather useful purpose.

"It upsets me that no one ever talks about Miriam. They just call her 'the girl' or say, 'oh that thing with the girl.' Does anyone know what happened to her?" Lucy asked.

She'd heard her dear, sweet grandmother lay all the blame at the feet of "that girl" her whole life. As in, "None of this would have happened without that girl."

While Lucy could understand her grandmother's need to point the finger somewhere, it felt particularly cruel to single out a fourteen-year-old girl as the culprit in that affair. Her grandfather should have known better. Because that was the start of the "bad blood" between him and the Ellis family, it didn't mean Miriam should shoulder any of the blame. From what Lucy knew, her grandfather didn't need much of an excuse to fly off the handle. Her own father, Lucas, told her plenty of reasons that Achiel had beaten him, and he was his oldest son.

"The thing with the trees. You mean to tell me that's real?" asked Noah. Oddly enough, the story of chopping the trees down was one that Uncle Lucas was actually somewhat proud of. Ronnie had taught his children that Uncle Lucas was a bit of a blowhard and prone to great exaggeration, so Noah didn't know what to believe. It was a surreal story, and Noah couldn't imagine the kind of patience it would have taken to cut down that many trees. He himself had never used a chainsaw, or an axe, but he imagined it would take a while and be exhausting.

"How many appeals did he attempt? And on what grounds? It seems like he should have run out of appeals pretty quickly," added Minnie. As a newly practicing lawyer of a year and a half now, she thought the legal aspects of her grandfather's story were fascinating. She was impressed that he had taught himself enough to represent himself for at least one of his appeals. Minnie had watched many prison movies and had seen examples of "jailhouse lawyers" and prisoners who spent their hours studying law, but she just assumed they were fiction created by Hollywood for dramatic purposes. Also, as a grudge-holder, she was impressed by her grandfather's ability to hold onto a grudge as long as he did. According to Uncle Lucas, Grandpa had been fighting the conditions of his incarceration right up to the day he died. She didn't know how to bring up her grandfather with Lucas by any means other than asking about the wrongful death case that Lucas had brought before the court. The case had failed, but he was still happy to tell Minnie about it and ask her opinions as a lawyer.

"There were really riots in his prison? That must have been scary. Did he start them?" asked Jasmine. This was completely new to her. Granted, she was born in 1981, the same year the riots occurred in Jackson Prison, but she was surprised she hadn't heard anything about this part of her grandfather's life. The family was still talking to Achiel in

1981 when she was born. It was before everyone started to erase him from their lives. She had received at least one birthday card from her grandfather on her ninth birthday. The birthday card envelope was beaten up and torn, and it had obviously been opened before and then taped shut. The stamps were cancelled, and there was a red stamp reading "from Jackson State correctional facility." The card itself was less remarkable. It said, "You're 9!" The "You're" was sideways, and the 9 took up the full height of the card. Inside, it read, "Happy birthday!" There was a short message, written in shaky handwriting: "Jazzy, I hope it's a great one. Love Grandpa." Jasmine hadn't thought twice about the envelope when she slid it from the mailbox, but later, as an adult, she wondered what would have happened if she hadn't been the one to get the mail that day. Would her parents have given her the card? Had Achiel written her other letters before that had been intercepted? Her parents had never taken her to prison to see him, she'd never heard his voice on a phone call, and her parents rarely mentioned him.

Paul and Leslie had questions of their own, but neither asked. They sat quietly taking it all in. All this had happened well before they came along, and as non-blood relatives, neither really had a right to ask their questions. But it was incredible to think they were connected, however tenuously, to someone who committed murder. Also, both were rather drunk and enjoying flitting in and out of the conversation.

Anton did his best to answer questions, but he didn't have all of the answers. He had reached out to Miriam, but she never responded to his phone calls or emails. Shelley and Miriam had long since moved, so when Anton finally got around to visiting the property they had once lived at, they were long gone. Lorraine had gone with him. Like the others, she'd had plenty of questions, but by now she'd asked them all. She was even with Anton one of the times he talked to his grandmother, so she had heard some of the stories first-hand.

Finally, the questions petered off. Lorraine had fallen asleep with her head on Anton's lap. The remaining Van Slycks glanced at the clock, around the room, and at one another.

Lucy broke the silence, "Anything else we should know about our family?"

There was a pause, before Noah said, "Ken asked me to marry him."

Several of them burst out with, "Congratulations!"

Randy, his brother, said, "I was there when Ken came and asked Dad for his permission. It was cute. I wasn't sure what Dad was going to say."

"I didn't know you were there," Noah said.

"Yeah. I was. It took Dad a minute, but he came around pretty quick. He said something like, 'Well, it took me four tries to get it right, let's hope it doesn't take him as many times.'"

Everyone who was awake laughed.

"I miss Grandma," said Winnie.

"She is pretty great," said Minnie. "I always wished we had gone back to Sicily with her, so we could see where she used to live."

"That would have been fun," said Jasmine.

"We should still go," said Georgie. "Maybe Mina would go with us?"

"I'm sure Mom and Dad would be up for it," said Winnie.

"Ours, too," said Carl. "Don't you think, Lucy?"

"Sure."

"What about Uncle Ronnie? Would he be able to?"

asked Georgie.

"I'll ask, but even if he doesn't, I'm game," said Jasmine.

Tentative plans were made, logistics hashed out, and then hugs were given as the next generations dispersed into the night. Anton felt great relief at sharing all he knew with everyone. He was no longer a keeper of secrets. Now they had the stories, true or not, that allowed Achiel to not be forgotten, because, knowing—even an incomplete truth—brought the closure of the mysteries surrounding the man the family had always talked around and never about.

As expected, they would never go to Sicily. When one generation was ready, the next was not. When one couple was stable enough to be able to afford it, several others would still be completing school or paying off debt or finding their entry-level jobs. Then the cycle would repeat, but with different players being ready and others not.

PART XVII: ANOTHER WAKE
(OCTOBER 2015)

People wanting to pay their respects lined up through the front doors of the funeral home, jammed up by the handshaking and hugging that was happening inside as they greeted the family. The immediate family—Sophia, Lucas, Ruby, and Ronnie—stood at the top of the stairs, which caused the log jam, and the visitors couldn't resist the temptation to hug and mingle right there, unaware of the people waiting behind them. It was only two weeks since the housewarming, when many of these people had seen one another, and yet they lingered. Unable to stop themselves from hugging, re-hugging, and saying how much Lucia meant to them.

The spouses—Gerry, Cristina, Kurt, and Lois—busily manned the logistics behind the scenes. Ensuring cards were gathered in a uniform place. Making sure people understood the layout and flow of the event. Periodically checking in on their partners, and interrupting conversations now and then to keep the logjam of arriving visitors as minimal as possible.

The grandchildren—Anton, Minerva, Winifred, Lucy, Lucas, Georgie, Jasmine, Randy, Noah, Paul, Julie, and Leslie—had no real responsibility, which meant they were rudderless and left to wander. Some lingered at the open casket. Others chatted with family members they knew well. A few chatted with family members they had never met before or had only glancing memories of.

All three of Ronnie's ex-wives were there. Hazel, Caroline, and Lila, all in the same room for perhaps the first time, even. If everyone wasn't so overwhelmed with emotions and the loss of Lucia, the gathering of ex-wives surely would have been the conversation on everyone's lips. Instead, the three ex-wives mixed and mingled. Lila had the smallest connection to the family, but even she paid her respects to Lucia and said how kind she had been (the few times she had met her).

Mina, Lucia's sister, wandered aimlessly. She examined each of the boards with photographs tacked to them in succession, went to the bathroom, and then started the loop again. Occasionally she'd make a pitstop in the family room, look at the food on the countertop, watch the others eat the food, and then leave, returning to the photographs.

Eventually, the call came for everyone to be seated. The soft organ music played as people continued to spill into the room and find seats. Eventually Gerry ran to the greeting area, interrupted all the hugs and greetings, and made Lucia's children take their seats. That dramatically reduced the logjam and suddenly people flowed freely into the larger space and took their seats.

The organ music played on, and on, but eventually the seats were full, save one or two awkwardly between couples and families, and then the priest began to speak. What he said and the hymns they sang together weren't particularly memorable. What was, were the grandchildren participating in the service. Not all did, or could. Several of them, including Lucia's children, said they simply couldn't speak without breaking down. But, Minerva and Lucy both did scripture readings. Carl read a short poem, and Jasmine performed "Amazing Grace" on her cello.

When Jasmine was done, the priest thanked her and then said, "and now, Anton with the eulogy."

He knew his name was going to be called to speak, because he had told his mom that he would, but he hadn't formally prepared a eulogy. What he had was a collection of memories about music and dancing, and a short poem he found in his grandmother's room. He had assumed his remarks would come at a point in the service when everyone was invited up to speak to say a few words. But a eulogy?

He stood, grabbed his notes from near his feet, and made his way to the podium. Once up there, he looked at the group of people gathered. He knew a lot of them, indeed most of them. It was an impressive gathering. He took a moment, looked at his notes, and then began to speak. With each passing moment, he made more and more eye contact with the audience, seemingly gaining confidence as he went.

"Thank you for all coming here to honor my grandma. It means a lot to see so many here for her. I'm her oldest grandchild. My earliest memories involve music and dancing. I don't remember who started it, but when I was at her house, someone would play Bob Seger and I'd sing and dance to it. I knew all the words and my grandma was so proud of me, she'd brag to her friends. I'm sorry to say, that talent, or confidence, or whatever, has faded with time, so no singing from me today."

"When I was going through her things, helping my mom, I saw her records and thought about that. Strangely, she didn't have any Seger, but a lot of other great classics. In her dresser drawer, I found a stack of papers including programs and invitations for weddings, wedding and baby showers, funerals, and several obituaries cut from the newspapers. At the bottom of the stack were two things.

"First, a tattered copy of Victor Silvester's *Dancing for the Millions: A concise guide to modern ballroom dancing*. When I say tattered, I mean, tattered. There's no better adjective to describe the edges of the pages. And, in truth, it was only about half of the book. The second half was completely missing. I couldn't find a publication date on it, but apparently it first came out in 1949. It's possible it could have been that old. It's obvious that book was well-loved."

"But, under that was this poem. I'll do my best to get through it without crying. We'll see."

Anton paused and took a deep breath and then let it out slowly.

"I'm not really one that believes in fate and all that. I know grandma definitely had faith in a way I didn't. But even I have a hard time denying the weird set of circumstances that allowed for this little poem to wind up in my hands today. I mean, what did I think I would find in her nightstand in the first place? And when I saw the invitations and programs and newspaper cuttings, what kept me digging to the bottom? Why didn't I stop? And yet, I kept going until I found this. Here it is."

He took another breath and fingered the corner of the laminated piece of paper.

"I mean, she didn't die at home. She was in the hospital until the end. And, she didn't say to anyone, 'hey, look for this little poem in my nightstand, I'd really like that read at my funeral.' And yet, it clearly meant a lot to her, because it was laminated. Which, I guess, is why it stuck out to me in the drawer."

"I tried to find out who wrote it, but most people who share it attribute it anonymously. However, after a little more digging—I know, Anton and his rabbit holes—I found it's likely Mosiah Lyman Hancock. He was born in 1834 and died in 1907."

Anton sighed and rocked slightly at the podium.

"Okay, for real now," he said, and read the poem.

When I am gone, release me, let me go
I have so many things to see and do
You must not tie yourself to me with tears
Be happy that I have had so many years

I gave you my love, you can only guess
How much you gave me in happiness
I thank you for the love each have shown
But now it is time I travelled on alone

So grieve a while for me, if grieve you must
Then let your grief be comforted by trust
It is only for a while that we must part
So bless the memories in your heart

I will not be far away, for life goes on
So if you need me, call and I will come
Though you cannot see or touch me, I will be near
And if you listen with your heart, you will hear
All of my love around you soft and clear
Then, when you must come this way alone
I will greet you with a smile and welcome you home.

"I love you grandma."

Sophie mouthed the words "thank you" to her son. And her siblings all dabbed at their eyes with tissues and attempted smiles at him.

Anton smiled at the front row, took the poem and his notes, and returned to his seat.

EPILOGUE

Here it is. Here is the moment in time that no one but Achiel and Clifford saw, but the family wondered about their entire lives. Some of the immediate family members heard an account of the events firsthand. Others heard accounts in the courtroom. The extended family heard versions of the story through whispers. And the truth of it all, the actual truth, is that it went down exactly like Achiel had said it did all those years before.

Clifford Ellis drove over to the property. He parked his vehicle directly behind the Van Slyck's vehicle, blocking their exit. He shouted things, haphazardly. He was drunk.

"You motherfucker!" "I don't want no trouble!" "What are you doing over here?" "Stay away from my family?" "My little girl! You—you—you, filthy, fucking, dog!"

Achiel told his sons to stay in the vehicle. He would go and see what was going on. He would make sure they were safe. When he approached Clifford, Clifford drew a paring knife. It sounds ridiculous, but it was true. It was a paring knife that Shelley had been cutting tomatoes with just earlier that day. After she finished cutting tomatoes,

Clifford cleaned it. He couldn't have told you why, but for some reason, Clifford put that paring knife in his pocket. It had a little cardboard sleeve that the blade went into, and he slid the knife into the sleeve before he put it in his pocket. And then wandered around the house as he did when he was drunk. He tinkered with this and that. He poked over here and looked at this and that. Sometimes he knocked something over, but for the most part he was careful and managed to amuse himself with his wanderings. And now that knife was drawn.

"Look!" he yelled at Achiel. "You ruined her! My Miriam!"

Achiel backed away as Clifford thrust the knife through the window at him. Backing away was completely unnecessary and a bit silly because Clifford's range was shortened by the window only being rolled down three quarters of the way. Clifford noticed this and rolled the window down the rest of the way.

"You're drunk," said Achiel. "Go home."

"You go home!" said Clifford.

Achiel didn't view drunks kindly. Men who lost control of themselves were not something he had a tolerance for. Clifford had a long history of losing control of himself. Achiel did feel bad about how everything had gone down with the girl, but that was a decade ago, and Clifford had to move on. He should have gotten over it. Clearly his daughter had. Besides, Achiel was the one who had spent the time in prison over the whole thing. He'd paid his dues. In fact, if he weren't an independent contractor who could pick up work whenever he needed, he probably would have still been paying for that crime because he'd be out of work.

"You go home!" Clifford said again, and Achiel laughed. This was his home. This was his property after all.

He was building a house here. He laughed again at Clifford and raised his gun slightly and touched the knife blade. They were fencing with ridiculous weapons. Clifford and his tiny paring knife versus Achiel and his rifle.

Was Achiel mad? Yes, he was. It had been a long day. Though he loved days like that, being outside with his kids, he was tired. It's hard to be in the sun for that long without feeling drained after eight or more hours. Achiel hadn't taken a nap like Ronnie and Lucas had. He spent almost the entire day on his feet, and most of it walking. Even though he did milk the disability benefit he received more than he should, he did sincerely have a back injury. Usually, it was fine. But on days like today, with him being on his feet so long, it started to act up. Now, he just wanted to go home, and this drunken idiot was standing in his way.

To make matters worse, he was being yelled at by a man that Achiel thought was far beneath him. This man had, in fact, caused Achiel to go to prison, which was something no one else had managed to do. Not even men smarter than him, and with better reasons for wanting Achiel locked up. So, yes, Achiel was mad. It was a long day, his back hurt, he didn't take kindly to being yelled at, he didn't enjoy being called names, and he had a history with this man. Achiel also knew Clifford was drunk and stupid, and he had Lucas and Ronnie to think about. For once, Achiel kept his anger in check and just wanted Clifford to go away, so he too could go away. He just wanted to get home, have some dinner, and go to bed. But that wasn't in the cards.

Clifford suddenly pushed the door into Achiel, bumped the rifle, and caused it to go off. Achiel watched in amazement as the bullet went straight through Clifford's throat. Bullseye. Achiel had hit many bullseyes before, but never one so unintentionally. He marveled at the shot. Clifford's body slumped back into the seat. Achiel couldn't see it, but the paring knife fell to the floor of the truck. The door closed most of the way, but not enough to turn off the interior lights. Blood oozed out of the dead man's body, and Achiel stood there wondering what to do. He'd killed people before, but he had been trying to kill them. This man he had no intention of killing. He was a drunk idiot, but Achiel had no intention of killing him. He only meant to knock the paring knife out of his hand and to tell him to go home and sleep it off.

As he and the boys drove away, he momentarily regretted not calling the police. It was an accident after all. Because of what had happened with Miriam, and because of the bad blood between him and Clifford, he didn't think anyone would see it that way. Besides, who would believe his ridiculous story about the gun just going off like that, and Clifford waving a paring knife around? It was laughable.

He'd fight his whole life to be heard and believed. Yes, he was a liar about many things, and yes, he had done many, many terrible things, but this, this was something that was entirely out of his control.

ABOUT THE AUTHOR

Originally from Michigan, Michael MacBride now calls Minnesota home. He has delivered newspapers, worked for UPS, delivered pizzas, done collections at a bank, was a roadie for a country band, was a grant-writer and funder-researcher for non-profits, taught English, Literature, and Humanities courses at universities and colleges in Minnesota, New Hampshire, Ohio, and Illinois, and held a few other jobs in between.

Now, he writes, helps others publish their books with Salty Books Publishing, and has a "regular" job, too. He thoroughly enjoys traveling and spending time with his wife and two boys.